IT WAS A NIGHTMARE
PARODY OF A HORSE—

a thing which had hooves and pricked ears and even a faint semblance of the long-ago Chinese artisan's clay harness upon its body, a jigsaw puzzle put together, jammed together, all wrong. It moved like a horse, heaving and digging to pull itself out of the earthquake-opened ditch. But its eyes, its eyes glowed a brilliant crimson, a demon's eyes, and they were fixed on him now.

It heaved itself one last time and gained the lip of the earthen gash, bucking out of the depths. It swayed on its pieced together legs, head down, looking, not to crop grass but to . . . what? Graze on human flesh? The creature snorted, aware of the terror which gripped him, laughing at him, and dark sooty clouds roiled from its nostrils.

He scrambled back, and the vermilion gaze stayed fixed on him. He could feel its heat, its hunger. It was *not* alive! It could not be. A demon! A demon animated the statue from within, and it wanted him, it needed him. And even as he turned to run, he knew there would be no escape. . . .

PHOENIX FIRE

by
Elizabeth Forrest

DAW BOOKS, INC.
DONALD A. WOLLHEIM, FOUNDER
375 Hudson Street, New York, NY 10014

ELIZABETH R. WOLLHEIM
SHEILA E. GILBERT
PUBLISHERS

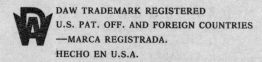

DAW TRADEMARK REGISTERED
U.S. PAT. OFF. AND FOREIGN COUNTRIES
—MARCA REGISTRADA.
HECHO EN U.S.A.

PRINTED IN THE U.S.A.

For Cheryl,
a true friend, no matter how many masks
I wear, with wishes for luck as you
embark on a brave new journey;

and

For Jessica,
with love and wishes of your own
as you, too, journey forward.

Chapter 1

The inner environs of L.A. never quite slept. It didn't have the frenetic pace of a New York or a Tokyo, Californians were much too philosophical and mystical about life, but L.A. still never quite shut down completely. Clint Humphreys, better known as Digger, liked the early morning hours when night's curtain was just lifting, and the smog hadn't gotten its acrid burn heated up yet. He wandered the cement pathways with a keen eye for the discards which were the mainstay of his life, snatching them up, a man-seagull of the inner beach of the city.

Begrimed and smelly, wrinkles etched into his leathery skin, his day was evening and late afternoon his night. That had proved best for him on the streets. No one beat up a dirty old man in broad daylight. He could sleep in relative safety then, once he went back to his hidey-hole in the thick oleander brush that fringed the freeway.

The last days of spring, when grayness held the heat down and the dirty air close, had gone. Now the summer began in earnest, a summer on the heels of a multi-year drought even for a Mediterranean climate. Digger meandered toward the museums. School wasn't out yet. The last few field trips were being scheduled. He got good lunches from field trips, impatient children discarding most of their food, though crunchy peanut butter stuck between his decay-gapped teeth. The children sometimes took pity on him and gave him their entire lunches. He could sell those he collected for a quarter and buy libations later. Digger looked forward to a profitable day.

He hunkered down across the corner, under a pansy-pink building which had been set up on massive round columns for a parking lot, its shops upstairs. The lot was scrupulously empty of refuse except for the oil and transmission fluid leaks patching the cement floor. He'd find nothing here, but Digger did not mind. He scratched his nose vigorously, awaiting the sun in its glory, and the screaming hordes of children descending upon the La Brea tar pits, bringing him treasure.

The ground shivered. He felt the tremor instantly, knew it was not another heavy truck lumbering by, and put a hand palm down to the garage floor to steady himself. The hairs in his ears quivered as if they were antennae. The shock was but a minor forerunner of another due that day. Digger knew these things. Hadn't he lived closer to the earth of California than any man he ever knew? Only the animals sensed more. He'd been holding his breath. He let it out slowly, his glance flickering overhead to the massive shopping complex balanced on thick columns. If it had been a major quake, he'd have been squished like a bug.

His bony hip had gouged out a dent in his backpack. Not a man to tempt fate, he reached for it now, with leaving on his mind, and hesitated.

The feeling stole upon him, a shivery, scared feeling, creeping across the garage floor shadows with a butter yellow glow. Digger held still, not amazed that he could see the oppression, the fear. He often saw things others did not, though he thought it was due to cheap wine as well as the keenness of his senses. But the color that began to bleed upon the slick flooring and wash toward him was not a color of fear.

Yet it brought a chill with it that raised the hair on his arms. His breath caught in his throat. He could smell brimstone, far sharper than any basin smog, and coughed harshly. His lungs rattled.

He got to one knee, cans and trash in his pack rattling, then froze in obeisance. "Lord God A-mighty," he got out, and raised a hand to protect his eyes.

The sheen increased in intensity to a white-hot flare, but there was solidity within the outline, and he saw it, saw the pinions outspread—and the fear became as hot as the sun, and the wrath for the Sodom and Gomorrah of the city burned.

Digger croaked out, "Forgive me, Gabriel!" before the white-hot tide of wrath crashed down upon him. He felt himself go, skin and muscle and bone and teeth, go like a taut band snapping, from life to death instantly.

Light fled to shadow. The garage stood empty once again. It cooled as much as it could in the morning temperatures which would reach into the hot, dry 90s before nightfall.

A pile of white ash marked all that remained of Digger and his discards, flesh and metal indistinguishable from one another.

Chapter 2

The quake shuddered through L.A. barely perceptible over the trucks rumbling through early morning traffic. It shook a few dust motes into the smoggy sunlight, little more, but underneath the pavement it sounded like cannons being fired across a bay in hopes of bringing bodies to the surface. An ancient superstition that, but there were those who understood that the thunder below the placid earth's surface would loosen its secrets, bringing them up out of the dark.

The raucous early a-yem voice of the local D.J. permeated the stillness, blasting out the open window of a modest silver Toyota, its owner driving with his left elbow nonchalantly out the window, and his head and shoulders bowed slightly forward over the steering wheel, a man almost too tall for his car. He swerved to miss a stray cat, but it might almost have been in reaction to the D.J.'s blaring voice.

"Hey, hey, what do you know? We just had a quake, folks, and the people over at Cal Tech tell me it was around a three point fiver, just a window rattler. Film at eleven, right? On the local front, El Lay fire marshals took to the air-waves last night, warning residents of the severe brush fire probability this year, what with that old drought and a hotter than usual June forecast. Campfires have been banned in the Angeles Crest forest, and all you firebugs, hey, let's be careful out there."

Harper drove into the back parking lot of the George Page Museum, turned the car off, and listened to it diesel for another minute before it staggered into silence. He didn't miss the absence of the D.J. as the radio lapsed as well. With a sigh, he looked out over the parklike grounds, grass holding a yellow-green despite water rationing, and watched a woman jogging behind the art museum, her fuchsia and violet outfit disappearing into the heat lines already radiating off the sidewalk. She was early even for the Hancock Park devotees and her fanaticism reminded him of his loss. He wondered if Debbie was going to come back.

Gut instincts told him no, frankly, not after four months. He didn't really want her to come back, it was just that the wondering was automatic. Loneliness bit at him and he didn't have a whole lot of other things to do with his life at the moment.

It was more than gut instinct, actually, he thought. She'd thrown her clothes vigorously into her suitcases, already packed brown cartons littering the apartment, and he'd surprised her, at that. When she'd finally spoken to him, it was like an eruption.

Her brunette complexion had been blotched with excitement, an excitement that had been almost sexual, her eyes sparkling with fervor. "I'm out of here," she said. "Finee. Ciao. And don't bother doing lunch. I held your hand all through your operation, I promised myself I'd do that much and I did—but now it's like living with some bloody old man. They opened up your chest and carved you up like a goddamn Thanksgiving turkey and then they put you back together, and all I do is wonder, every time we screw, if you're gonna croak on me. Not that we screw that often anymore." A silk blouse and a pair of jeans were slammed into the suitcase. A drawer kicked shut.

All he'd been able to say, feebly, had been, "It takes time. . . ."

Debbie tossed her head, her Paula Abdul mane of hair cascading about her face. "I don't have time to waste. You can lie around and sigh and hold your chest, but I'm going to live." And she was gone. Two tanned young men, who'd been waiting out in the hall and whose expressions were carefully bland as if they'd not heard a word of her tirade, filed in, took the cartons, and left in her wake. He'd not heard a word from her since.

A pigeon took off from a limb of the scraggly eucalyptus at the lot's edge. A long piece of bark sloughed off the tree from the bird's impetus. It fell to the ground and lay there like a snake's molted skin. He found himself with his hand resting across his chest, the leg the surgeon had stripped a vein from aching with a drumming throb, the gentle pound of his heartbeat echoing in his palm. He blinked and stared at the tree. El liked eucalyptus trees. There weren't many left in Southern California now. He thought briefly of the man who'd once claimed he could make a cheap substitute gasoline from eucalyptus and wondered if he'd gone the way of the trees. Even the koalas at the zoo didn't like California eucalyptus. They munched on Australian imports.

Elmore Harper swung his long legs out of his car and into the heat waffling off the lot, backwashed from the underside of the Toyota. It would be genuinely hot later, and smoggier, too. He yearned for February, with its crystal clear days of false spring. In February, the Angeles Crest could be seen clearly, purple peaks dusted with white, looking over the L.A. basin. Today, he could not even see the hills for the brown curtain of dirty air hanging low.

His briefcase sprang its lock again as he emerged from the car, and his notebook sprawled to the asphalt. He gathered it up as though it were a part of his courage, hugging it to his chest as he looked across the tar pits.

From the back lot, the tar pits weren't impressive. Most of the work here had been stopped for lack of funds and results. The acreage toward the front, with its ponds and the museum, got all the cultivation. On the back lot, there were small potholes here and there of tar seeping up through the grass, and one or two larger efforts with sagging chain link and wood fences cutting them off from public access. The jogger had probably sprinted over one as she crossed the boulevard without even noticing the saucer-sized hole.

The front pits, with their cement and fiberglass mastodons and dire wolves being pulled in even as they fought one another, were the big attraction. Harper smiled. It was Davis' day to take the high school kids through. He would get the first and second graders, who were scheduled later. Harper enjoyed the younger kids, but he could barely tolerate the ennui of the average high schooler. The museum couldn't compete with MTV.

He was early. It was the only way to miss the traffic and find a place in the lot before other joggers and visitors took the slots. It meant he had to start the coffeepot, but he didn't mind that much. It gave the others an excuse to talk to him, praising or damning his faint effort. Harper angled across the lot, skipping open seams, then stopped at the edge. His head turned against his volition.

A cool breeze pushed against his face momentarily. It did not carry the sound of traffic. It called to him.

"Oh, hell," Harper said. He dropped his notebook and briefcase where asphalt met grass and strode off across the grounds, in search of pit 29.

It was still roped off, but no one worked here

now. Excavating the tar pits was far more difficult than digging through layers of dirt and sand, difficult and expensive. But Harper leaned his rangy frame against the fencing of his favorite pit, for it was here that he'd been blooded. It wasn't much to look at—joggers paid more attention to it as a road hazard than the institute gave it—a blob of tar the size of mastiff's head coming to surface in the grass-covered creekbed. Despite the drought, the creekbed retained a threadlike freshet of water, runoff from the sprinklers. It trailed about the tar globule before disappearing into a cement pipe which looked more like a miniature arched bridge. Drawn to both the tar and the water, toddlers would duck under the chrome-yellow plastic ties fencing it off to poke a stick at the pit in curiosity.

It was here, while on a patron's tour, he'd experienced the thrill of discovery about the unknown and, while in its thrall, had looked across the workway and fallen in love as well. Debbie had been an undergrad at UCLA, brown-eyed, brunette with sun-streaked hair, a young lady who had changed lovers almost as often as majors. He thought he had brought constancy to her at last when she'd changed majors one more time and kept him, at least for the additional two years it had taken her to graduate. The love hadn't lasted. The dirt and tar, he reflected as he looked at it, had.

Not that she had been entirely wrong. His

heart surgery had thrown him into a pit of his own and he'd climbed out to be a docent as well as a patron, helping the Page Museum out three days a week. He was on sabbatical from the family firm, but he could not bear the emptiness of his apartment and the idleness of his mind, so, after bumbling about looking for appropriate work that matched his soul rather than his budget, he decided to volunteer at the museum, in gratitude for the heritage that had given him his income, the underground world of a million years past. It fit neatly into his sense of justice and balance. And it kept him from being lonely.

Harper smiled, the expression cutting across his angular and somewhat homely face. The gesture caressed the lines at the corners of his hazel eyes.

A thin layer of dusty water skimmed the patchy surface of the pit. A sparrow darted at the pool.

"Careful," Harper said. "Or you'll be caught, too." The loudness of his voice surprised him as well as the bird.

He'd already turned away when he heard the gurgle, and then a resounding BLOP! His astonishment caught in his throat as he looked back to what had erupted from the dirt and the tar. The sparrow broke away with a flurry of its smallish brown wings, its throat stretched in an unheard cry.

* * *

Susan Aronson zigged and zagged her car through the building traffic on the streets. She squinted a little because her sunglasses were busy elsewhere, holding her unruly curled hair away from her forehead and eyes, rather than performing the shading job they'd originally been designed for. The parking lot at Farmer's Market was already filling. It was tourist season in Southern California, ready or not. But most tourists were as anxious to save their feet as possible, so she found a spot at the outer edge of the dark red farmhouse restaurant, on the corner, and that pleased her because it was close to the side street she was headed for.

She hesitated, then locked her car. As she leaned over, her sunglasses gave up hair duty and fell down lopsided onto the bridge of her nose. She pushed them into position, straightened and looked around, taking bearings, fearful she might lose the car again. Then she shrugged. If she did, she did. She was in a hurry. Poppa Irving had called in a panic and she didn't want him out on the street any longer than necessary.

And he would be pacing the street, his bowed legs encased in worn black suit pants, wheeling his aged form back and forth, back and forth. Susan was used to these panicked calls from her grandfather-in-law, but she answered them, which was more than she could say for the rest of her husband's family.

She would catch hell from Sid and Maida later, she knew. Maida would say, in her slightly nasal voice, "Poppa cries wolf, you know that. You can't keep rescuing him or we'll never get him to understand that he's too old, that he has to give up that shop." Then she would give the phone over, saying, as if Susan couldn't hear her, "Sid, tell her. I can't tell her a thing since Geoff died that she'll believe me. You tell her." And if Susan were lucky, her father-in-law would only say quietly, "You're a young woman, Susan. You have a life of your own to live."

The light changed and she took the street in a lope, her own long legs flashing under her daffodil colored skirt. Someone honked, a polite beep-beep, perhaps in tribute to her legs, but Susan didn't look back.

The neighborhood changed, subtly, from the market tourism, signs becoming older, less neon, and bilingual, in Hebrew and English. She couldn't, of course, read Hebrew for all that she'd become an Aronson. But she knew the businesses. A used bookstore, a deli, a kosher butcher shop, a CPA with tax service, a men's specialty clothing store which advertised on TV, looking far vaster than its actual cramped interior, and as she sped past them, she could see Irving stop on the sidewalk, throw his head back, and spot her as well.

The morning sun glanced off his shiny forehead, and the breeze blew his fluffy white hair into a nimbus about his head. He might look almost Italian angelic if it were not for the powerful, hawked nose dominating his finer boned face. Susan slowed a little, to catch her breath, and she smiled. The old man waited for her under a hand-painted sign that read: ARONSON TAILOR AND SEAMSTRESS. The seamstress had since gone to her reward, but the tailor still labored here.

Irving smiled, too, and caught up her hand, pressing it to his chest. "You shouldn't hurry," he said, his patois accented heavily with what her deceased husband, his grandson, had once described as "heavy handwriting." "You should always drive and walk careful." He laid that burden on her, always, that she should never die suddenly as Geoff had, in a car accident, blood and flesh and bone in twisted metal.

"I do, Poppa. Are you all right?" His heart thumped under her touch.

"Now that you're here, I'm fine. Where did you park?"

"At the Market."

"Good." He smiled, brown eyes nearly disappearing in wrinkles. "We'll have lunch later."

She took her hand away from his chest reluctantly, for it had told her what he had not. She had felt his heart fluttering like a wild bird within his thin rib cage. "Poppa," she said.

He blinked rapidly, then looked up at the sign of his business. Like him, it was worn, faded, and proud. Plain and hardworking, Susan thought. She took his shop keys from his hand. "What is it?"

He hadn't even stayed in the shop long enough to take off his dark jacket, she thought, as she opened the door and two dead bolts. He hung at her heels. Susan looked over her shoulder at him. The nostrils of that proud hawked nose flared; a wary beast scenting danger.

"The gas," Irving said. "Don't you smell it?"

"Is the burglar alarm off?" she asked, pressing into the dim closeness of the tiny shop.

"Yes, yes. I was enough of a *mensch* to get that done before I called you," he answered in disgust. "I would not call, Susan, but—"

"I know, Poppa. It's all right." She dropped the keys back into his hand and closed his fingers around them. "It really is." She moved to the counter and took a deep breath.

Closed. A little chalky. A faint smell of old nicotine. Musty. But no gas.

She shook her head. "I don't smell it."

"Are you sure?" New York squeezed heavily through the "sure."

"Yes. Let me go to the back. Is the pilot on for the furnace?"

"At this time of year?"

"Never mind." She pushed through the red drapes and into the back where the tailoring workshop with all its clutter met her eyes. Irving still did a lot of work for a seventy-seven-year-old man. The machines looked as old as the man—there was one concession to progress in the corner, an almond colored sewing machine that did all the stitches one could imagine, all of which were diagrammed on its side, but she noticed its cabinet worktop was conspicuously empty of scraps and threads. She took two or three deep breaths at the sound of Irving's step behind her. She turned.

"Nothing, Poppa. It's all right."

The rims of his eyes sagged with age, and they filled a little now. "Is it, Susie?"

"Yeah, I think so." She gave him a quick hug. "Nothing's going to happen."

"I thought I smelled the gas. I dreamed—" he stopped hastily and shrugged off his suit coat. Underneath, his long-sleeved shirt had already been rolled up.

"Poppa, that was years ago, a freak thing, and it's not going to happen again."

"So you say. So they all say. How can they know? Indifference and ignorance, a Jew's worst enemy. They didn't know it was going to happen the first time. I, Poppa Irving, say I smelled methane. I should stand around and wait for Fairfax Avenue to go up in flames like it did last time?"

She didn't argue with him over that one. The spontaneous methane explosions which had rocked this old section years ago had had no parallel in L.A. history. The pavement and foundations of several buildings had just opened up and exploded into flame. It had taken months for the methane to burn off, to be drilled into release and capped. He'd known a store owner who was put out of business by the sudden fires.

Strange, she thought, that the event which had happened a block and a half away bothered him more here at the shop than it did in his little apartment which was even closer to the district. But she didn't question him. She smiled. "I think you've got gas on the brain," she teased him.

He froze. In the already gathering heat of the tailoring shop, his body went rigid. "That even you should say that to me," he said sternly. "Even you, little *shiksa.*"

The moment the words had left her lips, she knew she'd hurt him. She should have thought. Susan mentally slapped herself, punishing herself for something that ought to be as ingrained in her memories as it was in his.

His lips trembled as he said, "The only death camp to be closed down because of its failure. And what was that failure? They failed to kill us. We escaped, Susie. Hundreds of us. And I escaped twice, did you know that? I worked the Resistance, I was an underground soldier and when they picked me up, if they'd known," Poppa paused to spit a "feh!" of contempt for the Nazis through the fork of his fingers, "if they'd known I was Resistance, they would have killed me on the spot. But they didn't know. So I escaped death once and went to the camp. There I—we—escaped again. But this . . . this invisible, I can't fight."

She sat down wearily on a chair rescued from an old school. "I know, Poppa," she said. "I'm sorry. Please forgive me." Inwardly, she told herself that he ought to forget. For a little while. Enjoy living. Sometime. Just once.

He sat down, too, with a gusty sigh. He patted her hand. "I know, I know," he said. "It's a different kind of gas."

But infinitely more deadly. Her eyes met his.

Irving smiled. "Are you sorry you married into this *meshuga* family?"

Without a thought. "No. Never."

"Geoff is gone, rest his soul. You could leave. No children. No ties. What keeps you with an old cocker like me?"

"Love," she said, leaning over against him. The Aronsons were the only family she had left, however heavy their burdens of guilt and grief. Her own parents had turned their backs on her.

"Ah, Susie. Have I got news for you! I'm too old for you!"

They rocked in laughter for a few minutes. Then Susan stood up. "I've got to track down a dining room set that's late on delivery. My phone must be ringing off the hook and Angelo's in Vegas."

Irving did not get up. "You work too hard."

"I'm lucky to be working at all. You and Geoff almost made a princess out of me!" She paused, pushing the decorating business out of her thoughts for yet another minute or two. "I can't make lunch, but if you need me, call. Don't even think about it."

The old man smiled, even as he reached for a stubby piece of tailoring chalk. "Don't worry. Don't I always?"

She left him, head bowed over a pair of polyester/wool blend cuffs, but, before she stepped out the door into smog-laced sunshine, she took a last deep breath. Nothing. Why, then, did she feel uneasy?

Chapter 3

Harper looked at the object regurgitated by the tar. A cobalt and gold feather, as small as his little finger, floated upon the dirty water. He picked it up and looked after the sparrow which had fled. This was no sparrow's feather. A fine, knotted silken cord hung down from the quill, with a piece of a clay tablet attached. He palmed the clay. Dirt and tar obscured it. He scratched a fingernail through it absently, wondering what it was he had. A treasure from a hundred years ago or trash from last year?

Sunlight glinted off the brilliant feather. Dust motes only partially obscured its gleaming colors, and the tar had not touched it at all. He wondered what kind of New Age talisman it was and what the tablet would say when he cleaned it up. The thrill of a discovery all his own scratched through the tarnish of his loneliness. He could give it to one of the lab techs in the museum yet knew instinctively that he wouldn't.

This find was his. He curled his hand about it

and pocketed it. In an absentminded way, he glanced at the parkway and street, and the scent of smoke and fire reached him on the wind as it abruptly changed directions, a strong, choking scent that made him look for the source.

A dark green Jaguar pulled into the boutique center across the street and its driver got out, a petite, finely tailored woman with heels that seemed half her height. She carried a leather bag-case which bounced against her thigh as she started across the garage first floor. He'd seen her before, an older woman who ran one of the import boutiques upstairs. El had just bent down to pick up his things and return to work when her scream, patchy and hoarse, brought him running.

Her face was pale under its too early in the day heavy makeup and she pointed a shaking hand. A pile of white ash lay in the corner next to one of the massive support pillars. A battered and grimy nylon backpack, half-consumed, lay next to it. And a hand, seared off at the wrist, clutched a strap of the backpack. Harper squatted down to see if the truncated hand was fake or real. The smell of charred flesh told him it was real. He wondered what had happened to the rest of the body and looked at the ash. An aluminum can lay partially out of the pack. It had been seared in two, edges melted at the twinning, its other half gone to powdery ash as well. This had been one very hot fire.

He reached out and flicked some of the ashes aside. A dark outline had been scorched into the cement. He decided to disturb nothing further.

The woman had stopped screaming, but stood with her hand to her throat, eyes wide. Their gazes met.

"Can you call the police? I think this might be . . . remains."

She bobbled her head and clattered away.

El watched the pack with its single remain. Why a hand? Had it been axed away? And what fire could burn hot enough to powder aluminum—yet leave half a can untouched? He fought himself not to stir through the ashes again, possessed by a certain morbid fascination of wanting to know what had happened here.

By the time the police had arrived, the odor had nearly faded, the wind was threatening to swirl away the ashes, and he had gone through santaria rituals, gang initiation, spontaneous combustion, and countless other oddities as possibilities.

The patrolman looked down with dour lines etched into his face. "What happened? Touch anything?"

Harper stood up, his thighs cramping with the sudden stretching of muscles. Standing, he was taller than the policeman and something flickered through the other's eyes, possibly a reassessment of Harper. To El's satisfaction, it didn't include fragility. He said, "The Mercado

Boutique owner found it like this. We didn't touch anything."

The cop toed the artifact, grimacing. "Wonder what happened to the rest of the guy?"

"I think," Harper suggested slowly, "you've already got the rest of him."

"This stuff? Looks like somebody shoveled out my fireplace."

Harper shrugged. The wind had swept away and regathered part of the pile, revealing the scorched in pavement outline of a reclining man. He looked down at the silhouette. "Strange things happen."

He waited until the coroner's office came and collected the ash and other goods. The shopkeeper stayed beside her car as if its opulent metallic body could protect her from what she'd discovered, gave her statement, and then winged upstairs without another word to Harper. The police decided to put out an injured and missing persons report, pending word from the coroner's office on the ash content, and thanked him. He smiled ruefully when the police let him go and he loped across the street as the first buses began to pull into the lot. He gathered up his notebook and briefcase a second time. He wondered who had made coffee and if it was ready yet. He could use a cup. He watched as the first of the teens clambered out of the buses and strolled contemptuously across the grounds. He wouldn't be their docent for all the tea in China.

Xian, China

Tembo Chang watched the last of the big-nosed tourists file out of the site, holding his breath, grateful for the end of his day. The bloody Fourth Anniversary riots at Tiananmen Square had not slowed the flood of those who would pay to stare at the terra-cotta army of Huang, uniter of the Great Wall of China, dictator and emperor of ancient Ch'in. Even the dance of earth had not diminished the flow, through several of the statues had swayed dangerously in their places in the great, silent funeral army.

Tembo moved between the ranks of the army, his own compact peasant body dissimilar to these, the nobility of some twenty-one hundred years ago. He did not touch the figurines although the dark sleeve of his coat brushed them now and again. He found those who had swayed and looked them over anxiously, each different, each an ancient ancestor, as he looked into their blank clay eyes. This one had been an archer, his quilted coat a flimsy armor against ancient warfare, his quiver full of clay arrows. Like the tourists who looked over the army from their catwalks, he marveled at the artistry of the life-sized figurines. Hundreds in rows, all different, all individual, like souls frozen in terra-cotta, all to honor and guard Huang's victory and tomb.

He took a camel hair brush from his coat

pocket and dusted imaginary erosion from the archer. His ankles and feet had not yet been fully excavated. Tembo wondered how strong the earthquake had been to shiver him. Not strong enough to keep the tourists away or bring government relief workers in floods. A shrug, then, not a mighty dance of destruction.

Voices of fellow workers echoed through the site at Xian as they made ready to gather their lunch pails and leave. Tembo did not hurry to join them. He planned to hang back as the site was closed down and shut away for the evening. To do so would bring a penalty which could be severe, if he was caught, perhaps even the loss of his job. But he had something he wanted to do, and the desire of the forbidden burned in his breast like the flower of a red hibiscus, a flame which spurred him. Since losing his position in college as a student, he had only this work to study. But the mysteries of Xian were vast and Tembo happily lost himself in them.

He hid in the rear of the storerooms, in a dank, shadowy corner where the old tools of the archaeologists were still piled: peasant hoes and shovels, their shafts cracked by time, the wood oiled by the touch of many hands. He listened to the others as they gathered their battered pails, complained about the shortage of meat in the village market and the rudeness of the tourists, and shrugged their way out the museum front with its government store and showcase statues. Huddled in the corner,

Tembo breathed shallowly, listening to the silence fall as dusk lowered over Xian.

The site building was a huge shell, little more, except for the more elaborate front which held the showcased statues in their glass obelisks and the government store, the army itself still in the process of being excavated and refurbished, the size of the pit spreading ever outward, bare-bones catwalks to the fore so that the curious could see the size of the army. At night, darkness grew, fostered within the shell like a fog. Tembo had seen it before and it scared him, but the yawning poverty which stretched before him as a deposed student frightened him more. A major discovery within Xian would propel him to the fore of those waiting for promotion and perhaps even return him to the colleges.

And he had found something . . . a glimmering of something buried deep in the red dirt at the far-flung edges of the pit. It was beyond the perimeter established by the working excavators. If anything was to be found there, it would be his, all his.

Tembo woke suddenly in the dark. He had fallen asleep and wondered if he had been discovered or if he were still alone, his heart drumming as he listened. There were frequently work crews at night, but since government bonuses had thinned, so had the fervor for overtime. He thought he was alone except for the night watchmen, and those he could easily circumvent. They would be upstairs, playing with their tiles and dice.

He found his hand trowel and lantern and stole out of the storeroom, making his way to the rear of the site where the shadows were deepest and darkest. There he knelt and carefully began to dig down. Already at the level of those statues with feet revealed, standing up on bricks and tiles, he began to remove the dirt below. He thought of those whose first goal had only been to dig a well and who found, instead, Huang's legacy to the world.

The dirt was loose. He had already dug down once and then replaced it, so his task went quickly for the first hour. Then, as his nails grew tender and packed with dirt as he did his fine handwork, the dirt grew hard again. Tembo blew his breath out, thinking of sweet riceballs and warm tea, soothing and filling. He moved the lantern into line and leaned over the hole he was creating. He took his whisk broom out and smoothed the hard dirt, just to make sure he was not troweling into something.

The trough all but swallowed his arm. If he found nothing concrete this night, he would have to find another way to dig, because his efforts would be noticeable. He whisked away, then the lantern's dull light caught the edge of what he'd found before. Tembo's breath quickened. His blunt cut dark hair fell across his forehead into his eyes as he leaned close.

This was not dirt. This was fired clay, the edge of something, a shield rim perhaps. Tembo's fingers brushed it. A shock thrilled through his fingertips and he yanked his hand back in surprise. He grabbed up the lantern and lowered it down, to see what he had found.

A rim, yes, and fired terra-cotta, like that of the army. But not a shield rim, no. The line was straight, with no curvature.

Tembo sat back on his heels. He looked across the silent army, and though they were hidden in the night he knew they were there.

Did they stand on yet another tiled plain? But why then was this half a man's body length under their sandals and boots? What was it? How had it shocked him, like an exposed electrical wire?

A snatch of conversation from beyond the catwalks made him freeze. The night men were making rounds. He could hear them grumbling about the luck of the dragon throw. Tembo hastily filled in the trough and shuttered his lantern. His back ached and his belly grumbled as his mind raced. What had he found? How had it bitten at him, stinging at his touch?

The watchmen went away. A door banged at their heels. Tembo crouched on the loose dirt, waiting for their return, but no one came.

A cold fog crept out of the ground, invisible, but he felt it rising up. It carried a smell with it, one he had never scented before, foul and greasy. Tembo grimaced and scrubbed his tongue over his teeth. He thought of the garbage the many visitors left behind and how the refuse stank until it could be hauled away, but this was not the same.

It slunk about his limbs, numbing his feet, bringing a fiery ache to his knees and twining its way up until it clutched at his throat. Tembo swallowed convulsively. He would be ill. He could hide no longer. Clutching his tools against his workcoat, he got to his feet and scuttled through the dark pit. Even as fear and loathing drove him away, he planned another midnight return.

Chapter 4

Her phone was ringing madly when she got in. Susan slung off her shoes as she raced to pick it up before her answering machine kicked in, but she was too late. Angelo's distorted voice came on and she paused to listen before picking up.

"The tables have done me wrong," her partner complained, without introduction, "so I'm staying over another night. I'll be home late tomorrow. Don't forget to call Mrs. Lerner for me tomorrow morning and explain to her about dye lots when she places her order for those custom drapes. I know she's going to want to coordinate her slipcovers, even if she doesn't. If you can't get her to order more fabric, cover my ass anyway. She's going to come back to us on this one, I just know it. Adios, baby."

Susan felt her mouth settle into pouty lines, but she refused to answer and instead let the machine ring off. Crap tables or no crap tables, Angelo had promised she wouldn't have to work with Mrs. Lerner. Now she was obligated. She sank into the wingback chair next to the phone and watched a yellow leaf drop from the potted ficus beside her and drift slowly to the tiled floor. Not enough water or too much—she could never remember. The yellow leaf joined several of its branchmates.

At least it hadn't been Poppa again. She expected another call from him before the day was done, remembering how frail he'd felt and how hard his heart had pounded. It wasn't unreasoning panic though the rest of the family might think his terror irrational. She knew. He feared because he sensed something to fear and it bit at him, stung him, drove him until he had no choice but to call for help. If his mind had been dim in any other way, she might think it due to his age and the frailties all men were subject to. But no, this seemed to be Irving's own private devil, and she couldn't leave him to battle it alone.

Her answering machine blinked at her, willing her to listen to it before she opened the bundles of letters in her hand. The letters held messages she was all too familiar with, bills upon bills. She played back the previous messages. Golden Nail had called to tell her her oak reproduction table set would be on tomorrow's truck. She blessed the conscientious traffic manager who'd called after hours to let her know. That lessened the blow of having to deal with Mrs. Lerner. Sid had called, instead of Maida, telling her there was to be a family council about Poppa and of course she was invited and she should call and let them know.

There was an ominously casual tone to his voice. And there was an impersonal message from Nordstrom's, reminding her she was a payment overdue. Susan sighed and erased the outside world from the tapes. She sat in the wingback chair for another long moment, letting it be her spine and hold her up.

A snub-nosed face, chin high to the doorknob, peered in through the front door which had been left ajar.

"I fed your cat," said the child's voice attached to the face.

Susan brightened. "Come in, Nina. Where is he?"

"Out on your back patio. He's lying under the hibiscus, waiting for the hummingbird to get close enough to catch. But the hummingbird's too fast, isn't it?"

"I certainly hope so." She curled her feet under her and leaned forward to catch up her purse. "How much do I owe you for this week?"

"A dollar fifty. Okay?" Nina stood, her ten-year-old form a living monument to her artistic ability, the thigh long shirt decorated within an inch of its life with plastic thread and glitter and paint, the laced edges of her leggings peeking out down below. Even her shoes had been decorated. Susan half-expected to see the word "Chaka" emblazoned somewhere across the T-shirt, graffiti style.

Domino did not need to be fed on a regular basis, but Nina had taken the chore upon herself and Susan thought it charming to be held up once a week by the artistic entrepreneur. Had Rembrandt started this way?

She picked through her wallet for the crispest dollar bill she could find, added two quarters to the total and dropped the money into Nina's paint-stained fingers. "So how's it going?"

Nina's eyes rolled. "We got to go on a field trip this morning. I didn't have enough money to buy a stuffed woolly mammoth, but Peter Latier almost pushed me into the tar pit in front where the big lake is and I could either have drowned or died in the tar, but he did it for attention, Mom says."

Susan blinked. "Right," she murmured, determined not to be overwhelmed by this flood of information.

Nina took another long breath. "And this neat guy showed us around, he was real tall like Abraham Lincoln and funny-looking like him, too, but he told rad jokes and he let me hold the head bones of a dire wolf and he knows all about the pits and the tar and the gases that make it bubble up and everything. And there's this neat skeleton of this woman on exhibit who got pushed into the pit a long time ago—and the light changes and she's all dressed like an Indian and then she's a skeleton again. He said she was a *sacrifice*." And Nina's voice lowered conspiratorially.

"She was?"

"Uh-huh." Nina made a fist about her money. "Well, gotta go. Mom's going to take me down

to buy more puffy paint. Thanks a lot, Susan."
She disappeared in a blur of fluorescent colors.

Stunned by the surfeit of information, Susan
remained in her chair. The front door had still
not shut, and a chocolate paw fished through it,
and then the rest of the Himalayan slunk in,
eyes still slightly crossed from the intensity of
the hummingbird hunt. Domino flung his tail
up in the air, plumes to the winds of fate which
had decreed he'd go empty pawed that day, and
made his way to the chair, where he arched his
back and fell over on her ankle.

Susan reached down and pulled him into her
lap. His pale blue eyes in a chocolate mask
stayed crossed in ecstasy as she scratched a
well known G-spot under the cat's chin. "And
how was your day?" she said quietly to the cat.
"Mine just came to a crashing halt."

She put the cat down and got up to close her
door before anyone else decided to cross her
threshold. Domino took up residence in the
wingback chair and began to groom himself vigorously.

Susan picked up the swatch book she'd left
on the floor and spread it out on her dining
room table, looking for the Pindler and Pindler
fabric Mrs. Lerner had been partial to. She'd
have to call the factory to reserve the dye lots
as Angelo'd requested. She stood on one stockinged foot then the other as she leafed through
the fabric samples. She tagged one or two possibilities if Mrs. Lerner changed her mind again.

This was work she'd hoped to do at Il Mode but hadn't had the time to get to.

She should be thankful, she knew, that she had work, and work aplenty, but Angelo had not taken her in out of the goodness of his heart. She'd proven her talent and she'd more than doubled the business of the firm. The sense of color and balance that Geoff had mildly scoffed at when she'd picked out his ties and socks and suits or redone his office had stood her well in his sudden absence.

And it had been sudden, shockingly sudden, a little over two years ago. Where had Sid's solicitous voice been then, she wondered in sudden bitterness. Wrapped in his own grief and guilt, like Maida and Geoff's brother David and sister Karen, no doubt. She had been ill, but the family had coaxed him to a charity affair at the temple, something she might have hesitated to attend anyway, and he'd gone. He'd bought her a painting at the silent auction, eaten the best brie, drunk fine wine, and they'd let him drive away even though he'd drunk a little too much wine. He was a grown man, they'd all told her later. A grown man responsible for his own choices.

Poppa told her they knew they'd failed Geoff and her. They couldn't say it, but they knew. The unspoken hung between them like a curtain. Only Poppa had pierced it, unafraid in his unabashed grief over death, abrupt and unfair. He was conversant with death. He'd faced it too often in his youth. He and she shared an understanding about it. If the family took Poppa Irving away, made him retire and then leave his apartment for some senior home somewhere, she would be truly alone. And so would he.

The condo was silent except for the sound of Domino's muffled purr and grunts as he groomed his fluffy and ample body. She looked up once, thinking that she should plan a dinner, did not feel like cooking for one, and went back to paging through the fabrics. Maybe she'd pick up Chinese.

When, and if, the call came from Poppa Irving, she'd welcome it more than he could know. There was nothing left of Geoff's spirit in the condo, nothing lingering even in the shadowed corners, nothing left at all, and she could not bear it that night. Domino in his cat-ego-eccentricity was no help. The fabric patterns clouded before her eyes, and the corner of one piece dappled with sudden teardrops.

Jasper Trenton, the Old Tar himself, helped El clean the clay tablet scrap. The elder doctor came in to the museum irregularly, a benefit of his age and his schedule on the charity circuit foundation. People who have been tuxedoed until one at night raising money are not generally required to come in at seven the next morning. Or so Jasper told him in dry tones as he painstakingly cleaned off the layers of tar.

Dr. Trenton had been only a boy in the early 1900s when the pits were first opened and researched. A gopher, really, but he was the most distinguished archaeologist still working at the Page Museum who could remember those old times when Hancock Park was still a munificent rancho instead of Wilshire Boulevard and gleaming office buildings. Trenton's finely groomed beard was more white than gray, and his pate was a weathered brown. His glasses had been worn for so many years that he had permanent purple shadows under his eyes from their weight, but his eyes were still a lively, snapping blue.

"Like peeling an onion," he said, wiping off another thin veil of tar. "And you can't go any faster or you might obliterate something. So who found this, umm? You did?"

Harper had already told him. He just nodded and leaned on his elbows, watching the doctor work at the white linoleum lab table. Behind them were enough dire wolf and coyote skulls to pave Hollywood and Vine, stacked in open drawers from floor to ceiling. "Out on one of the little pits," he said. "Came to the top with a blob and a bubble."

"Unusual, that." Trenton wiped again. The air was poignant with the smell of solvent. He put his once white now dirty rag down and passed the tablet fragment under a standing magnifying glass. "Chinese. Cuneiform, almost. Couldn't tell you anything more. Not my field." And he passed the object back.

Dr. Ellington wouldn't have passed the artifact back. He would have held onto it with an obsessive light in his eyes which could be misconstrued as greed, but then, Dr. Ellington was young, preppie, and upwardly mobile in the ranks of local archaeology. He was the sort of doctor who would have relished Egypt's glory days. Harper wouldn't have asked for Ellington's help. He couldn't have afforded the eventual payback.

He took the clay tablet back. The feather and the silken cord lay in his pocket. The tar hadn't stuck to them, although how it could not have, he could not have explained. Chinese. That gave him a good excuse to visit a close friend, one he hadn't seen a whole lot of lately, unsure of how the friend would take his metamorphosis from high-powered businessman to mild-mannered docent. Victor was not a social friend but a genuine friend with common interests. El hadn't seen Victor since Debbie had walked out of his life. He turned the clay tablet over in his hand. "Not a laundry ticket, eh?"

Trenton laughed, a sharp bark. "Good one, El. Probably an amulet of some sort. It might go back to the early rancho days here. Go to the museum and get a Chinese scholar to tell you what it says. You've probably got a talisman for good fortune and health."

"Probably." Harper rewrapped the tablet, uneasy at having shared it and even more uneasy at the thought of having to expose it further. Then he thought of his friend who might help, and felt a little better. The awkwardness of seeing Victor would be swept aside by his friend's passion for artifacts of his heritage.

Trenton clapped Harper on the elbow. "Good to have you with us, El. Give your family my regards." He pressed his glasses up his sharp, thin nose and launched himself across the lab, in search of further business in the rear, out of the windowed public viewing, more obscure and satisfying. Harper watched him leave, thinking that the Old Tar would probably see his family far sooner than he would.

The Chinatown gates had been repainted again, their red-lacquer poles impossibly bright in the late day, the gilt rims at the top catching the sunlight. Harper eased his Japanese car through the Chinese economy streets and parked in the lot beyond the gates. On foot through the cement mall, he passed small Chinese delis, windows draped with barbecued ducks hung by their long red necks. Soap shops fragrant with ginger and jasmine aromas that drifted out half-open front doors. There was a video store with garish kung-fu posters and one with the current beautiful Chinese actress, her red headdress dripping with crytal droplets upon her hair and forehead, looking wanly into the sunset. He wondered what that epic was about. Her beauty made him pause a moment. Dirt and tire soot besmirched the streets, and the long towered shadows of sky-scrapers across the freeway and to the southwest began to finger across Chinatown.

He'd come for early dinner, because it was the only way he could catch Victor Jue at the

Jade Pheasant. American born Victor was none-theless one of the best Chinese restaurateurs in Chinatown and the Pheasant would be packed long before twilight and not empty until nearly midnight.

Entering the Pheasant was entering another world, cool, dim, smog and heat forgotten, the massive aquarium to the front filled with ere-wons and dempseys, silver, green and red in the water. El took a deep breath. The air smelled of garlic and scallions and ginger. He paused by the front cashier's register and waited for his eyes to adjust to the dimness. Then he saw Victor in his gold jacket at the small bar. In a world of constant changes, Victor seemed immutable. He smiled.

Victor wore his hair in a conservative pompadour, combed his eyebrows upward as if they were luxurious caterpillars, conspicuous in an ethnic face which was normally devoid of much facial hair, and liked to sing to his dinner crowd. He had his back to Harper now, but there was sheet music upon the bar next to his drink, which would be no stronger than Perrier with a lime twist, and El knew he was studying his evening's repertoire. The lounge lizard facade hid a deeply committed scholar and businessman.

It was for the scholarship, as well as a good meal, that Harper had come. He fingered the bit of clay in his pocket as he approached Jue's elbow.

Another Chinese gentleman leaned close to

Victor's shoulder, the man older with hair the color of iron, and deeply sunken cheekbones. He saw Harper first and abruptly stopped whispering, sitting back, dark eyes hard.

Victor swung around. The expression in his glance changed gears and then a smile creased his moon face. He reacted as if it had only been days, not months, that separated them. "Harper! You're late for dim sum." He wore a crisp white shirt under his gold jacket, with a metallic gold bowtie at the collar.

"You're wearing your Saturday night tie," Harper said dryly.

"Trouble! This man is always giving me trouble," Victor said to no one in general as his unintroduced companion moved a bar stool or two away and paid a great deal of attention to his drink. Victor stood up. "Come for dinner?"

"That and help."

"Oh?" One of the fuzzy caterpillars arched its back in interest. "You need Dear Abby?"

"No." Harper's face heated up. Victor had known Debbie almost as well as El, and her absence was glaringly apparent. "Debbie left."

"Ah. I am not sorry to hear that. You've been through a lot, El. You need to know your friends from your enemies." Victor stood, appraising him.

El felt something melt inside of him. He reached for Victor's hand and pounded his arm. "I missed you."

"And I, you. So how about dinner? You can use the feeding up."

"Actually, I need someone who can read Chinese."

Victor laughed. He looked about the Pheasant and said, "Well, you've probably come to the right place." He crooked a finger, took a menu from the waiter who approached, and led Harper into a smaller, more private dining room, off the larger and more crowded central room. He sat Harper down with ceremony and perched opposite. "What is it?"

Harper brought the talisman out. "Just curiosity. I found it by the pits." He laid it down on the crisp white linen tablecloth, next to the vase with its single daylily. He'd reattached the silken cord. The cobalt and gold feather shone in its brilliance.

Victor's hand shot out and then paused, cupping the air over the find. He blinked, then drew it to him by the knotted cord. Harper sat back in mild surprise, watching.

The man eyed the talisman, then took the lotus-folded napkin in front of him, opened it with a snap and laid it over the top. "Where did you find this, El?" Victor asked in a subdued tone.

"I told you, by the pits."

Victor eyed him. The restaurateur sat back in his chair. He rubbed the corner of his mouth. "It's old, El. This tablet almost looks to be a forerunner of porcelain."

"I've brought you an artifact? I thought it might, at the most, be from the turn of the century. A laundry ticket," and Harper smiled apologetically for his bad joke.

Jue shook his head. "There's part of a seal here for good fortune. The rest I can't recognize." He pushed the napkin back across the table. "I can't look at it now. Why don't you keep it for a few days?" He got to his feet. "It's good to see you again. We need to talk. I want to know what you've been up to. Since you stumped the master, dinner's on me. Okay? I'll have Lum bring pot stickers and you tell him what else you want." He squeezed Harper's shoulder. "And next time, bring a new lady friend with you." He left, in a hurry without having appeared to be. El watched him go and wondered what it was about the find which had frightened him.

For it was terror which Victor had covered up by snapping open the napkin and tenting the talisman. Nor would he touch it again. He and El had met over an import deal and El knew that few things unnerved Victor Jue. Harper drew the object back and pocketed it as the reed-slender Lum approached the table with a bamboo steamer of pot stickers. He gave Harper a smile which did not warm his almond eyes.

Outside, in one of the alleyways that connect the tourist Chinatown with the old residential neighborhood, a young lady walked, her silk dress tight despite its slit up one supple thigh, her ankles curved tightly on the stack of impossibly tall heels. Her long black hair, a wig, hung to her rounded buttocks, and she walked with a sultry, steady click click along the pavement. She wore *Opium* and its scent drifted sleepy sweet behind her. She passed one of the very large bank buildings dominating the corner of Chinatown and paused, pensively, by the rear parking lot where Jags and BMWs dominated the slots. She saw no drivers.

After a generous study, her kohl-lined eyes blinked and she began to walk on, the night very young and her prospects still very good. The emerald silk dress rustled and slid a little farther up her thighs. Something stopped her. She pivoted on one spiked heel, looking back toward the lot.

A cold feeling shivered up her spine. It pierced her sexual arrogance with fear. She looked about, to the sky, to the rooftops, in sudden dread. A yellow white eye of blazing intensity in the velvet dusk streaked out of nowhere. It hurtled across the arc of twilight, descending on her.

She screamed as the night flamed with white light, a comet's tail of heat, and the fireball hit, two, maybe three cars exploding into flame, white-yellow flame. The explosion knocked the wig from her pretty face and baffled her against the squat bank. Her tiny purse rattled to the ground. As soon as she could catch her breath, she began to scream. The mascara ran from her eyelashes as her eyes teared from the blast.

Sirens tore through the night.

Chapter 5

Victor's sentry met him at the alley doorway. He was young, hardened, an L.A. man, nothing of the mainland left in him, four generations gone from China. His hair was oiled back and his eyes dark as flint. He wore a sharkskin suit that spoke of money and tailor shops in Hong Kong.

"Tong," he said, as the glow of the parking lot fire reflected off the tall buildings surrounding the mall canyon.

"Are you sure?"

The sentry's clipped answer was drowned by another explosion as another gas-filled car caught despite the efforts of the fire department. They did not see the lot, but the second explosion rocketed upward like a launch at Cape Canaveral, fluming between the buildings. Victor's eyes smarted. He said, near the sentry's ear because the noise was deafening, "My car was in that lot."

Tam Chen responded, "I understand."

There had been a lot of cars in that lot, Victor reflected, as his sentry moved off to consult with his own hierarchy of underlings. He wondered if it had been a pipe bomb or perhaps a Molotov. He wondered if it had been the long arm of the mainland reaching out to daunt him, or extortion efforts of the local tong, or whether he had even been the target. He stood in the tomblike safety of his own doorway and watched the orange reflections dancing in the summer sky.

Harper watched, too, the warm glow of his dinner and tea gone to a leaden knot in his stomach, the harsh wash of the fire against his face. He saw the girl leaning against the bank building, flanked by policemen who talked vigorously. Her long, oval face was smooth, expressionless, streaked by long black bars of mascara. She'd had emotions once. She'd cried earlier. Now, nothing.

He stood back from the curious crowd, listening to the rapid singsong of Cantonese as they watched and speculated. A massive red truck cannoned fire retardant across the pavement. The parking lot was a field of white foam and orange flames despite their efforts, but he didn't think another car would catch now.

A police officer drew close to him, attention directed to a fellow officer.

"She won't budge. It's probably gang activity, but she says it just came out of the heavens, like a comet or something. She's scared stiff. Closed up like a clam on us."

The other man made a rude noise and turned away, speaking softly. El couldn't hear any

more and let it go, thinking that he was in another world anyway. He turned back to the mall
lot, to the safety of his own modest vehicle. His
hands curled about the talisman in his pocket,
and he felt a vague comfort, like he had when
he was a kid with his garishly dyed rabbit's foot,
unaware at the time that an animal had died to
give him good luck. The thought came back to
him now and he wondered what lay in the talisman's past, what violent karma had been ex-
ecuted, to seal good luck within the piece.

The phone rang after midnight. Susan flung
out a hand, searching for the receiver, her
thoughts in the deep, dark well of sleep, her
stomach vaguely hungry, as she finally retrieved the phone and answered it.

Poppa's voice, gravelly and apologetic. "Are
you all right, *shayna?*"

She touched her bedside lamp, flooding the
room with its subtle glow. A long time ago,
she'd perfumed its lampshade, and the aroma
still drifted with the heat of the lamp. *Joy*
flooded her senses as she scrubbed a stubborn
eye open. "I'm fine, Poppa. Are you all right?"

Across town, in an aging apartment as different from her condo as night from day, with
wallpaper curling, yellow and brittle at the
edges, and the phone a plain black instrument,
the old man sat propped up in bed, his balding
pate decorated by stiff hairs which refused to
either fall out or lie down in an orderly manner.
The only light in the room came from a bare

bulb, its chain cord trailing down the wall over Irving's headboard. How could he be all right? He dreamed at night, terrible dreams, of fire and death and the sweet, almost unsmellable odor of the death gas. How could he sleep, with dreams like this? And this time she'd been with him, like Joan of Arc, surrounded by the flames. He knew then he did not dream of the old death camp, but his future . . . whatever future an old cocker like him had, and Susan was as doomed as he was. It frightened and paralyzed him. He had had no idea of how to save himself and now Susan was involved as well. But at least he would not steal away her dreams. He would bear the burden alone as long as he could, until he knew how to warn her.

"I'm fine, fine," he rasped back.

"That's good, Poppa."

There came a rustle over the wires. His hearing wasn't good enough to tell him if there was static on the line or if she'd moved in her bed, the sheets rustling. "Would you like me to come over tonight and sit up with you a while?"

"No, no, I'm fine."

"Angelo didn't come back today," Susan said. "Now I've got to see Mrs. Lerner in the morning. Poppa, you should come with me. Give up tailoring and help me in sales. You could charm her. She's not going to be able to make her mind up again, I know it."

"Now, Susie," Irving said, and relaxed a bit, her troubles fading away the acute terror of his dreams. What harm could come to her while planning new carpeting and slipcovers with fussy old women? "What would I do wearing a pair of fancy pants, eh? An old man like me? A little chintz here, a plastic slipcover there fixes everything, like your grandmother, rest her soul, used to say."

He was rewarded by her breathy laugh. "Poppa! Plastic slipcovers in L.A.! I'd be drummed out of the decorating corps!"

Irving said, out of habit, "I remember when my mother used newspapers for hall runners. . . ." His voice trailed off. Gone, all gone. From the poverty of 1930's New York, they'd returned to help their relatives in Poland and been caught in the same net of hatred, swept up and interred, and most of his family had not survived the war either in the underground or in the camps. "You're a child, a baby. What do you know?"

"I know it's . . . almost one o'clock. Can't you sleep, Poppa? Are you dreaming again?"

"Ah, Susie, Susie. What are a few dreams to an old man like me, as long as I can wake up? Every dream is a blessing. You go back to sleep now. I'll be fine."

Her voice sounded faint, or perhaps it was his hearing, "All right, Poppa. You go back to sleep, too."

Irving hung up. He pulled his thinning blankets up to his chin and stared into the murky corner of his small apartment. Shadows did not frighten him. He knew every angle and curve of the apartment, day or night. But he did not know what he would see when he closed his eyes. White hot fires burning, L.A. inexplicably in flames, and the sweet and sour smell of gas. . . . With a sigh, knowing that sleep would be gone for some time, he got up and padded across the linoleum floor to the old and warp-sleeved bookcase across the room. His gnarled hand went to the Old Testament, but his knobby fingers brushed past it and, instead, came to the *Cabala*, which sat in the shadowed corner. He brought out the old and well-used book of mysteries. When he lay back in bed and settled himself to read, the book fell open across his lap without his turning the cover.

Domino clearly thought she'd brought home the swatch book for his comfort, Susan thought, as she padded out of her bedroom in the morning and found him curled up on it, paws across his masked face in a vain effort to shut out the morning sun. Feeling a bit wicked, she poked a finger into his ample Himalayan rib cage. "If I'm awake, you're awake."

The cat yawned and gave her a jaundiced look. It was obvious she ought to know cats and people kept different time clocks. Just to be mean, she pulled the catalog out from under him and flapped it in the air a few times to rid it of cat hairs. Domino rewarded her by pretending to flee in great alarm, disappearing down the hallway to the second bathroom where his litter box, and privacy, was kept.

She called Poppa's apartment from the kitchen while microwaving a cup of herb tea, but no one answered. He was customarily up early, taking in coffee and bagels at a small deli down the street which opened at dawn's first light and attracted little old Jewish men like a candle flame did moths. She'd been there with him many times, and thought of all the wives left in peace to sleep in a little later. It was a kind of sweet, benevolent social gathering. She had been flattered, flirted with, and even pinched. If she'd still had Geoff, she would not have felt like an outsider.

She worried about the family meeting. They would argue again about Poppa and she would not be given the chance to have an opinion, but in the end, they would lean on her to make Poppa see the sense of it. All the disadvantages and none of the advantages of family membership. Still it was better than the totally silent cold shoulder of her mother, and the quiet acquiescence of her father to her mother's will.

She pulled outfits out of her closet and spread them across the bed, like a squire choosing armor for his knight, outfitting for the skirmishes of the day. Heavy armor or light?

She power-dressed for Mrs. Lerner, double-breasted blazer, with matching pin-striped shorts that did a nice job on her legs, a simple blouse and pearls. The gray pin-striped suit gave her an opportunity to wear her red scarf knotted nicely at the neckline and a red-feathered hat, sporty and tilted for a jaunty look. She needed jaunty to charge her up after her half-sleepless night. Her glasses rested on her nose. She took them off and slipped them into a breast pocket on the suit jacket.

Domino emerged from his solitude to ask for breakfast. She fed him and changed his water. He flipped his tail in disgust.

"You'll want to eat that later."

His pale blue eyes told her otherwise.

"Then," she said, "burn in hell, because that's all I've got and I'm not buying you that fancy stuff with four bites' worth in the can."

The Himalayan cruised past her with an air of unconcern. He had other caretakers with better taste and a deeper sense of obligation. He went to the patio door.

"Not today," Susan said. "Today you stay inside." She grabbed up the swatch book, watched a few more hairs waft into the air, and left the condo.

Mrs. Lerner wore Evan Piccone slacks, a Claiborne blouse, heavy makeup and platinum blonde hair neatly done. She also had her face pulled tight in one of those scalp clip maneuvers, the "surgery-less face-lift" which Hollywood actresses had made famous. Her hairdo hid the procedure, but Susan knew the look. It came with the polish of Hancock Park money, which was like Bel Air money, quiet and powerful. She wondered if Mrs. Lerner would have the jowls of a bloodhound when she let the clips out.

Her condo had been done in the peaches and slates of the Southwest, but she was unhappy with that now and leafed through the swatch book looking at the pages Susan had paper-clipped for her attention.

She stabbed a French-tipped nail at one. "This is it. What do you call it?"

"Royal Albert," Susan said. "Like the famous English china."

"Yes. Yes . . . yes, but—"

Susan leaned forward quickly. "Angelo wants me to tell you about dye lot differences. Did he explain that to you? It didn't matter in the hues the Southwest look was done in, but it can make quite a difference here."

Mrs. Lerner blinked. She had light brown eyes, with a faint rendition of California crow's-feet at the corners, and now a vagueness came into her expression. "No," she said slowly. "I don't think so."

"Well this red, this crimson border, is very distinctive. Every bolt run of this fabric will be of a certain hue. If we order the draperies and wallpaper from one run, they'll match. But if we go back later to order enough fabric for matching slipcovers, there'll be a difference in the red. Or any color, for that matter."

"Oh, dear. Perhaps I should just—" Mrs. Lerner's voice trailed off as her attention flickered across the room. She frowned as she tried to think just what she should do.

"What we should do is order enough for covers now."

"But I'm not sure yet if I want covers. I wanted to wait and see the whole room made over before I decided."

Susan pressed. "We'll take the fabric back if it's not used. But if we order now, everything will match. If not . . ." she shrugged, a Poppa Irving shrug. *Oy*, she thought, to go with the shrug.

Mrs. Lerner's eyes faded back to her. She smiled. "Oh, all right, Susan," she said. She leaned forward and clasped Susan's hands. "You've never done wrong by me."

Susan met her smile impulsively, calculating the orders she would have to put in. "Now, about the deposit—"

"Oh," and Mrs. Lerner dimpled. "Didn't Angelo tell you? He lost to Carl last month, poker again, and this is what I wanted." A knowing look smoothed her face. "Oh, dear, you didn't know."

"No, I didn't, and I apologize," said Susan awkwardly, feeling like a fool. "I had no idea. But," and she stood up, "you want a new room and you'll get one. I'll phone you in ten to fourteen days when everything's in. We'll schedule workmen then."

Susan left the condo and frowned as she reached the grassy sidewalk and the too brilliant day hit her sight. The fatigue from last night's late phone call came flooding in, filling the void the adrenaline rush of closing the sale had given her. Fatigue and seething anger at

Angelo. It was bad enough that Il Mode was doing the job for free, but now he had her working off his debts. She could not afford to work for nothing. Then she saw the museum complex and parkway across Sixth Street.

The bas-relief front of saber-toothed tigers, woolly mammoths, and other creatures came into focus with a sudden intensity, as if she ought to remember something and couldn't quite. The small parking lot was jammed with big orange school buses.

The man, she thought. *The tall and homely man like Abraham Lincoln who knew about tar and bubbling gases and everything.* With sudden purpose, Susan put her swatch book and briefcase into the trunk of her car, threw her hat on top of them, and sprinted across the street to the back lot of the George C. Page Museum. If she were going to spend the day tilting at windmills, she might as well tilt at some useful ones.

Darkness flooded the Xian site like ancient water trying to reclaim land which had escaped it. Tembo stood, back ramrod straight, in his hiding place, his throat closing up as if he faced being drowned. Sweat trickled down his face. The day had been very warm and still, oppressive, and there had been heat lightning that evening, the flashes flickering like faraway warfare.

The palms of his hands itched. A dribble of sweat behind his left ear traced its way into his already sodden collar. Gas built uncomfortably in his stomach, but he could not wind it, not from his hiding place, lest he give himself away.

The last chattering and grumbling voices faded away.

Tembo blinked rapidly. It was foolish to do what he planned, but the discovery drew him. Despite the fear which twisted around his heart, snaked through his lungs, swelled in his gut, he had to find out what lay beneath the dirt and Huang's army.

When he at last became convinced he was truly alone, he edged out of the back of the storeroom. He had his tools in a cloth bag slung at his hip. Now he let wind, carefully, but found little relief in it. His guts continued their hard swelling and he thought he would be ill from the pressure.

His fingertips were still numb from the stinging they had taken last night. He had burned himself on his morning's teapot, without notice until the white, watery blisters welled up. Now he blew on them in the dark, which did little to help or soothe the injuries, flesh that was now raw where he had scraped off the blisters during the day.

It lay under the dirt waiting for him, like a massive snake coiled underground. He could sense its dry coils moving, scraping, rubbing against one another in anticipation, readying for the strike. It was evil. He put his hand to his chest, where an amulet crafted by his peasant grandmother was hidden beneath his work-shirt. He had not worn it in years, not since college admittance exams. It did not seem to hurt to wear it now.

Even the night workmen had gone for the evening, taking the weekend off. He was totally alone within the dig. He and thousands of terracotta statues, each individual, each the portrait of a man who had fought for Emperor Huang and Ch'in hundreds of years ago.

Tembo Chang swallowed hard and began his foray into the dark. Catwalks stretched overhead like the rib cage of some vast, dead dragon. His single-eyed beam grew yellower and yellower, dying as it tried to dispel the night.

He heard it before he felt it. The dance of the earth, the great shrug of the beast which carried the earth on its back, the footfall of a god, the shifting of the serpent ... the quake rumbled like a freight train across the ground, headed toward him. Tembo grabbed for a stanchion of the catwalk and held on. The pressure in his head grew dense like the skin over a drum would if someone stood on it, sinking in, building until it ripped apart.

Then the tremors hit. The building creaked and shivered, the catwalk swayed, the soft earth rippled under his feet. Jolt, jolt, jolt, pause while the ground buckled, then another sharp jolt like a battering ram into a gong.

There might have been another. Tembo did not know, for suddenly the catwalk screeched like a cat whose tail had been stepped on and began to sway wildly. Then, as the weak yellow eye of his lantern pierced overhead, he could see the catwalk come apart and rain downward like a toppled stack of sticks.

Chapter 6

Betsy's sun-tanned face split into a grin as Harper came past her desk. "El! I didn't know you were coming in today, but I'm glad you did. A certified letter came for you this morning, plus I'm to deliver a message from Dr. Ellington. He says if you spend any of his grant money, he'll hunt you down like a dog and kill you." Too many years of sun had leached away looks which might have been spectacular in her youth and now, in middle age, left her merely pleasant looking. But, with her blonde-streaked dark hair held back behind her ears by a strategically placed pencil, that was good enough. Her humor was infectious.

Harper smiled back. "Nice. Sounds like he's already been working with the kids today." The young lion of a paleontologist didn't frighten him and well she knew it.

"How'd you know? The Nature Company brought in a special excursion. Want your letter?"

"Yes, and tell Ellington that no, I didn't spend any of his grant money. I merely placed a much

needed order for toilet paper and hand towels."
El watched as Betsy unabashedly held his certified letter up to the overhead fluorescents before giving it to him with a shrug.

"Any guesses?"

Her frank blue eyes assessed him. "Well, I don't think it's an answer to the Singles ad we placed for you last week. But maybe it is."

"You did what?"

Betsy pealed with laughter at having caught him off-balance. She did not answer, but waved him away as her phone extension rang and she had to stifle her amusement to pick up the line.

El went to the tiny, impermanent cubicle that he shared with two other volunteers. The movable walls flexed with every earthquake or passing truck on the boulevard and had even, on occasion, been known to topple. There were no messages waiting in his mail slot and his third of the table looked fairly uncluttered. He sat down and spread out his hands on either side of the letter, debating whether to open it or not.

He knew the handwriting on the address, of course. It was his elder brother Cal's and its contents were personal enough that he had not even charged his executive secretary with typing or addressing it, and El knew what the interior message was, as well. They'd given up writing him at home because he'd stopped accepting the letters.

His sabbatical was over. The firm wanted him back. And not opening the letter would not help him any, even if he did not wish to go. Almost unconsciously, El put a hand over his heart. He didn't think he was ready. He didn't think he'd ever be ready.

His palm left a damp smudge on his shirt. His scar ached a little as he took his hand away. He opened the letter anyway and found, in Cal's terse wordage, the message he'd known would be there, plus all the words he hated to hear: wasteful, idle, prodigal, duty, obligation, potential, cowardice. He folded the crisp business sheet back up and replaced the letter in the envelope. Not hope, faith, or charity. Or even need. Certainly never love.

He was not the person he'd been before his illness. He was no longer a hard-ridden executive en route to somewhere upward. That was the person Debbie had wanted to live with, he thought, and she'd left when he was no longer available. That was the person Cal wanted back. That was the person whom El had left lying on an operating table at Cedars Sinai and could no more retrieve than he could bring back their mutually dead father. He found it ironic that Debbie and Cal had finally agreed on something: they had had a use for the old Harper and none for the new one.

He swept the letter into the wastebasket. Not that the old Harper had been so despicable, but he remained unreachable now for El. The desire to be buried eyebrow deep in deals and intrigues making an honest buck in spite of the competition had left him. It was as though all the blood they'd given him during surgery had been entirely different, so different that every cell of his had been transformed, metamorphosed into—what? He didn't know. He only knew that he could no longer get fulfillment out of that sort of life. Calvin did. Cal could not understand how El could walk away. The partnership would have to be settled, his vacancy filled, the power struggle stretched in yet another direction—but El was afraid to commit to that just yet. What if he were wrong about himself? What if it was just an effect of the anesthesia, like occasional forgetfulness and flare-ups of anger which he'd been warned about and did suffer, though less and less frequently. What if he woke up one morning and found out he wanted to return to the hunt and the kill again? And so he postponed the inevitable breakaway as long as he could. Not now. He wasn't ready yet.

No confrontations. Not to keep Debbie. And not to let go of his career and seize a new life. Not yet.

His phone chimed with the interoffice tone. He picked it up. Betsy said confidentially, "No answer to the ad?

"No." He felt himself grin sheepishly. Her desk was behind him now and he could feel her impish grin impaling him. But he'd be damned if he'd turn around and look, to give her the satisfaction.

"Too bad. Oletha needs some help changing the register tape out front. Could you. . . ?"

"Of course," he said smoothly. He hung up,

grabbed a role of the self-carbonizing tape, and left the back offices for the front of the museum, where school children were busy lining up in the outer lobby.

Oletha was a big, comfortable, dark woman whose no nonsense looks kept the kids in line at least as far as the turnstile. The turnstile was built into part of the display case for the gift shop. They entered past the cases, looking at dinosaurs and North American mammals and left through the same area as well—getting them going and coming, as she would say. The voices of children filled the air now as he crossed behind the rain forest inner courtyard, cutting across the main floor, and she had someone trapped in the turnstile, locked in, the black woman's ample arms crossed over her bosom. Changing the register tape seemed the farthest thing from her mind. There was a stormy look on her face as though she'd caught a thief.

Her captor looked anything but cowed under Oletha's glare. The woman glared back, high color blazed across her cheekbones, matching the crimson scarf knotted about her slender neck. He knew the type, he thought, almost in dismay, as he approached, and as Oletha's voice rose and the young woman's chin went even higher.

"I told you," Oletha said huffily. "One free adult per twenty kids, and you'll have to come in at the end of the line. You have to keep these younguns in order or they'll be scattered all over the museum—"

"And I told you," the young woman said, "I'm *not* with this group and I'll be happy to pay, but all I want to do is talk with someone."

"Well, if you're not with these children, who is?" Oletha's coffee brown eyes panned the lobby for anyone taller than four foot six. "Someone has to be in charge." The noise level of the unchaperoned children rose in unre-hearsed agreement.

"I don't know. Maybe they're not off the buses yet. All I know is," and a pin-striped sleeve came up, revealing a graceful hand holding a ten dollar bill, "I just want through."

"You'll have to pay full price if you're not coming in with a group."

"That's fine. I just—" Stormy blue eyes swept over El and he felt stunned, like a nocturnal creature pinned by spotlights in the dark. Then her gaze swept by, having dismissed him, and he felt slighted and unhappy. "I'm looking for someone who can give me some information. A tall man, somewhat Lincolnesque—"

"No one like that here," declared Oletha. "And with all these groups coming in this morn-ing, none of our docents are free." She snatched the ten dollar bill from the young woman's hand in triumph and let the turnstile open, its chrome bars propelling the captive forward. Then, as Oletha turned to ring up the admission, she made a face. She looked up as El moved for-ward again, finding his feet functioning again.

"El! Betsy said you'd come in. You're a savior. I can never get this tape loaded proper." She paused. "And maybe, since you're not supposed to be here anyway, you can help this lady."

Glad to be in motion and useful, El opened up the computer register and loaded the cartridge of paper tape. Oletha worked around and under his elbows, drawing out the change she needed. She dropped the young woman's money in her palm just as El said, "Done. You're open for business again, Oletha." He came around the counter and drew the woman away carefully as the chaperones for the school group emerged from the masses now filling the lobby.

He smiled and half nodded toward the children. "You don't want to get in their way."

"No," she said, with a smile and a slightly wistful look. The color in her face bled back to normal, seeming a little pale by California standards.

She likes kids, he thought with faint surprise, and realized he didn't know her type at all, not really, despite the sharply fashionable clothes she wore and the sun-streaked hair and carefully applied makeup. There was a beeper clipped to her purse, but it remained silent. "I'm not here officially and I'm only a docent, but can I help?"

She was still looking backward abstractly but directly at him now. He had the impression he was only vaguely in focus. Her gaze narrowed. "Actually," she said, "I'm looking for someone with a scientific background. A geologist, perhaps, who can tell me about the tar and the gases . . . Tall and rather homely, like Lincoln, but I don't know his name."

El flushed. He gave a slight bow. "I'm afraid I'm probably the only volunteer who fits that bill."

"But you're not homely—" She looked at him sharply and had the grace to blush as well.

"You and my mother," he said ironically, "are in the minority. Anyway, I'm only in for a short while today. What can I do for you? I'm Elmore Harper, but they call me El."

"Susan Aronson," she said. "I'm sorry. This is getting worse and worse. First she trapped me like a criminal sneaking in and now I've insulted you."

"I blame Oletha," he said, drawing her farther along with him, toward the courtyard. "She started us off on the wrong foot. What sort of scientist do you need? A paleontologist? Did you find a bone in your backyard?"

She shook her head. "Nothing that simple. Besides, I think I'd know whether it was something Fido buried back there or not. No, it's a little more complicated than that." She took up residence on a concrete bench, tucking her shapely ankles out of sight.

"Now it's my turn to apologize. It's just that pretty young women usually don't wander in off the street looking for help."

"Ummm. And it would be useful if I knew what kind of rescuing it was I needed?" She smiled then, and the expression lit up her long, oval face, transforming its perky prettiness into a kind of sublime beauty only he could see. He decided then that he'd walk across the vast pond in front of the museum for her, if need be, despite the deadly and treacherous tar that lay just below its surface. Or whatever else she might ask of him.

She looked embarrassed, however, and began toying with the beeper attached to her clutch purse, unclipping and then replacing it. "I don't know if you can remember the spontaneous methane gas leaks years ago—"

"In the old Fairfax district? Near Farmer's Market? Sure I do. Fascinating. Like dragons erupting from under the street. My dad's favorite clothing shop went up in flames." El laughed at the memory. His mother had died of disgrace for years because of his father's insistence on buying discount clothing when he could have afforded anything from anywhere.

"Could it happen again?" Susan asked.

"Well, there's a kind of underground lake or layer of methane under that section, but no . . . I wouldn't think so. You see, they piped into it to draw it away. Otherwise we'd have little spigots of eternal flames all over that area. And with the new mall being put in, I think they even drilled out to channel it away. I'd say it was unlikely."

"Would you . . . I know it's an imposition but could you . . . could you come somewhere with me and explain it all, reassure someone who still lives and works down there . . . just tell him it couldn't happen again, like you told me? It's important to me."

That was it? Never had a rescue been so easy. Still, he thought he could press for a fee. "Dinner?"

Susan smiled slowly, and the look in her eyes told him she was aware of his ploy. "All right. Dinner for three."

"I'm free tonight."

She didn't consult the kind of massive date book which usually accompanied her banker/upper management style of dress, but she did think a moment, as if recollecting. "All right, then."

"Good. I'll do some more research on it to convince your—"

"Grandfather," she said, getting to her feet.

"Grandfather." He tried not to let his dismay at being chaperoned tonight show. "How about the Olive Garden?"

"All right. Seven too early? Poppa Irving retires early."

He put the time into his watch. "No, that's fine. I'll meet you there. Meantime . . . you paid for it—wouldn't you like a tour of the museum?"

She put out her wrist with an almost identical watchface upon it. "I've got appointments," she said.

"Ah. Well, get a rain check from Oletha."

A streak of mild fear passed over Susan's face. El reached out and plucked her ticket from her hand. "Never mind," he said. "I'll take care of it. Tonight, then."

And she was gone, out the rear exit from the courtyard, so gracefully and quietly, compared to the massive tour of schoolchildren tramping in his direction that he almost wondered if she'd been there at all. He blinked once or twice and put the ticket to his nose. The faint smell of her perfume was upon it, just from the few moments she'd held it.

He thought of her eccentric grandfather, whoever he might be. He had a nice granddaughter.

El turned away.

Tembo woke with a throbbing at the back of his head and across his neck. He lay still, blinking, unsure if he were blinded or not, then the thin, pale golden beam of his flashlight pierced the cloud of darkness around him. He put his hand out, grasping, and found the torch. To save its meager beam, he clicked it off. His legs felt pins and needles numb. He'd lost a shoe; one foot was icy cold. Or—and he sucked his breath in—perhaps he'd lost the entire foot and didn't know it?

One pylon lay across him, its weight heavy but not crushing, and Tembo dug his hands into the dirt, slowly dragging himself out from under it. Every movement brought stabbing, bruising pains that racked his body. As he wiggled out from under, fiery shocks lit his feet and he welcomed this return of sensation though it brought tears to his begrimed face. It was good, he told himself, his body was of sturdy peasant stock. Otherwise he might have been crushed. He had merely been pommeled.

The great structure remained silent. No one from the village or town came to see the damage. Tembo counted himself fortunate to have not been discovered and yet . . . he wondered why no one had come. He wondered how much devastation had hit. He lay still, panting.

He flicked the flashlight on and feebly examined himself, hands shaking, the pale light wobbling. He seemed all right, no cuts or gashes. He would be black-purple tomorrow, he thought wryly. But he would have a tale of survival to tell over a pot of warm rice-wine. If he dared to tell it. If he dared to reveal his presence at the site.

The earth under the catwalk structure lay gaping open. The flashlight caught it as he swept it one last time over the foot which hurt so badly, and Tembo froze as he saw what it illumined.

An orange light, the rim of it like a corona in an eclipse, answered his pale yellow beam. It flared from deep in the earth, a man's length downward from the bricked floor below the first emperor's army. From the depth at which Tembo had first discovered . . . something. It swallowed up the light he aimed at it.

Tembo dropped the flashlight in cold fear. He levered himself to his knees, every injured muscle crying out in pain which he ignored, so afraid was he. He watched the leading edge of something begin to crawl out from under the earth.

An aftershock hit. Tembo could feel it, hear its dull pressure in his ears, before he knew what was happening. He dropped back to his elbows and knees, covering the back of his head.

But he watched the chasm in the earth move, twitch, slip-slide its edges against one another. A terra-cotta horse, a single chariot mount at the edge of the excavation, began to teeter. Then it fell into the gash, crumbling into shards as it hit.

Tembo caught his breath sharply at the damage. The animal had been one of his favorites among the statues needing restoration. The fire in its eyes had been almost real. He mourned its loss even as he prayed for the earth to become still. Another portion of the catwalk crashed to the ground, iron bars bouncing with terrible clashes and screeches. He winced with every note, expecting to be hit.

The orange flare grew bright, creeping out toward the terra-cotta fragments. The pinpoints of the corona sparked blue-white when they touched. Tembo thought of fingertips, experimental, reaching out tentatively. The orange aura flowed into and around the shards. The site went dark momentarily.

His heart did a rapid rabbit thump in answer. The ground had stilled. Tembo straightened from the ground again. He narrowed his gaze, drilling his sight into the midnight surroundings. Then the glow began again, duller this time, more red than orange—but that was because it now emanated from the ... thing ... crawling up from the chasm!

More red because the terra-cotta shards hued it—the shards which had been cobbled into a nightmare parody of a horse—a thing which had hooves and pricked ears and even a faint semblance of the artisan's clay harness upon its body, a jigsaw puzzle put together, jammed together, all wrong. It moved like a horse, heaving and digging to pull itself out of the ditch. Its eyes glowed a brilliant crimson, a demon's eyes, and they were fixed on Tembo.

Its clay lips curled back. Light shone from the broken, tile plate-like fixtures which made it. Its ears stayed pricked forward, alert. It heaved itself one last time and gained the lip of the earthen gash, bucking out of the depths. It swayed on its pieced together legs, head down, looking, not to crop grass but to ... what? Graze on human flesh?

Tembo felt himself quivering all over and a sudden heat washed down one thigh. He realized he'd wet himself in the terror which gripped him. The creature snorted, laughing at him, and dark sooty clouds roiled from its nostrils.

Tembo scrambled back a step or two, clutching his flashlight to use as a club if need be. The terra-cotta horse snapped at the air, teeth clicking. The vermilion gaze stayed fixed on him and he could feel its heat, its hunger.

It was *not* alive, it could not be. Yet it seemed to be. And it clip-clopped a step toward him. The orange-red light which bled out of its fragmented pieces grew weaker.

A demon! A demon animated the statue from within. There could be no other explanation. His head throbbed until he thought his own skull would explode. The broken catwalk was to his rear and right. He could run only to the left, but already the demon horse had taken a step toward the left, head down, watching him.

Prepared to cut him off if he tried to bolt.

It wanted him. It *needed* him. Tembo tried to swallow, felt dust in his throat. He coughed. The phlegm he spat out he could not see, but he could have sworn it would be as red as the terracotta clay which faced him. "Go away," he said. His voice sounded weak and spindly.

The horse demon pawed the ground. It snapped teeth at him again, swinging its head up. He smelled its breath then, heavy with carrion and foul decay. Tembo let out a squeak and then clamped his own mouth shut lest the demon try to steal his breath.

He felt nailed to the dirt. The hot crimson stare of the beast followed closely as he inched his way to the left a shuffle at a time. One shuffle. Another. Pain lanced through his left hip. He sucked his breath in sharply. The horse's eyes flared as though feeling and enjoying his agony. It swung about and stomped a step closer to him. Its carrion smell hung heavily in the air. He tried to hold his breath.

Pain watered his eyes and he dug at them with a dirty fist. But through the watery blur he could see the unmistakable dimming of the light which burst through the horse's many seams. The farther away from the ditch, the dimmer it got. Its power, whatever it was, came from below.

Tembo took a deep breath, trying not to feel the hurt of his ribs. He steeled himself to run, run as far and fast as he could. He flicked on the flashlight and shone it away, into the dark recess of the dig, away from the silent, strangely menacing army which watched him struggle with the demon horse.

The horse struck abruptly, like a snake uncoiling. Its teeth met with a shock upon the barrel of the flashlight and yanked. Tembo fought to keep it from being pulled from his hand. He tugged back with his meager strength and finished with a twist. Clay bits flew as the head of the flashlight came free. The motes halted in midair and slowly wafted back to the toothy smile of the beast.

Tembo bolted. Knowing he had not only his life but his soul to lose, he thrust himself into the dark, his pencil-thin beam his only lifeline. The horse demon made a choking trumpet and lunged after.

His head felt as if it would explode with each jolting step. His feet screamed their bruised flesh and pain. His lungs ached with the greasy, evil rot of his last deep breath. He coughed and wheezed and pumped. His ears sang. He could hear the beast thundering after him. The clay jaws clicked on the air next to his ear, missing. The drumming drew nearer. He would be stomped to death if he faltered. The aura of illumination rose over his shoulder like a sunrise which would bring his execution.

No more cherry blossoms. His caged birds would pass to his careless brother. His hopes of scholarship, dashed. His destiny of taking a bride and fathering children, torn away. His family shadowed by his disgrace, should his body be found here.

But he did not think his body would be found. The demon would consume him, bones, gristle, and all. Not even his torn and dusty peasant's coat would be left.

As if in answer to his thoughts, something grabbed his shoulder and bit, hard, fabric tearing away as he staggered and swerved. Tembo sprinted with renewed terror. His heart felt as if it would explode with every step. He could not hear for the roaring in his head.

The earth moved again. It reared up under his faltering steps, sending him to the ground. He rolled as it jolted sharply. The demon horse plowed to a halt and reared, hooves flailing the air, coming down to crush him. The crevice behind him, now opening clear across the hall of the site, the crevice which glowed orange into the night, closed abruptly with the earthquake's movement. The terra-cotta horse collapsed simultaneously, in pieces and dust upon his feet.

Tembo lay trembling for long moments. Finally his gasping grew quiet and he sat again, looking at the mound of broken clay. His shoulder ached where the beast had marked him with its inanimate teeth. His body ached where the dance of the earth had pounded him. He put the palm of his hand to his jaw.

What had his meddling loosed? What had he done?

Tembo sat, his flashlight across his thighs, and felt the dark sooty cloud of evil welling up in the night. Possibilities crowded through his mind, superstitions of his parents and grandparents and theories of his professors. Two worlds halved him.

He did not know which he would answer to when he returned to see what lay beneath the emperor's army. He only knew he would return. It was as if the horse had snatched up his soulstring and he, puppetlike, must dance to it.

He would return.

Chapter 7

Tam Chen had been Victor Jue's man for so long that he'd almost ceased to think of himself as a separate entity. His devotion to Victor extended far beyond the loyalty of a paycheck. If a paycheck were all he needed, he had long ago earned his law degree and passed the state bar. He had financial possiblities vastly greater than that of business manager to a restaurateur. But Victor was more than that, and Tam was but one of the many shadows he cast, and all of the legions of shadows owed Victor much.

Which was why Tam was determined that the tong would not bother Victor again. He did not know which hand bothered them, but he had a fair idea, and also knew it would be useless to negotiate at this point. A demonstration of equal power would be in order. It irritated him that such a thing needed to be done, that the members of the branch of tong which he suspected were all, like himself, American born, and should value what their birthright had given them and not hinder Victor in his workings. But the tong was greedy, the illegal smuggling of immigrants had always meant money, and the tong was not willing to share.

It did not matter that what Victor did was humanitarian. It saw only the lost revenues. It did not care that Victor sweated day by day to see that Hong Kong, when freed, would cast itself free of China as well. That also meant lost revenue from the darker paths the tong traveled.

Tam—meant to have been born Tom, but his mother's crabbed English handwriting had been misinterpreted at the crucial time—Chen sat at the cold marble bar of the Jade Pheasant, idly sketching his thoughts on a bar napkin. The front door opened a slit, late afternoon sun flooding in, and then closed. Before Tam's dazzled eyes could adjust, the newcomer stood at his elbow.

"Mr. Chen?"

The voice of Victor's friend and good customer El Harper sounded out of the dazzlement. Chen gave a thin smile and bowed his head. "Victor is out just now, Mr. Harper."

"I know. He asked me to drop this by. He said he'd like to take a second look at it."

A handkerchief-wrapped object was placed on the bar next to Chen's napkin battle plan. He hastily disposed of the one and picked up the other. He slipped it in his pocket with another nod. "I'll give it to Victor when he comes in."

"Thanks." The lank man smiled to second his gratitude and left. The lowering sun blazed his silhouette for a moment on Tam's sight. Then his thoughts went back to his plans for the evening, object forgotten in his sharkskin suit. Chen thought of himself more as a barracuda than a shark, teeth just as deadly, but even more difficult to detect amid the reefs and treacherous barriers of the underworld. Tonight he would threaten. In three days, he would strike.

Susan closed Il Mode with a sigh born of relief and an effort to blow sweat-plastered bangs from her forehead. The late June day heat was stifling in the shop, something seemed to be wrong with the air conditioner so she'd shut it down, and she did not feel she could deal with any more crises that day. Whatever had gone right with the Lerner deal she'd paid for with a multitude of other events going wrong. The dining set had not been delivered and the person who'd called to guarantee it was suddenly unavailable for comment. The Alexander Carpet mills had sent a nasty overdue notice and cut off a necessary shipment for a job Angelo had scheduled, and the shop phone machines were overflowing with nearly indecipherable messages, thanks to something garbaging their systems.

She sat down at her Duncan Phyfe desk, its mahogany surfaced skritch-scratched from years of work, her papers scattered across it. She'd always meant to get her desk refinished. Now she hadn't time or money . . . and no place to put all her work if they took her desk away. Her neck was stiff and her head hurt. She leaned on an elbow, massaging one ache and then the other.

Putting out fires, Geoff had called it, when he'd run across trouble. Today there were so many hot spots she scarcely knew where to turn and all of them, save one, Angelo's accounts. His earnings, her time and effort. She began to sort the mail into piles. Overdue shipments, overdue bills, overly impatient clients. . . . Those stacks sorted and put aside, she began to work on the answering machines, playing the tapes over and over until she had garnered sense from most of them. Both machines, her number and Angelo's number, had run amok. She had no idea what could have set them off, perhaps a temporary power brownout, but she knew that it would be easier to invest in a new machine than to have these repaired, unless it was a simple matter of exchanging worn tapes for new ones. Angelo would use the trouble as an excuse to pitch for voice mail again, but she detested the system. Il Mode still had a small, intimate touch and voice mail would obliterate that.

Immersed in the garbled, ghostly voices, she did not hear the intruder until his warm hands were on her neck.

Susan let out a scream, followed closely by Angelo's surprised holler. She twisted in her chair as her partner hopped up and down, protesting, "You scared me! I come in offering a neck rub and you scream like a *bruja*."

"I . . . scared you?" She gasped for breath. "Oh, God. Don't ever do that to me again!" She grabbed a sheaf of papers and began to fan her face.

Angelo laughed. He perched on the corner of his own desk, handsome and insufferably male-looking in his Latino way, his thick blue-black curls brushed back, their bounty touching the open collar of his polo shirt. "No matter. We should have the *policia* here in a minute, the way you screamed. I thought you heard me come in!"

"Not the way I was concentrating." She made an effort to compose herself. "How was Vegas?"

"Hot and cruel, as always." Angelo wrinkled his face. Strictly temporary, the lines fled abruptly except for several creases around his eyes. Asphalt eyes, she thought, like a newly poured street, eyes that would take you on a journey somewhere deep and dark. Geoff had been jealous of Angelo when she'd first started working with him part-time. Neither of them knew then that the jealousy would be unnecessary but the job would become crucial. Like many in the decorating business, Angelo's proclivities ran in another direction. He tapped the cleft of his chin. "Keep frowning at me like that and you'll have wrinkles, *carita*."

"You left me with Mrs. Lerner."

He lifted a shoulder and let it drop eloquently. "It's a long drive. I would not have made it in time. You did well enough, didn't you?"

"I did. Once I wiped the egg off my face. You

didn't tell me this was a gratis job! And we've overdue bills you told me you'd handle. And don't give me that shrug. I can't pay my bills on your charm."

"Ah." Angelo looked down at his desk, along the line of his muscular thigh, enclosed by sleek white summer pants. "I did forget to mention that, didn't I?"

Susan gathered her frayed nerves. "Angelo, your time is yours and mine is mine. But I've spent most of the day tying up your loose ends. That means that neither of us is making money."

He looked up. "Don't raise your voice at me. You brought this all on yourself. There was nothing that could not have waited until tomorrow, no? Not even Mrs. Lerner, if you had insisted."

"Well . . ." she hesitated. "That's true enough, but—"

He put up a palm. "Susan, you borrow trouble. The world will still turn if you stop twirling it around, eh? Next time, let it lie."

Lie to fester, she thought. She took another deep breath. "I can't. That's my part of the partnership, evidently, to mop up what you've spilled. If I didn't have to borrow trouble, you didn't have to go to Vegas."

"Ah. So that is your problem. I got a day off to play and you didn't. I will make it up to you, *carita*. As soon as we've caught up with the bills." He quirked a brow. "Perhaps you need a weekend with a beautiful boy, just like I do, eh?"

She sighed. It was almost impossible to stay angry with him. He swung his legs off the desk and stood up. "But the bills. . . ."

His eyes flashed. "We're creators, you and I! That's why neither of us works buried deep in files and some stuffy huge company. Breathe deep. Lose that creativity, stifle yourself and me, and we both lose the freedom." He glared at her, daring her to say one word more, to utter one more syllable of protest about the unfairness of the partnership.

She shut her mouth tightly. She knew better than to argue further with Angelo in this mood. She stood. "In that case," she said. "I need fresh air. I've appointments tonight." She grabbed up her purse and brushed past him to the rear door, where her car was parked in the back lot.

He called after. "And then tomorrow we'll make sense out of the chaos, eh? You can go charging in and slay whatever dragons you want and I'll hold Mrs. Lerner's hand."

The back door banged shut on his last words, but Susan smiled in spite of herself. She could not stay mad at him, a Latino Peter Pan, whose normal good humor had buoyed her up more times than she wanted to remember.

And, no, she had no desire to be buried in some huge, stuffy company, wearily shuffling papers. Charm or not, Angelo knew which of her buttons to push, she thought ruefully as she swung into her car, and never had he hesitated to push any of them. She cursed herself for being afraid to push back.

She was still worrying about Angelo when she got home. Domino met her at the front door, pretending she was an intruder, letting his back ruffle and his already plumed tail fluff out suddenly, before arching his back to rub against her ankle as she kicked off her shoes. One sailed by his silently flat nose and he ignored it with Persian aplomb, a heritage from his father's side of the cat tree. She looked at the time and let out a muffled "Damn."

Poppa Irving answered her call with a, "Don't worry. Am I going anywhere without you? Then all right. Take your time. I'll be here," when she phoned to tell him she was late.

No sooner had she hung up than the instrument vibrated under her palm with a ringthrough. Maida's brisk voice said accusingly, "Where are you? We're all here at Steamers waiting for you."

The click and bustle of a busy restaurant was evident in the background. "Damn," Susan answered. She flexed her stockinged feet. She'd forgotten the council meeting. No one had ever asked her if the scheduling had been convenient for her.

"You forgot," Maida said. Her voice was slightly flat, atonal, part of her inheritance of her husband's New York accent. She raised her voice and Susan knew the next remark was directed at Sid and the others. "She forgot." Then, "How long will it take you to get here?"

"I'm not coming. Poppa's waiting for me now." In her mind's eye, she could see Maida's elegantly manicured hand at her throat, one finger loosely entwined in a loop of pearls. "I've found someone I think can help, someone who knows about the methane and the fires and . . ."

"Susan, dear," her mother-in-law answered. "If it wasn't that, it would be something else. He's an old man. You can't treat his fears like they were rational. We have to do something."

Susan steeled herself. "Mai, I'm not coming. I've made an appointment with someone who's very busy. Please, just have a pleasant dinner with everybody and we'll have a council in a few days, when I know a little more. Please?"

A sigh. "Sid, she's got an expert. I don't know, somebody who knows about gas . . . what, should I know what she has in mind? Sid wants to talk to you, dear," and the phone abruptly changed hands.

"You're letting Poppa manipulate you," Sid boomed in her ear. "You can't do that. You've a life of your own."

No, she didn't. Through the phone lines, she heard something she would never have heard talking directly to Sid Aronson, a subtle tone of fear. What was he afraid of?

Sid pressed. "He cries wolf and you listen. You can't do that, Susan."

"Why not?"

"I know my own father."

She realized that he didn't, or at least, not as well as he thought he did. Or maybe he knew he didn't, and that was not fear she heard, but guilt. The times when one could catch Sid Aronson off balance were few and far between. She said hastily, "I'm late. I'll call you about it as soon as I can," and hung up.

Sid said something, inaudible, sundered in mid-syllable as she put the phone down.

Domino had taken up residence at her feet and was grooming her nylons. He evidently liked the raspy feel of the material against his tongue. "It's a late dinner for you," she said. With an "ugh," she put her moist foot back into her shoes, ran a comb through her hair, and bolted out the door. With light traffic on this early summer evening, she just might make the restaurant on time.

Tam Chen found the narrow street, with its frame and stuccoed houses, gang graffiti abundant upon flat surfaces everywhere, small yards fenced in with chain link. Not clean, no, the gutters full of refuse both human and inorganic. The stink of asphalt rose in the heat. His nose wrinkled slightly. His American-born Chinese grandmother would have been appalled by the filth. For that matter, any of his family would. But this was a gang neighborhood in Monterey Park, the leading edge of a plague crowding that city, as it did almost all cities within the L.A. basin. Would that the next earthquake opened up a giant crevice, he thought, and sucked them all down.

He wore his gun on the inside of his jacket,

where its flat line was barely perceptible due to the excellent cut of the suitcoat. He touched it now, to make sure it was secure and yet easily pulled, as he moved into the shadows of the garage off the alleyway. The shadows were long, but sunset was still an hour away. He would wait.

But there was a chorus of voices inside the garage. The door must be up and the young men crowded inside, working. He winced at the sound of harsh Chinese, slurred and improper, sprinkled liberally with English gang slang. Not even a proper tong, this bunch. Tam licked dry lips. It would be that much easier to impress them and teach them a lesson. He and Victor wanted no interference. After the bloody Fourth Year riots at Tiananmen Square, there was a new flood of students and others preparing to travel the pathway they had prepared to freedom. He wanted the tong to keep their hands off. His younger brother was even now in Hong Kong, smoothing the way. For his brother's safety, and the safety of all their plans, this must be done.

Tam listened. He smiled a thin, wolfish smile. He was in luck. They were building incendiary devices, the crude tools of their trade. He would not only impress them, he would wipe out their inventory at the same time. That could set them back weeks. He listened to their rough talk and savored his own sardonic humor.

As he leaned his shoulder against the stucco garage, the heat of the building infiltrated to his flank. Shadowed now, this slab of stucco must have taken the full brunt of the afternoon sun. He put a palm to it. The rough textured cement coating was cool to his hand. Tam frowned. Why then did his jacket and hip grow so warm?

A shout inside the building. In Chinese and then strident English. "Fire! Fire!"

Tam took a few strides backward, into a massive lantana that grew wild at the fringe of the alleyway, and squatted in its dusty embrace. The shouts of fear and amazement increased.

Chen decided that something had gone terribly wrong inside the garage and so retreated even farther, to a tall, almost weeping willow sized oleander and knelt among its deadly pink flowers. His flank remained hot, as if iron scorched him, but the outpouring of youths from the garage across the way drew his attention.

They abandoned the garage with screams of hysteria and, on the heels of the last youth, a massive BOOM sounded and the garage exploded in white-hot flame that tore away Tam Chen's sight.

Tears gushed from his eyes and as he blinked to regain his vision, high calls and shouts followed the explosion. He could hear the crackle of the flame and a hissing sound which tailed away. The stink of sulfur and brimstone filled his nostrils, obliterating the dusty sweetness of the oleander. He dug fingers into his eyes and prayed that he was not blind, that he would not be found here, to the disgrace of all of Victor Jue's plans.

A moaning, trembling call cut through the smoke and flame and debris. Not all the tong had gotten out in time. He could smell the burned flesh.

His sight came back in blurry outlines and that was enough for Tam. He withdrew from the oleander, backing away through those who now began to fill the alley, not watching him, but pushing and shoving to see what had happened.

Inside the safety of his car, he brushed dried cobwebs and oleander leaves from his blue-black hair. He looked at himself in the narrow rearview mirror. The tears had left tracks on his face. He grimaced at this weakness. He put a hand to his flank, which still felt warm. A hole in the fabric met his touch. He pulled up the suit jacket and stared in astonishment. The handkerchief wrapped artifact, forgotten, fell from the seared pocket with a clunk. He put his fist through the hole, its edges curled and crispy black as if torched.

The object within the plain white handkerchief had its cuneiform writing and remnant of a seal burned in sharp black outline upon the white linen. Tam touched it with trembling fingertips.

Heat lingered in it.

What was it? And what did it have to do with the fire and explosion within the garage? He traced the brand on the handkerchief. He was not a superstitious man, but now he wished he had listened more closely to his grandmother and her tales of the Chinese gods and demons. Here was something Cal Tech could never explain. He put the car in gear and drove away in the other direction as sirens began to wail. He had been told to put the object into Victor's hands and the sooner the better.

Chapter 8

"So tell me," Poppa Irving said. "What sort of dinner is this?"

Susan glided the car through street traffic. She thought a moment. "Well, this dinner is mainly an accident."

"An accident? You want me to give up brisket and mashed potatoes at Norm's for an Italian dinner that will probably give me heartburn all night *on accident?*"

She felt herself smiling. "Give me a break, Poppa. I had a chance for a date and I took it."

"So why'd you bring me along?" He looked over at her, eyes shining over his proud nose. "You need me like an extra hole in the head. So who is this guy, anyway?"

"A friend. Someone who offered to help."

Poppa settled in the car seat. "You can always use friends." He sniffed, as if reserving his judgment for the value of the dinner host's friendship. "So where'd you meet him?"

"At the tar pits."

"At the tar pits?" Irving echoed, in New Yorkese astonishment.

"Yes."

"If only we'd known," Poppa muttered. "We could have met a nice someone there sooner. The tar pits? The deli, the laundromat, I can see—"

"I do my laundry at home. What are you complaining about? It's a free meal."

"A free meal with heartburn, I can do without." Her passenger stopped looking at her and looked out the window at the traffic. It had begun to ease up. They wouldn't be too awfully late.

"You won't get heartburn! I promise. If you lay off the garlic bread." She finessed a lane change and saw the restaurant sign two blocks down. "We're almost there."

"So who is this miracle man?"

"El Harper. He promised me some answers to some very important questions." She pressed her lips into a thin line of silence and Irving knew he would get no more out of her.

But he never knew he'd given himself away. "We could have met a nice someone sooner . . ."

With the tiniest of smiles, despite being twenty minutes late, Susan pulled into the parking lot.

El passed up waiting at the bar. He wanted all his wits about him when Susan and her grandfather-in-law, if he remembered correctly, joined them. The dinner reservations were bogged down and their tardiness didn't bother him. He knew what street traffic could

be like at seven o'clock on a summer evening.
He leaned against a Roman pillar in the lobby
entrance and occasionally jousted with a phil-
odendron leaf which seemed determined to
wander down from its post and caress his forehead from time to time. Behind him in the
atrium, a small fountain trickled into its basin,
reminding him that he was thirsty. He had almost given up on them when he saw a flash of
peach and dusty rose at the doorway, accompanied by a slight, fierce-looking older man. He
straightened immediately and told the hostess
his party had arrived.

Susan had changed from her austere business
dress of the day into a sundress of peach and
rose with a little jacket over the strapped bod-
ice. She looked fresh and cool. The older man
who accompanied her wore a black suit so worn
its threads were shiny and there were three
straight pins lined up in a row on its cuff. Neither Irving or Susan seemed to notice them and
so El said nothing. Either a mortician or a tailor, he thought, as they all sat.

Over the menu, Irving put up a knobby finger.
"Do not have the Caesar salad," he warned.
"Raw eggs are bad for you."

El gave him a fond look which he promptly
hid behind the menu board. Susan looked
around to see if any of the waiters had heard,
then ducked her head as well. Irving snagged a
waitress going by with a tray of hot cheese
bread, made scone style. He pressed a five dol-

lar bill into her hand. "And a basket of bread sticks, too," he said. "While we're waiting. That way if you forget us, we won't starve." He looked over his menu at them. "You can't take the New York out of me," he said in challenge.

"Who would want to?" El Harper answered, laying his menu down on the table. "You may have saved us from certain death. I've eaten here before and the service is leisurely. But the food is good," he added appreciatively about his hot scone.

Susan leaned forward. "Poppa, you don't even know if that girl is going to be our waitress."

He shrugged, and answered with a twinkle in his eyes, "If she isn't, she'll take our table anyway. You'll see." He made a mouth. "I wonder how the veal is."

"Tender," El reassured. "Like it's supposed to be."

A basket of warm bread sticks appeared along with the young woman and a broad smile. She took Poppa Irving's order cheerfully while Susan scanned her menu a moment longer. El paused, saw that Susan wasn't quite ready and gave his order, precisely. "And I want the pasta naked, the sauce and cheese on the side, all right?" The waitress nodded, undaunted and looked to Susan who ordered chicken marsala.

El waited until the girl had gone before responding to the question in Susan's eyes. He touched his throat, at his open-necked shirt. "Heart surgery," he said. "I have to watch the fats and calories. Putting everything on the side cuts down a lot."

She hadn't noticed the scar, but now she saw the purple-blue mark under his fingertips. Her stomach went queasy as she realized the scar probably stretched from his neck all the way down to his navel. But he was so young, and then she blushed as she realized part of what she'd thought she'd said aloud.

"It's not the wear and tear," El answered easily. "A minor birth defect. They tell me it's the kind of thing not usually detected until too late. Like the college athlete who suddenly drops dead. So I'm all patched up, good as new, with a hundred thousand mile warranty. But it's not the kind of thing you want to go through again, so now I'm careful about the other stuff as well." The lines in his face crinkled as he smiled at her.

Susan saw the expression in his eyes and knew as clearly as if he'd told her, he didn't trust his warranty. She saw the fear of his own mortality and knew the reason for the underlying streak of sadness this man carried, the Lincolnesque streak young Nina had characterized so clearly. It wasn't the structure of his face, though he was a tall, gaunt man. It was the fatalism underneath his expression. She looked away quickly before he thought she was staring.

"Young people shouldn't die," Poppa said suddenly. Then he cleared his throat. Susan covered his hand, found it trembling under hers, and gave it a warm squeeze.

"My husband," she explained to El, who now looked puzzled, "died very unexpectedly in a car accident."

"Ah," he said. "I'm very sorry," to both of them.

Poppa nodded gruffly. "It happens." He looked across the garden room of the Italian restaurant, gaily bedecked in red, white, and green. "And it shouldn't."

"Does this have anything to do with what you needed my help on?"

Susan shook her head, saying, "Not exactly," but Poppa interrupted her. "I know what sudden death is," he said. He pushed up his suitcoat sleeve, unbuttoned his well starched cuff and rolled it back to expose the crude numbers tattooed on his forearm.

Sid and Maida had tried, any number of times, to convince him to have the tattoo removed. But Poppa Irving had staunchly refused to and now he displayed it like a badge of courage.

El nodded. "I understand," he said, and there was such a depth in his voice that Susan, with a flooding feeling, dared hope that he did. Harper put his arms upon the table, leaning forward. "Let's talk about the gas."

Victor Jue leaned on his desk, green shade lamplight the only illumination in the room, and looked at his second set of accounting books, the set of books which contained all his hopes for his projects. The money which had been carefully culled had finally amassed to figures of importance, needed for important work. He heard the click of the door behind him and did not stir until a slender shadow fell across his pages. Tam Chen smelled of herbs, and smoke, and subtly of wild flowers, and Victor wondered where he had been.

"The tong," Tam said quietly, "should not bother us for a while. Not that bunch, anyway."

Victor looked up. Reed thin, barracudalike, Chen stared back. "You did," Victor said carefully, "nothing illegal, I hope."

Tam only inclined his head in answer.

"Good."

"They did it to themselves," Chen said, suddenly garrulous. "You'll probably see it on the eleven o'clock news, if you care to watch." He reached in his pocket and extracted a bundle wrapped in white linen. "I suggest you be most careful with this. What it is, I do not know . . . but," and he laid out the artifact, with the char-branded handkerchief straightened next to it. His fingertip brushed the insignia and then its twin seared into the fabric. "They were manufacturing pipe bombs, crude devices, and a sudden combustion among their materials caused a very damaging explosion."

Victor had his hand upon the linen, drawing it into the spotlight of his lamp, and looked up in shock. "You were caught in it?" Now he saw the scorched hole gaping in Tam's right side pocket and he smelled the smoke more strongly.

"No. And if I did not know better, I would suppose that this—" and Chen jabbed his index nail at the clay tablet—" had something to do with the combustion. How I don't know . . . but I was on fire before the tong was."

Victor's hand shook, but he continued drawing the linen into bright light. He traced one of the signs. "Great evil," he said. And another. "Great hope. What has El Harper brought me?"

Chapter 9

Victor pored over the artifact again, rubbing his eyes, blinking them to rid them of exhaustion, and not finding the action much use. Tam had long since left, keeping to his own hours, bored by Victor's scholarship.

He eyed the surface under his hand magnifying glass. A porcelain tablet, of poorer quality, made by the masters of fine china. *We had to start somewhere.* Victor thought, as he sat back in his chair and stretched to ease his back muscles. But if it was a forerunner of the kiln's ultimate artistry in, say, the 1400s, then it was old. Very old. Far older than Chinese ancestry in Los Angeles.

What had El gotten hold of? Was this something stolen from a museum? He found it hard to believe. El was many things, perhaps even a hesitant man since his surgery, but Victor's friend was not a thief. Never a thief. But gullible perhaps. Yes. Perhaps someone had stuck him with guardianship of this until a black market collector could be found.

And the pity of it was this was only half, perhaps even only a third, of the complete tablet. Victor added to that pity his inability to decode the writing other than two symbols which had not changed much through time. He could bring it to the attention of another scholar, but that might endanger El since the tablet's origin would then be questioned. It would take time, which he had precious little of these days since the bloody Fourth Anniversary, but for El, he would make it.

He traced a character, the cuneiform slashes in the tablet imitating a fluid brush stroke. Classical Chinese form had changed very little in the two thousand years since the Ch'in dynasty when Huang had standardized it shortly after proclaiming himself first emperor.

The strangeness of the item made him wonder. He could not discount Tam's story because his assistant was not given to the fanciful. But neither could Victor understand what might have happened. How could this simple tablet give off enough heat to burn its ideograms into its handkerchief wrapping? Or ignite objects through a stucco garage wall?

He would have to start with translation. That would bring the beginning of what he needed to understand. With a sigh, Victor got up from his chair and desk and went to the book-lined wall. He browsed in the dim corner, picking out three volumes. His slim hand hesitated over the fourth, then finally he drew it off the shelf: *Mysteries of Ancient China*. He already had an enigma. He wasn't sure if he wanted a mystery.

He reseated himself and opened the first book. *So we begin again,* he said to himself, and began to read.

Poppa sat back and watched the man watching his granddaughter-in-law. He was used to men watching her, he himself looked at her with appreciation, but he was not used to her looking back. She had not done that in years. So he put his chin up, wary of this stranger, who listened to his tale of his youth and horror but who, he felt sure, had not really heard. In turn, he had heard the young man's story of his father losing his favorite clothing store. It had been told impersonally, but Irving did not hear it impersonally. He'd known that man for many, many years. He'd even done alterations for him when his own tailor had too much work or had been ill. Now there was nothing. No business. Zilch. As if it had never been.

"So we're not talking flashback here?" Harper asked.

"No, no," Susan said hastily, but Irving himself did not answer. He merely looked back.

"I mean," pushed El, "you're not trading one experience for another?"

"And if I did, what would you do with me?"

Harper gave a thoughtful blink. "Perhaps counseling. There's a Holocaust Center in town. I'm sure they'd know of someone ... but if not. ... Well, if not, I don't know what more I can tell you. A methane lake is pooled under that part of town. They've drilled to draw away the mounting pressure. It shouldn't happen again. You've nothing to be afraid of."

"So am I crazy?" Irving felt his voice sharpen in intensity and he leaned forward on an elbow, fork stabbed into his veal piccata.

"Poppa," protested Susan.

He frowned at her. "I want to know what this total stranger things. My own family thinks I'm *meshuga*. What does he think?"

"I think," Harper said, "you've had a frightening experience, out of the blue, and it set off echoes of other bad memories. You're perfectly sane to have these unsettling feelings. But I also think that, if someone tells you it's going to be all right, you need to accept and trust that it will."

The two men stared heavily at one another. Poppa felt an unspoken communication between them, but he did not like it. *This* goy *is going to take my Susan away from me*, he thought. *And then who will I have?* He sliced off a bite of the tender veal and jabbed it into his mouth. *Then who will I have?* He waved the empty fork in the air. "That's easy for you to say."

"Yeah." Harper grinned. "Unfortunately, it is. *I* didn't just almost spontaneously combust into nothingness." He choked suddenly, as if he'd remembered something, and Susan pounded his back once or twice.

"Are you all right?"

"Fine," he got out. "Swallowed wrong."

"You shouldn't talk with your mouth full," Irving observed.

Harper looked as if he did not know whether the old man was offering advice or was teasing.

"I think he liked you," Susan said. She'd driven Poppa home and was pleased to see that El had followed her directions and had been parked, waiting for her, in the condo lot. He stood in the villa archway now, as she unlocked her door.

The corner of El's mouth quirked. "Maybe. I don't think I performed much of a rescue. You know, Susan, you might seriously consider some counseling for him."

The lock clicked as she looked sharply back over her shoulder at him, the wounded look on her face cutting across what had been an expression of pleasure. "You think he's crazy."

"There's a wide field between being overly anxious about something and being totally, off-the-wall crazy. We all play in that field from time to time, I think. I know I do. Usually when I'm stuck in gridlock on the 101 at five in the afternoon."

That brought the smile back. The door swung open. Susan stepped in, tripped over something that protested, and the lights went on. A nimbus of illumination haloed her hair as she picked up a rumpled looking cat. He put his ears back, blue eyes in a seal point mask of unhappiness.

El looked down at the beast. *All she's got is*

an old man and a cat, and they both hate me. They think I'm poaching in their territory. What am I doing, sending out signals? He reached out and scratched the cat just under the chin.

The cat made a disgruntled noise and, betrayed by its own pleasure instinct, put its chin up at the same time for easier access. At least he had a chance of winning some part of her family over. He scratched a few more minutes, then moved past Susan into the condo.

"Where is it you want to take me?" Susan asked, after introducing Domino and putting him down. The cat hit with all the delicacy of a forty pound bag of feed and wandered off in search of a quieter sleeping spot. "Give me a hint."

"No, that's cheating. But wear something comfortable. Jogging shoes, if you have them." What was he thinking? This was El Lay. Who didn't own jogging shoes? El looked around the living room. Comfortable, green and strawberry and primary blue country. A little cluttered. He didn't see room to stretch out to watch football, but nice. She'd bucked the Southwest trend and the austere black and white anti-yuppie trend nicely. A woman who decorates after her own heart, he thought, remembering what she did for a living. He put his hands in his pockets.

She came out in old jeans, a hand-painted sweatshirt that looked as if it might have been done by a schoolchild, and joggers that had just enough wear on them to show she could be serious about her exercise. The jeans looked good on her. She had what he thought of as a pert behind. And she looked as if she'd shed some extraneous personality as she bent over to tie her laces. "I assume we're not going dancing."

"Not tonight, anyway."

She straightened after tying the last knot. Her light colored eyes stared at him, assessing him. "Does that mean there'll be another night after tonight?"

He said lightly, "Maybe not. I'm going to show you a bit of my insanity. It could be a tough decision."

"Um," she answered. "Maybe I'll let Poppa make it. Tit for tat."

"Then I'm dead."

"Not necessarily." She grabbed her purse and breezed past him.

The boulevard was never quiet, but most especially not on a summer night. Susan sat beside him in relative silence but he wasn't accustomed enough to her to know whether or not she was at ease. Was this a comfortable silence or was she on edge?

As they neared the museum, her head turned suddenly. She frowned at the pink Mediterranean center on its heavy pillared legs. "That's where the old man died, isn't it?" she asked, as he swung by it to get to the back parking lot. Her head shot back as quickly. "No wonder you choked at dinner. Did you know about it?"

"I was here when they found him. I didn't

even know it was old Digger until they ID'd him from the backpack. He used to mooch off the kids who came to the pits for field trips."

Susan shuddered. Even amid all the area's gang shootings, the strange death of one old man had been unsettling. "They said he'd been torched."

"Combusted is more like it. The tabloids next week will probably say an alien death ray killed him." El turned off the motor. "Want to leave?"

She considered him. Then, "No. If you're not worried, I'm not."

"Well, it's a little like getting struck by lightning. I never had been, and it doesn't seem like much of a danger around here, but if you were to ask Lee Trevino, he'd disagree with you."

She laughed. "How many times has he been hit? Once, twice?"

"I think it's been three times, but that's a golfer's occupational hazard. Still, it can give you pause if you want something to worry about."

She opened her car door. "Like Poppa," she said as she got out. "I think sometimes he wants to have something to worry about."

El got out his police force flashlight. "From what you told me, he doesn't like change. That's why he left the studios, probably, he and his wife. Hollywood types too unstable."

"Maybe." Poppa Irving had told them both stories of when he and his wife had worked for the filmmakers. Sylvie had even sewn for Edith Head, but that was back in the early '50s. They had endured those glory days only long enough to build a nest egg. "You could be right. And that's what unsettles him now. He can't control the changes the fires have done to his business, his home."

"See? A little counseling could help."

She smiled brilliantly. "It could. Thank you, El."

Her expression lit up the night. He put out his hand. "Now come see what changed my life."

They were getting ready to dig at the main pit. Temporary fencing had been set up and the overhead gallery where onlookers watched was also lit. El played the beam over it anyway. "We'll have about a hundred workers in here, off and on, in the next three weeks."

"Why?"

"It's summer. The heat softens the tar enough so the digging's a lot easier. They'll pack all those drums—" and he showed her the metal drums waiting—"Once those are full, they've a year's work ahead of them going through all the artifacts."

"There's a lot?"

He nodded. "The pits have been pulling in unwary prey for about forty thousand years. Dr. Ellington has all he can do with two weeks' work of excavating. Most of it will be small stuff . . . birds maybe, and rats' skulls. Coyotes and wolves. We've enough canine type skulls to fill the museum top to bottom. Most of it is in storage. The summer dig is fun. A lot of students and patrons get to help."

She looked at him. "You helped."

"Yeah. I found a California lion's jawbone. Long as this," and he measured the night between both hands. "Bigger than African lions, they were. Makes you wonder what happened to them."

"And you quit your high-powered executive job for this."

For a moment he almost regretted having shared information with her over dinner. But she'd not dug deep and she had no idea that a Debbie had even existed. So he'd not told her everything. He felt safer. "No. Not exactly." El's chest hurt a moment, but he did not touch it, a gesture that was both comforting and superstitious, like crossing oneself against evil. "I think my job quit me." He leaned on the fencing. "It's just that everything is in layers, like the pits. I felt like peeling things down a bit, to find out what was important and what wasn't."

"And?"

El paused. "I think I'm still peeling."

"And I thought Chippendale's made it look easy." Susan looked away, across the grounds. A sudden night breeze set the eucalyptus trees shivering. Her hair was borne aloft a moment. Then the fencing they both leaned on began to tremble.

She backed off, alert. "What is it?"

He stood, feeling the earth vibrate under his shoe soles. "Quake, I think. Not much of a rumble. Probably an aftershock of the one the other day."

Susan took a quavering breath. "Part of Southern California I just can't get used to."

He took her hand. He could feel the tension in it. "Let me show you 'my' pit."

"You have a pit?"

"Indeed I do." He steered her across the park-like grounds. The grass, as hot and dry as it had been, had collected a faint sheen of dew. It sparkled as they strode across it.

Susan laughed and then put her hand over her mouth to hide it. "Oh, my," she said, as she leaned down.

"It's not the size that counts," he said.

She let out a muffled sound, then said, "I should hope not. It doesn't even rate a fence."

"Well. Most people out here think it's just a tar blob. The joggers skirt it. Maybe a stray bird now and then gets deceived." He leaned over, trying not to feel offended, and skimmed the dirty water over the ebony face below with his outstretched hand. "It's a deceiver. This is where I found my lion jaw."

"Here? Not back there?"

He shook his head.

"Well. Well."

El felt compelled to defend himself. "Under-neath, this was a massive lake and river of tar. This is just the finger of an arm which draws back into," and he gave a jab with his chin in the direction of the main pits.

She looked up impishly. "This is the rough part, isn't it?"

"Rough part?" He suddenly lost her train of thought.

"Debriefing. You don't talk to anybody for years and then suddenly, somewhere, you meet someone you want to know everything and you have to tell them . . . but you don't want to scare them away, you don't want to tell them too much, just in case you've made a mistake and this is the wrong someone to be talking to." Susan straightened. She had her hands on her hips. "I make Jell-O and fudge using only a wooden spoon. My grandmother taught me that one."

He caught her drift. "Really? No plastic, eh. Well, I can only tie a Windsor knot looking in the mirror, because I learned tying my older brother's tie. And my brothers and I all have unusual names .. Calvin and Donovan and I."

Susan grinned again, across the tiny pond of his pit, when the ground began to gurgle. He reached across and grabbed her in sudden, unknowing fear, and brought her to his side.

A mockingbird screamed across Hancock Park from one of the shade trees edging the walkway. The small pit roiled and bubbled like a witches' cauldron and then gave birth. He saw it heaving forth and then bobbing to lie floating upon the waters which grew quiet and deadly still over the tar's surface. He bent down. It was a twin to the piece of tablet he'd found earlier, across the break line, and he knew he'd found the second half. A seal stretched across the edge, prettily wrought in metal with jade embossed in it which came to light as he scratched his nail over it. There was a bit of wax on its underside, which had probably affixed it to the tablet.

"Come on," he said and drew her with him back to the car, where he found a can of WD-40 in the cluttered trunk and cleaned the seal off. It lay upon his palm like an ancient coin with a slot in it to carry upon a purse string. The tablet he would take to Victor. The seal he strung upon the cord he had in his pocket, the pretty feather accompanying it. It looked like a talisman as he held it out, stretched between his hands. It had no value, except for its prettiness, but he wanted to give it to her. "To keep you safe from things that go bump in the night."

Susan bowed her head and let him drop the necklace around her neck. She fingered the coin and eyed it in the moonlight. "Even blind dates?"

"They'd have to be pretty blind not to see you're a lovely woman."

"Woman," she repeated. "I was a girl when I met Geoff." She sighed. She wrapped her fingers about the seal. "Thank you."

"It's nothing. Victor and I think it's probably a Chinese laundry ticket from the 1870s or some such."

She laughed. "And who's Victor?"

"Let me save this one for . . . talking over expresso?"

"Yes. That sounds nice."

He held the car door open, thinking that Debbie had never liked expresso and she had never been what he could classify as fully grown. He liked that thought as he got back in the car.

Back in the night, Victor Jue stretched restlessly and a chill stirred the back of his neck, as if some quiet voice whispered in his ear that his name was being spoken. He set aside his heavy books, thinking. Of the some ten thousand ideograms, Victor had forgotten far more than he had remembered. It would take some time for him to refresh his memory, and the task of translating the tablet clearly was insurmountable without its other fragments. But the ideograms which spoke loudest to him, he should never have forgotten.

Great evil and great hope. If he were correct, an incantation perhaps even reaching from a time beyond the birth of Christ. How El had gotten the tablet was no longer the question. How much danger he could be in possessing it now nagged at Victor. What had happened to Tam Chen and would it threaten Harper as well?

Chapter 10

The wallpaper of the tiny apartment was yellow-stained, from years of the nicotine smoke which had eventually killed the seamstress and forced the tailor to abstain from one of the few vices he enjoyed. At night, the wallpaper harbored a twilight glow in the meager lamplight, and it issued its faint cigarette perfume, so that Irving could almost feel the presence of his lost Sylvie. He took small comfort from it. At his age, he was glad for even small comforts. Waking up in the morning was a comfort. Falling asleep promptly at night without too much heartburn was a comfort. *Go for the gusto*, he thought, as he padded about the apartment in his mule slippers. *Slip-slip*, the noise of his shuffling like the flow of years.

It seemed like only yesterday Sylvie had sat at the breakfast table with him, her old chenille robe wrapped about her birdlike frame, her hair yellow-white with age, complaining about the wallpaper. "Irving, we need to strip that paper. It makes me nauseous. I've looked at it so long."

"So we'll strip it," he'd answered. "What do you want to put up instead?"

"Nothing fancy, Just comfortable. I'll pick something out," she'd answered, surprised by his sudden capitulation.

But the job had never been done. Her various aches and pains had suddenly coalesced into a fatal illness and she'd weakened quickly once she'd discovered it. Lots of people lived years and years with emphysema, but not his Sylvie. It was almost as though she needed an excuse to fly to heaven. In the hospital, fading quickly, she'd looked at him one last time and said clearly, "I never did get the wallpaper stripped."

He'd put his callused hand over her forehead. "I'll take care of it," he'd told her.

But he never had. Like Sylvie, slip-slipping away, time and effort were eluding him. He gave up smoking, although it was too late for his dear wife, but he kept the paper. It reminded him of her.

He sat at the breakfast table, patiently slicing up a bagel the way some men did apples, chewing a piece and readying the next bite, thinking about Susan and her new boyfriend. Susan was the only ally he had against the march of time. Without her, Sid and Maida would yank him up by the roots and put him in one of those retirement condos, which weren't even as roomy as this old apartment. In those places everything was plastic and the only view was of the neighbor's garage. No cars, just golf carts allowed. A nurse on twenty-four hour call. Meals in the cafeteria. He'd have to get a pass to leave. Under Sid's and Maida's thumbs day and night. He'd half-reared Geoff, but no kids were allowed in those places. He knew it. The thought of them raised what little hair he had left on his head.

As if he didn't have enough trouble in his life, now he had to sit up and ponder this Elmore Harper. It had been inevitable, perhaps that Susan had gone back to her own kind, he thought. God knew that Sid and Maida and even his other daughter Naomi had not welcomed a *shiksa* into their family with open arms. But the girl had been an angel, an absolute angel, and she'd made Geoff happy. Stern, tight-lipped Geoff who'd weathered the bad years of his parents' marriage like a soldier in an undeclared war. For those years of happiness alone, Irving adored Susan. And he'd cried when the end had come, all too soon, all too unexpectedly.

Irving sighed and carved off a last piece of bagel. He stuffed it into his mouth, chewing on the side which bothered him least. He got up and shuffled around the kitchen, looking for a bag to put the remainder in. He would have a full bag of trouble to take to bed. Trouble instead of company. He sighed again. Maybe he should get a cat.

He thought of the plump, dumb furbag Susan kept and laughed at himself. He should have a cat? He turned off the lights and made his way to bed by memory, kicked off his mules and tucked himself in. As he always did, he said goodnight to the silent spirit of his wife, who had occupied the right side of the bed where he never slept, not even to this day.

His heavy breathing faded to a mild snore, then a deeper, unconscious snore. His body drifted into the mild paralysis of deep sleep.

Then, as he traveled into fear, his old gnarled hand began to twitch.

He awoke, bolt upright in the bed, sweat streaming from his seamed face, his jaws stretched in a silent scream. He brought his shaking hands to his face, mopped the sweat away, and said, "Susan."

The fires came not for him, but for her.

Imprinted against his retinas was the image of her, surrounded by flames, calling, crying for him to save her. He could feel the sheets of heat, hear the crackle of flame and glass bursting under the pressure of the fire, smell the wood, the metal bubbling, the flesh about to be branded. He'd answered but she could not hear him, could not see through the smoke and flame to know which way to turn.

Irving took a deep, shuddering breath. In his dream, he'd known how to save her.

Her only hope was for him to find out what he'd known in his dream.

Her only hope.

Chou came early to his job as janitor at Xian, puffing in the muggy heat even in the purple of dawn, his child on his back. The young girl slept despite the bicycling motion of her father, a man old enough to be her grandfather, and he marveled at her tiny mysteries. Toy Moon, he'd named her, because her face was as round and brilliant as a new moon. Also because it did not hurt to invoke the goddess of the moon to keep away his wife's weaknesses.

Chou knew himself to be a fortunate man. His first wife and children swept away by treacherous summer floods, he had been lucky enough to marry a second time, a sweet, young village girl. And he had been able to obtain this job working at the emperor's tomb, where the longnoses came to gawk, the Americans and French, British and others, to gape like idiots and drop money if they felt awed enough about what they saw. He had been even more blessed when his wife told him she was expecting. But his fragile wife, malleable to anyone's will, had cowered under the anger of the neighborhood grandmother whose job it was to preach birth control for the government. Chou had had his children. It did not matter that none had lived.

Unluckily for Chou, his second wife did not have the grit his first wife had had. Luckily for Chou, she had knuckled under as quickly to pressure from him, threats of daily beatings and displeasure if she got the abortion being offered her. And then Toy Moon had been born, beautiful, precious, perfect.

He did not trust his second wife with her care and keep. Slavery of unwanted girl children was a dark secret in China. He knew of whispered rumors that families had disposed of unwanted young girls, of children beyond quota. He did not trust his second wife not to bow to the criticism and sell their child away. So whenever he felt her weaken, he took Toy Moon with him. It was not a disastrous thing to do. The tourists liked to take pictures with her, cooing over her china doll prettiness, clothed in peasant garb. The extra money Chou made he pocketed and kept hidden from his second wife. When old enough, Toy Moon would go away to school.

There had been many rock slides along the roadway, like hump-backed monsters waiting in the predawn, and Chou guessed that the quake which had awakened him during the night had been much stronger near the site. He churned his legs and brought his bicycle skillfully around the obstacles. He would have to call for help in clearing the road.

He steered his bicycle into the workers' rack and left it. Toy Moon stirred and made a tiny noise at his shoulder. He kept her in her wrapping until he was inside the building. A cloud of darkness denied the lavender sky lightening outside. Chou paused, his hand on the light switches. He could see that part of the catwalk must have come down, its partial silhouette at the building's far end. He turned the lights on, fearing to see the terra-cotta army in pieces, his livelihood smashed by the spiteful dance of the earth.

One statue had fallen. He saw no other damage. Chou's impassive face allowed a twinge of a smile. He knelt down and unslung his three-year-old daughter. She did a dance upon the earth, too, reaching up for him, wanting to be back in his arms. He hushed her. He dare not take her with him into the office area where he must use the phone. If his superiors heard her prattling voice, he could be in much trouble. He sat her down upon the ground and gave her his keys to play with. He would be right back. Chou straightened and made his way across the grounds to the interior offices.

The child sat for a moment, jangling her father's keys. Then, with rump in the air, hands to the ground, she paused before standing up. She looked about with a toddler's curiosity.

The earth quivered. A bird caught inside the large structure gave a cry and winged across the expanse before disappearing among the girders. The unnatural light threw dark, blade-sharp shadows behind the emperor's clay army. The tremor was not enough to unfoot the youngster, but she hesitated, eyes growing large in her round face.

Toy Moon watched as the ground opened, ever so slightly, and a sullen red light began to creep out, creep forward. It looked like fireworks, a fountain of sparks and darkness, bubbling first slowly, then swiftly across the floor toward her. She put out a hand and gurgled.

The red stream came to a halt, then tugged, and it separated from its leash, its comet tail of crimson snapping back into the crevice from which it had issued. The remainder balled and then bubbled and then formed.

Toy Moon waggled her fingers as the creature made stubby legs and tottered toward her, as unsure as a newborn lamb.

But it looked liked no lamb. Thick-jowled and sharp-eyed and well-clawed on each paw as it staggered near. It grew surer with every step, eyes turning yellow and knowing, blood-red body of light transparent and yet solid.

Toy Moon pulled her hand back. It looked like a big dog and big dogs frightened her. Her mother was afraid of big dogs and dogs sometimes chased her father on his bicycle. She curled her arm tightly to her side now as the thing approached, and it made a rumbling noise deep in its chest. It gnashed its shadowy teeth and they clicked inside heavy jaws.

The little girl turned to run, screaming for her father. The creature gave a bound and a snarl, its translucent body thickening. The blood demon jumped twice. It caught her on the second jump and she screamed no more.

It fed deeply, tearing the clothing from soft flesh and, with every chomp, it grew. When the blood demon had finished, it left nothing but damp rags upon the ground. It raised its head, listening, understanding the desire of its master still trapped below. It was to seek, to scout, to know the enemy, to look for Huang's troops, to clear the way for its master's return and vengeance.

It was also to search for the second master,

for power divided was power weakened, and Huang had planned well when he brought the master down.

With a whine, the blood demon signaled its understanding of its mission. It pressed its heavy, mastifflike body through the warehouse door and trotted into the dawn, unaware of how much time had passed, not yet realizing that the age of monsters had gone.

Chapter 11

Susan woke slowly, aware that she had had a full night's sleep, that there had been no panicky call from Poppa, and she thought for a moment how blessed that was. She wondered how parents of babies lived through nightly awakenings. There were mornings when she awoke feeling like a zombie and had no choice but to get up and stagger to work. She didn't have weekends off—sometimes weekends were her most lucrative appointments, when the working wealthy squeezed out a moment of their time.

But today she woke feeling brand new and looked at the ceiling of her bedroom—she'd had it stenciled, its curling vine beginning to burst ripely with flowers—and thanked God for El Harper.

Domino called from the dining room which, condo-size, was more of a breakfast nook. "Aack-aack," he cried, his hunting cry and Susan got out of bed, shrugging into her cotton duster, wondering what prompted her normally lethargic cat into a relative frenzy of morning activity. The early morning was full of birdsong and warbling. She padded into the dining room, squinting a little at the bright dawn, for she'd left the shades drawn, to find Domino sitting flat nose pressed to the glass doors, his chocolate tail switching back and forth angrily.

Birds sat on the walled, shaded patio everywhere there was space to perch. They filled the trellis and the passion flower vine, the stucco wall and the redwood patio suite she and Geoff had bought in Ensenada years ago. Susan stood, taken aback by the sight. There were sparrows and robins and starlings, grackles and goldfinches, mockingbirds and scrub jays, and the flighty, darting hummingbirds angrily buzzing at all of them. They sat and chirped, sang, mocked, teasing the cat at the glass door.

Their bright, hard eyes flicked glances at her. They dipped beaks and bated wings, filling the air with their quills.

"What do they want?" Susan murmured, talking to no one, her voice furred with sleep. She knelt over Domino, who ruffled himself with indignity as she scratched behind one ear. "This isn't natural." She wondered if Nina had scattered bird seed last evening. But these birds weren't feeding and, besides, she knew the species to be territorial and incompatible. Mockingbirds habitually chased all other winged creatures out of their area, even crows and redtailed hawks. Only the mild dove seemed to be beyond a mockingbird's fury. And the hummingbird, so tiny and fragile-seeming, was only a clawmark behind the mockingbird in aggression.

Domino grunted deep in his chest again, his muted hunting instinct frustrated. She straightened. A moment of fear pierced her, then melted. Stranger things happened, like the flock of starlings which had darted down a Pasadena woman's chimney, chasing her and her family out of the home before the wayward birds could be evicted.

"Maybe it's been the quakes." She pulled her duster tighter and slid the glass door back gingerly, knowing the nylon screen couldn't hold back all of them if they came at her.

But the sound and movement of her approach sent them into the air, with a *whirrr* and a beat of wings like pheasants taking to the sky, knowing gunners were behind them. They separated like chaff in the wind, each species darting its own way, and then she and the cat were left alone except for a goldfinch.

She looked at it. "You don't even belong here," she told it. She hadn't seen a goldfinch since leaving her Ohio home. It blinked, onyx eyes gleaming, a male, its brilliant yellow marked by black flashes. Then it, too, launched. She thought for a moment of her mother, her Shaker Heights society mother, whose own hard eyes had flashed at the thought of her marrying a Jew and with whom she had not exchanged a word since. Those unsaid words lumped now in her throat. Susan blinked fiercely and turned away.

Domino pushed himself against the kickplate at the screen's bottom, grunting his anger. She reached down and picked up the ruffled feline. "Not yet," she told him. "They might come back and I can guarantee you they'd kick butt. There're too many of them for you!" She scratched his ears to tickle him into a good humor as she walked to the kitchen.

Domino would have none of it, so she let him go his grumpy way. He waddled back to the breakfast nook and sat at the screen, growling little cat growls and threats. A handful of birds came back, perched momentarily, and then took to the air again. Susan found herself watching with the fear that her patio might fill again, unsure of what she'd do if it did. Was it a sending, a premonition? Did her thoughts of her estranged family mean anything? Her fingers itched to pick up the phone, but she knew what her parents would do if they heard her voice. They would say, "Wrong number," and hang up as they'd hung up before. She didn't think she could stand the pain, but what if something awful had happened? What if the birds meant something?

But the strange thing did not happen again and she returned to the kitchen to fix cereal and muffins.

She checked her date book and calendar watch as she sat eating breakfast. Brushing aside the talisman necklace Harper had given her, she spread out the morning paper, seeing the news without really reading it, concentrating on planning her day.

"Oh, my God," said Betsy. "He's whistling. He's making coffee *and* he's whistling." She put a hand to her forehead. "I can't stand it. I'm just not a morning person."

El made a face at her and whistled louder. His grin won out over his pucker then, and he had to settle for an off-tune hum. Oletha looked at Betsy.

"And if this isn't bad enough, this is the second batch of coffee. He's already poured a round for ever'body in the lab. My," she said. "What a difference a day makes."

"And it isn't even the weekend yet." Betsy sat at her desk. "Are we allowed to ask?"

"No." El stood back and watched the coffee maker do its magic.

"But, honey," Oletha countered. "We're *women*. We'll burst if we don't ask." Her brown eyes shone in her face.

"Burst away. I've got a broom and dustpan around here somewhere." Harper made a show of looking in the cabinets.

Betsy laughed and then said, "You don't need to ask, Oletha. It's obviously a woman. And it's not Debbie because he's not gloating . . . he's just happy."

Oletha put a finger to her pursed lips. "Umm, ummm. And I bet I know who. That uptown lady I had trapped in the turnstile yesterday. Uh-huh. That's it. Lancelot came roaring up like a knight in shining armor." The cashier raised an eyebrow at him. "Am I right?"

El said nothing as Betsy pointed at him in triumph. "That's the one. Look at the color in his face. El, you didn't give her one of your famous *private* tours around the museum, did you?"

He put a hip to the counter. "All right, you two. Yes, it's her and no, I didn't give her a private tour, and there's really nothing to talk about because nothing's happened."

"*Yet*, honey," said Oletha. "I think that's the operative word." She got out her coffee cup and cleaned it. "Remember who said it first."

Betsy shook her head, sun-streaked hair bound back in a clip. "Well, at least you're awake, El. I was beginning to wonder about you for a while."

He put his mug down on the counter and answered sheepishly, "So was I."

Oletha gave one of her rich, booming chuckles. "You'd better be wide awake, Lancelot, because you've got eighty second graders comin' in 'bout half an hour." She poured her coffee dark and steaming and walked away, ample hips swaying. "Thank God for year-round school," she said and laughed again.

El looked at Betsy. "Was I that obvious?"

The middle-aged blonde sat back in her chair. "Well, it wasn't that you walked around tripping on your jaw before, but you've always been the quiet type, El. I could never quite picture you as that fired up corporate man you were supposed to have been, and, mind you, I see our patron lists. But, yes, it's obvious. And don't you think it's time? I didn't even see this glow before Debbie left."

He shrugged. "Debbie had hit the end of our relationship long before I knew it, but I guess I knew it all along." He poured himself a cup and painstakingly measured the dab of nondairy creamer and sugar he now allowed himself. He looked into its swirls, divining, without being given any knowledge. "She's just really nice."

"What's her name? Seeing her again?"

"Susan Aronson. And I'm not sure. We didn't set anything up."

Betsy checked her watch. "Well, even the uncivilized in L.A. are usually up by now." She raised an eyebrow.

El curled a lip at her. "As if I'd call with you listening." He took a deep sip of too hot coffee, made a face, and downed it anyway.

Betsy pretended not to notice. She pulled out a stack of paperwork. "Our amateur diggers will be here in force in a couple of minutes. Call now or forever hold your peace."

Dr. Ellington's eighty or so paleontologist wannabes qualified more as a herd, but Betsy was right. With the second graders coming and Ellington's people on their heels, the museum and its environs would be chaos. He sat down at his desk and picked up the phone.

Maida said patiently, "Do you think this will help Irving?"

"I think he listened. Mr. Harper brought

copies of the geological maps, showed us what had happened and where." Susan was nearly dressed and cradled the phone between her neck and shoulder as she selected shoes to wear. Maida had that patronizing edge to her voice, the one she used when she was irritated but didn't like showing it. Susan had deliberately not checked her answering machine until after her shower, knowing that Sid would have called at least once. And he had. Now that Sid was at the office, Maida had come charging in in his stead.

"You could have told us earlier," her mother-in-law said now as if reminding a petulant child of good manners. "We were all there, even Naomi, and you know how she hates to miss her bridge group."

Not Sid's fault he'd bullied them all into going, but her fault for failing to make the quorum. Susan swallowed back a remark. "You know my schedule, Mai. It gets very hectic. And then this opportunity came up. You know Poppa's not senile."

"He's a manipulative old man and who knows if he's senile or not? He won't go to the doctors Sid's lined up for him."

Susan thought silently that if Mai or Sid spent more time with him, they'd know whether Irving was senile or not. "He's not," she answered quietly.

"Ah, Susie. If you only knew what a burden it is. With my mother not feeling well—" Mai's mother was in Florida and their only contact was by phone—"and not being able to leave Poppa by himself. . . ."

"Who says? Poppa's fine."

"Susan, Susan. Calls three, four times a day. That's fine? You don't know, he doesn't call you like that."

Of course he didn't. Susan usually came down to see him after the first call. "Mai, I really think this man helped. I don't think Poppa's going to be so frightened about the gas. Listen, I can't talk any longer, I've got an appointment."

Mai said indifferently, as if mouthing a pleasantry, "You work too hard, dear," and hung up.

Susan hopped about, one shoe on and one shoe off, heading for the cradle to put the portable down. She was late, late, late, and Angelo would have a snit. He was taking her in with him to see one of his more important clients, a well known TV sitcom star and time was of the essence.

The phone toned before she even set it down and Susan answered, saying, "I know I'm late, doll-face, I'm on the way."

A deep, pleasant voice said, in puzzlement, "Susan? This is El Harper."

"Oh God," she said, muffled, then cleared her throat. "El! I'm sorry, I thought it was my partner." How could she have done that? She never called Angelo doll-face except when she needed to butter him up for something. She felt her face glow with embarrassment.

"Ah. I won't keep you if you're running behind. But I thought . . . I've got tickets for the

Greek Theater. Do you like John Williams? He's doing their Fourth of July *1812 Overture* show this weekend. Can you make it tonight?"

She checked her watch calendar. "I've got a late appointment at 4:30. You'll have to pick me up at the shop about 5:30. Do you mind?"

"No!" The sound of a cleared throat. "That sounds good. I'll see you later."

Susan put the portable back in its cradle. Domino sashayed through the bedroom. "You're in luck," she told the cat. "Nina gets to feed you tonight." She grabbed her purse and ran for the door.

"Wow," Betsy said. "I'm impressed. The Firework concert series? I thought it was all sold out."

El looked at his phone as if it had betrayed him. "It is." He put his hand to his sternum for a moment, quelling whatever pain might well up. He had season tickets, as did Cal and Donovan, through their company. El's had gone unclaimed for months. Now he would have to restake his territorial rights. He took a deep breath and put a call through to Amber, his brother's executive secretary.

"Amber, it's me, El."

"Oh!" He could hear Amber taking a deep breath as if to herald one of his brothers.

"Don't tell them it's me."

Again, "Oh." Then, softer. "What can I do for you? Did you get your mail?"

He pictured Amber, perpetually young in the

California style, eyelids tucked here, legs sucked there, hair a carefully curled firebrand red, eyes an indefinite hazel, smarts undeniable: She could probably run the company without Cal, Donovan, or him—and she knew it. "I got it. If he asks, later, I don't have an answer yet."

Amber made a breathy sound, one of her camouflages for her intelligence. "They're not trying to force you out. They want you back. Cal needs you."

His chest squeezed. He took a difficult breath. "I'm not ready."

"All right. Just a minute." He could hear a ring of the other phone before she put him on hold and, in the silence, he took a necessary moment to compose himself. He thought of the cannon salute of the *1812 Overture* and how it resounded through the natural hillside amphitheater of the Greek. He hadn't been for years. He realized he missed the traditional summer show. Amber came back, brilliantly cheerful. "The lines are busy and your brother is headed this way," she nudged him.

"I want my tickets for the Greek tonight."

"Ooooh." Amber went silent and he knew she was thinking. "That's going to be tough. Cal had them doled out to a client."

"Tell him I asserted myself and claimed them. Send them over to the museum by messenger. I want them by three this afternoon."

"He'll be angry."

El smiled slowly. "No, he won't. He'll think my

style is coming back. He'll be glad. Just do it, Amber," and he hung up before she could protest more. And he knew, as he sat back and felt the mild adrenaline surge, that he was right. Cal would be angry at first, but then hopeful. He wanted El to have that old piracy edge back. He'd take the aggressive action as a signpost of hope.

Just as long as El got the tickets.

Angelo was waiting on the street side of the gated mansion on Laurel. He leaned against his car, white summer suit glaring in the too bright light. His dark hair had been layered again recently. It gleamed with the same blue-black polish as the feathered crows which had been cracking open seed pods of the jacaranda trees and had scattered as she drove up.

"I know, I know, I'm late." She grabbed an armful of swatch books from her trunk. They'd ride up the gated driveway in his Jag.

Angelo smiled. "Just fashionably." He got in and pushed the door open for her.

Leather creaked as she scooted in. Dark shadows flitted across her. She looked up. The crows were shooting across the skyline.

"Cross your fingers," her partner said as he brought the Jaguar purring to life and eased it into the driveway. He announced who they were to the call box and, after a second's pause, the gates rolled open. Angelo goosed the car and they were inside one of the more secluded estates in the area.

The 1920s faded coral mansion was not a

teardown, resisting the trend to buy property and pull it down, rebuilding homes to two or three times the size of the original mansion. She knew the history of the house vaguely: it had belonged to a silent screen comedian, then a forties and fifties Western film star. She was glad it had been kept in more or less its original exterior state, for it had a Mediterranean grace the newer Spanish style homes could not match. It was used occasionally for location shots and its backyard reflection swimming pool held an elegance that bespoke an earlier era of Hollywood when stars were royalty. A thrill ran through her at the possibility of working on the interior.

The Jag curved around the front drive. The six-car garage was actually on the first floor and a sweeping outside stairway to the left led to the entryway. Bougainvillea had been trimmed aside to leave the stairwell clear, though it claimed the rest of the wall.

"He's expecting us. No staff today, so we've got him all to ourselves," Angelo said. He popped the trunk release. "You go on up and I'll get my samples."

Gary Dimitri, star of big and little screen. Susan had met several well-known names since she'd started working for, then with, Angelo, but Gary was undoubtedly the biggest. She resolutely began to climb the shaded stairwell, hoping Angelo would not be too far behind. This was, after all, his client.

Halfway up, a C-AACK brought her to a stumbling halt as something darted at her from the tiled roof. She felt the crow coming at her face and ducked her head. Claws snatched at her hair. A rough yank and strands parted company with her scalp. It smarted. Susan looked up in surprise as the crow flew off, its trophy in curled toes.

Yet it had not seemed as if the bird attacked, but . . . but what? She couldn't put words to it. She took a deep breath and climbed the rest of the stairwell, finding the heavy oak double doors open and awaiting her. Gary Dimitri stood with his back to her, young, lean, wearing black toreador pants and a flowing white shirt. His chestnut hair was shorn just at the billowing collar of the shirt and when he looked at her over his shoulder, she felt a quirk of the sexual attraction this magnetically funny yet sexy actor held over his television audience. He pivoted about when he heard her come in.

The famous brown eyes went wide. "Who the hell are you?" A black marble and mirrored table nudged the back of his knees, its surface marred by razor blades and powdery traces.

Susan knew instantly she was in a situation in which she had hoped never to be. Her glance startled away from the table, flew up to the man's face. "I—I—" she stammered. The swatch book spilled over her arms.

"Oh, my God," the man said. "Chintz, for crissakes." His eyes raked her up and down in scorn. "He's brought Jane Fucking Pauley to do my house!" Dimitri's voice soared higher with every note. "I make an eight figure income and I get Pollyanna for a decorator!"

Susan's face went flaming. She knew the crow's dive had left her with her hair disarrayed and she stood with her arm full of country fabrics that now, as she looked into Dimitri's home, were as inappropriate as polka dots. Her stomach clenched. "Mr. Dimitri—" To her further horror, she could not stop stuttering.

"Get out! Get out!" the actor charged at her with elaborate gestures waving his arms about.

She backed up to turn and run. Angelo caught her by one elbow.

"What is it, Gregori?" he said soothingly. "She just got here. What can she have done?"

"The little prig has got it written all over her face. I won't deal with it, with her smarmy, prissy morals. Get her out, out, out."

Susan swung on her partner. "Angelo, I never—"

He nodded. "Gregori, my dear, she's my partner. Pull yourself together and make believe she's from *TV Guide*. Give me something to work with, eh?"

Dimitri threw his head back, reminding Susan of a skittish colt undecided whether to bolt or not, the whites of his eyes showing. "I won't have my name bandied about. Get her out," he said finally, breathing hard.

Angelo sighed heavily. He reached over and took the weight of Susan's swatch books from her arms. "Go on," he said softly. "Wait for me downstairs in the Jag."

Her composure came flooding back. "I'll not," she answered back. "It's ninety degrees out there."

"Then go on back to the shop. It's not your fault. He's got a noseful, from the looks of him, and coke always makes him paranoid. We'll get the job, don't you worry, and a little guilt money will give us that much more profit."

Susan fled. As she went down the stairwell, she could hear their mingled voices.

"Gregori," echoed the actor's sulky voice. "Only you know me, Angelo."

And, coaxingly, Angelo's response. "Gregori, Gregori . . . I thought we talked about this. I thought you were going to Ford's while we re-did the house, before shooting started. All the pressures, I know, but Susan's a sweet girl and one of your fans . . . you'll feel differently to-morrow. . . ."

Susan pounded down the driveway. Her nails dug into her palms as she realized that Angelo had used her. Used her to take the brunt of the temperamental actor's paranoia over his well-hidden lifestyle and to jack the price of their service up with what he aptly called "guilt money." With every drum of her heels upon the tiled driveway, she told herself she didn't need that. With everything else she had to deal with, she didn't need to baby an actor's drug prob-lem. She'd always told Angelo she refused to be involved with his clientele who indulged themselves and he'd always smoothly sworn that he would respect her wishes. He hadn't minded. It meant that he would always get the lion's share of the plum jobs, for L.A. was the capital of spoiled, indulged, and destructive people.

Black lightning streaked above her. Crows again, gliding silently. She smoothed her hair into place and watched them warily as she came down the slope. The driveway gates had been opened. She jogged through and pressed the call box button to signal she was by. She never looked back until she was settled in her car.

The two birds landed on the hood of the car, heedless as she started its engine to frighten them away. They stalked to the front windshield and perched there on the recessed windshield wipers, staring in at her. Susan stared back, held by their onyx eyes. The crows clacked their beaks once or twice, dipped their heads several times as if bowing, then spread wings and lifted off. One still had a long, silken thread of her hair stuck among his toes. She watched them leave in bewilderment and for some reason thought of El Harper's favorite tar pit, deceptive, dirty water hiding the secret face of the tar below.

Chapter 12

The day had been a nightmare for Tembo. His body stiff and half-broken, he hunched in his dark clothes and worked despite his aches. The routine had been shattered by the events of the night before and something new, which Tembo was only vaguely aware of. One of the janitors, Chou, had been stricken, heart attack or stroke, the rumors flew around the site. He'd been borne away, catatonic, grieving, unable to tell what had happened to him. Tembo had not seen the incident and with the clean up of the quake damage still going on, leading the tourists around and out of the way of the area with its temporary limited access, had been troublesome.

He returned to his home at the end of the shift, cycling on the road down to where crews were attempting to clear the rock and dirt slides. He noted that they were nearly done. There would be no work at night. Good. He did not wish to be observed when he returned.

He came to a halt as he observed an altercation between a local farmer and the man in charge. He knew the farmer, a thin, wiry, complaining man whose voice rang out stridently.

"My best bull slaughtered, and no one will do anything about it. A wild thing, I tell you. Bring your machines, your guns."

"I'm here to clear the roads. Go to town if you wish to report something," the authority said. He frowned heavily, his brows like bushy caterpillars. He rested his hand protectively on his hip where he wore an army pistol. It was the only weaponry of any sort to be seen and, at that, was unusual. Tembo wondered if he wore it to protect his machinery from theft or sabotage.

"I have my cows and calves to protect," the farmer shouted. He waved his arms akimbo. "What good are any of you? We ask for help and it never comes."

Tembo said mildly. "We can't run from your beast if the roads aren't clear."

Now the farmer glared at Tembo. He made a cat-hiss sound of disgust and spat in the road. He picked up his own battered bicycle and mounted it, spindly legs a match to his wire spokes as he pedaled away furiously.

The road authority looked at Tembo. "And what can I do for you, citizen?"

"Nothing, honored sir."

But the road authority did not seem inclined to let Tembo by that easily. He looked after the farmer. "Do you know of what he speaks? A great, red claylike creature, a wild dog perhaps?"

Tembo thought privately that such a beast would starve to death. Animals of most any kind, save farm animals, were rare in the towns and villages. Forbidden in the cities. He himself had only a bird for company. He could honestly say he knew nothing of such an animal and did.

High atop his equipment, the road authority shifted weight uneasily. Then he waved to Tembo, passing him by without another word, and his machine roared into life, its exhaust grazing the back of Tembo's calves as he pedaled past.

After his dinner, Tembo brought his bird to the market where the other men sat. He took the cover from the reed cage and listened as the birds sang, sweet warbling notes, the birds sometimes harmonizing with each other and sometimes battling for the loudest melody. He sat until his bones ached in the hot summer night and the sky began to grow dark. Then he took up his songbird and made his way to his room again, determined to sleep for a few hours before returning to the emperor's army.

The alleyway was shadowed deeply by the time he reached the row of huts and rooms where he lived. Cage swaying gently in his hand, he stopped before his door, and saw that it was pushed slightly ajar.

He had left it firmly closed.

Tembo thought. Could he have offended the road authority somehow and earned a visit from the neighborhood bureaucrat to scold him? He had little in the way of worldly goods for anyone to take, so he discounted a burglar. The thin open line between the door's edge and frame seemed an ominous portent. He hesitated to cross the threshold. He could almost smell someone, or something, lurking within. Awaiting him.

Inside its cage, the songbird gave a sudden, lurching flutter, setting the cage to spinning wildly. It also pushed Tembo's heart into a skipbeat. He took a deep breath to settle himself down. He put a foot out and toed the door wider.

A darker shape in the gloom shifted. A glint lanced toward him. Tembo's voice throttled in his throat. His hand, weakened, opened and bird and cage crashed to the floor.

Light flared and the slim Chinese girl sitting in the corner held up her cigarette lighter. "Oh, Tembo," she said. "Is he all right? I didn't mean to startle you."

"Rose Wine!" Tembo kicked his door shut before retrieving his songbird. The resilient wicker cage had suffered no damage and the bird was only slightly ruffled. Tembo put his embroidered coverlet back over the bars and hung the cage on its rack.

He took his lantern up and lit it, having used his allotment of electricity for the month. Rose Wine snapped her cigarette lighter shut and smiled palely at him.

"I know I should not have come—"

He drank in the subtle beauty of her face and figure. One look was all it took to know that this was the daughter of learned people, merchants and nobles, people from a house with a high door. Even her hands, stained by scholars' ink, were finely shaped. She was a poet, had been born to be a poet, and now she stood, her face shining at him. All his work, all his hopes to return to his former position, had been crafted so as to earn her love and respect back. And now, to his shame, here she was in his village hut.

She put a hand out and took the lantern from him, setting it on his low table, which served as eating table, desk, and occasionally an extra chair. "I apologize, Tembo. I endanger you."

"Never. How can you say such a thing?" Yet he hesitated to embrace her. Something about the way she stood—her clothes, different, her hair . . . she was the same and yet changed.

Rose Wine sensed his hesitation. The corner of her mouth curved back. "I should not have come." She made as if to brush past him.

"No." He caught her arm. "It's like a dream, having you here."

She shook her head. He could smell her now, his delicate, sensitive student, covered with the aroma of the road and hard days, travel on the back of a poultry truck and worse. He took her awkwardly in the curve of his arm, fearing to be more intimate than that, fearing his heart would burst if he did . . . and she rejected him. He could feel her trembling within his light hold.

"What is it, little one?"

Rose Wine shook her head again. "I should not have come. I place you in jeopardy. But . . . I could not leave without seeing you." She raised her face to him and, in the lantern's soft glow, he could see the tear streaks across her cheeks. "I have not . . . eaten or slept much in the last few days."

He lowered her to his only chair. His teapot stood out, cooled, left from his dinner, but she had not touched it. He poured her a cup now and she took it. For a moment their fingers entwined. She drank and then, over the rim of the cup, their glances met again.

"What is it?"

"I must leave the country. I was one of the students in the riots. The authorities have my face on film, my voice. . . ." Rose Wine's words trailed off.

Tembo blinked once or twice, uncomprehending, and then he understood. The Bloody Fourth at Tiananmen. "Oh, Rose," he murmured.

"Do you understand now?"

Yet his dismay turned to joy, for it was to him she turned, not her high-ranking father or mother. It was his hut she sat in and him she begged for shelter and understanding. With all his love, he would give it. He fixed her a cold dinner, light meats and fruits. She ate quickly, birdlike, reminding him of his adored songbird. She wiped her fingertips delicately on his napkin.

"Will you come with me?"

Tembo rocked back on his heels. Fleeing

would take money for bribery and travel, as well as cunning. He had only his one meager fund, his savings for a small television set, and it would not take the two of them very far. Rose Wine, however, was already en route. She must have already made one or two contacts. He bowed his head. "I will follow you when I can," he said. "I promise. But I cannot go with you." He went to his secret place and removed the stock of money he had hidden, and pressed it into her uncreased palm. "Promise you will wait for me."

Unshed tears sparkled like gems in her deep brown eyes. "Oh, Tembo," she answered and flung her arms around his neck. "I don't know if I'm strong enough to go without you."

As soon as he uncovered what he had to at the emperor's tomb, he would have money and contacts enough to follow her anywhere. He might even be able to catch up with her in Hong Kong. He whispered into her ear, "Leave word for me in Hong Kong. At the bank where your father has done much business . . . you know the one?"

She nodded.

"All right. Leave word there. You're going all the way to Canada?"

Rose Wine nodded again.

"Then I will come. Soon. I'll have an easier time of it . . . no one is looking for me." Tembo felt a strength he had not known he could muster. "We must sleep a bit and then you must leave. Will you . . . share my cot with me?"

Faint color came into his pale love's face. Rose Wine nodded a third and last time, as her free hand went out and dimmed the golden lantern.

He arose just after midnight, when even the summer sky over Xian was purple dark. Rose Wine breathed lightly and gently as he left her side and dressed. She knew the roads she must take and she had told him the names of two of the contacts who would help transport her. He had forbidden her to tell him any more, satisfied only that there was indeed a vast, underground network dedicated to helping the students flee. She was in danger, yes, but she had an excellent chance of getting out.

Tembo pushed open his door so that the slightly cooler night air could flood his tiny abode. He took a deep breath. His fortune was changing at last. He could feel it.

He did not notice the two slanted, glowing eyes watching him from a doorway across the alley. The orbs quickly shuttered themselves from detection as Tembo strode out into the night and relieved himself, before returning to his hut and bringing Rose Wine out.

The blood demon could smell the difference, as well as the bonding, between the two. The little one it knew, from the memory of another it had absorbed on the road that morning, its first taste of human flesh since its long sleep. From that taste, it knew what its master did not—that centuries had passed, that Ch'in had greatly changed, as had all the world. It knew of students and riots for democracy and abortion and computers and Western music and all that the hapless student had known before he had devoured it. He also knew that this one was headed east, toward the rising sun, just as the second master had been sent.

Therefore, he would not devour either of these two, but follow the little one. At least until the road eastward ended, and he had more knowledge to report to his greater master. Yes, the world had changed much in his sleep and the greatest of it all was this: flesh and blood were in much abundance and had not the magic needed to stop him from taking whatever he wished. And if they could not stop him, then his master would have dominion over everything when he rose.

Satisfied, the blood demon settled back onto its haunches and waited for the little one to begin her travels.

Chapter 13

Portents filled the silence shrouding the emperor's army. He could feel it welling. His vision filled the blind eyes of the terra-cotta hundreds. Tembo had felt the fortune riding the night wind as he'd sent Rose Wine on her way. That same fortune now swelled him with confidence. He'd come armed with several flashlights and his lantern. Workers had cleared away the debris from the fallen catwalk.

The crevice which had gaped open in his nightmare visit was now closed over with soft dirt that would be easy to shovel away. The emperor's men stared impassively at him, arrayed hundreds deep across the site. Below their feet were crude bricks and dirt. What was below that, Tembo knew, was for him to discover for once and all.

He found a shovel dropped in among the janitors' supplies and thought for a moment of old Chou and what might have befallen him to strike him mad and senseless. The rumors were rampant, his young wife gone and the child sold, or even that he had murdered his child and come to work, thinking the blame would be put on his second wife. Or perhaps that he himself had sold his pretty young daughter to a Western tourist. No one knew the truth of it and twisted old Chou was in no condition to tell the story.

Tembo tightened his hands upon the shovel's shaft and hefted it to his shoulder. The glow of his lantern set upon the ground was like the gleam of a harvest moon, yellow-orange against the midnight. It drew him back like the beacon of a lighthouse for fishermen. Tembo took a deep breath and began to dig.

The shovel sank deep, deeper than he drove it, as if dipping into the fresh ground of a new grave. The head was reluctant to be pulled back, laden with dirt, sucking down as though into quicksand. Tembo fought to remove the shovelfuls. So heavy were they that his face began to run with summer sweat and his heart pounded. His ears roared with every load he tossed aside and the shovel sank deeper and deeper, swallowed by the eager ground.

He looked up once as his lantern flickered. He could feel the sight of the statues upon him, watching him. What secret did they hold beneath their feet? What would be his reward for discovering it?

Tembo thought of old Huang of the Ch'in Dynasty who had consolidated what was to be China. The Great Wall, he brought together and ordered completed, to hold back the more barbaric tribes to the West. He fought and conquered, withstood assassins and rivalries. What treasure had he buried below his victorious army?

Tembo mopped his steaming forehead with his sleeve. The harvest moon of his lantern shrank a little. He did not notice. If what he brought up could be pieced out through the black market, he might even catch up with Rose Wine before she made it to Hong Kong. She was going to the coast and by junk from there. It would take her several days unless she was stopped by authorities or pirates. She had taken his money and put it in several purses secreted all over her body, hoping that one or two might not be found if she was stopped. Tembo had thought her terribly brave and beautiful as well as pragmatic. She had clasped his hand as though never wishing to let it go before finally leaving in the night.

A dull thunk interrupted his memories. Tembo stared down in surprise. So soon he had dug through. He reeled his shovel in . . . something clung to the head of the spade. He pulled it off and clambered out of the hole to the lantern and held it up.

Terra-cotta and gold . . . he was right! There was another layer a man's height below the army. He looked at the clay piece. Not bricks or tiles as were below the army's feet now, but slightly rounded. From its curvature he could predict that the entire site underneath the army would have this layer below. Yes. Perhaps a gigantic battle shield. He would have to wait until the entire piece was excavated to know if he were right—and he had no intention of waiting. But he sucked his breath inward in excitement, regardless. He had discovered something none of the honorable doctors and scholars had even guessed at. He alone!

The gold sparkled atop the molded rim edge, an insignia, a seal, or perhaps an imperial coin, with a few pieces of jade embedded in it. Not much in the way of treasure, but the antiquities market would see him paid handsomely for it. Yes. Tembo licked his lips, tasted the salt of his hard labor upon them, and turned the coin over in his hand. A few daubs of wax obscured the ideograms. He picked at them and a chill wave of uneasiness went down his spine, under his shirt and jacket, chill in spite of the heat of his work and the close summer night.

He examined the clay segment again, like a turtle's shell, welded together piece by piece. It must have taken the artisans months just for this flooring. He turned it over. The underside had dirt clinging to it. He brushed it away from the dry clay surface and found ... slime ... clinging to his fingertips. With a shudder, Tembo flung the phlegm from him and wiped his hands dry upon his knee. The wet slimy stuff felt disgusting and ... evil.

He held the piece close to the lantern. The shard bit off the light as though eclipsing it. His gaze narrowed, sharpened, upon the clay. The whole underwall of it was covered with the glistening, gooey material. He shuddered and put the clay shard upon the ground. He pocketed the coin, picked up the shovel, and jumped down into the ditch.

He landed with a solid thump that set the whole world trembling. His gaze shot up to the lantern as the earth roiled beneath his feet. His lantern danced above him. The catwalk leaned and groaned, the metal whining. Overhead beams CRACK-CRACKED with strain.

Tembo put his hands out to steady himself. The soft dirt rained in about him, covering and filling his shoes. The immense hangar groaned and cried aloud. He could not see it swaying in the dark, but he heard its movement.

He would die here, in a grave he'd dug for himself. Tembo kicked his feet free of the dirt and flung himself at the side of the ditch, preparing to claw his way out. The earth continued to rumble and ripple, and he sank another half length into the dirt until his waist was even with the rim exposed by the gaping crevice which opened up.

Tembo rolled over, saw the black maw yawning, heard a suck of something moving, and wildly swam his way toward the pale moon of his lantern. It had ceased to tremble, but its light was sickly, the oil spilled out perhaps, or the wick too short. . . . Tembo, for his life, knew he had to get to the light.

Another rumble began, a sound vibrating from deep within the earth, a sound he felt rattling in his bones, his chest, pressuring his eardrums long before he heard it. He thought of the train which roared through the night of his dreams, but the sound grew higher and higher until it beat at his senses, an immense laughter. As he kicked and clawed his way up the soft dirt, something caught his ankle and held him.

Tembo kicked wildly. He thought of his shoe catching on the now jagged edge of the rim— catching him up, a fish on a hooked line. Sound baffled him, a dull roar, and when Tembo fetched over on his back to see what had caught him, his heart stopped.

Silver planes screamed in low over LAX as Victor eased his car into the parking garage of the Bradley International Terminal. Tam Chen sat for a moment, reluctance to get out tensing his slender frame. Victor fished about in his pocket, found a handkerchief and passed it to Tam. Tam absently wiped his palms without looking at the cloth and did not notice the brand imprinted on it. He wiped his palms a second time before he shoved the handkerchief away. Their heads turned and they considered one another.

Tam spoke first. "I do not like leaving now," he said.

"We haven't any choice. The students are filtering into Hong Kong. We got them that far. I don't trust anybody but you to begin getting them out." Victor's broader, rounder face was the opposite of Tam's chiseled, long face, but they reflected each other's concern.

"The outbreak of the young tong has me worried."

Victor laughed without humor. "From what you told me, that hand is out of business."

"I could be wrong," Tam said flatly, "about who endangers you."

"Or you could be very right." Victor slapped a hand down on the car seat. "We're talking a week, two at the most. I can do without you."

Tam gave an unconvinced grunt, but he grabbed the door handle and opened his side. Victor hid his smile of genuine humor and got out the driver's side.

Despite the length of the flight, Tam had dressed as dapperly as ever, his trouser legs in sharp creases, the gleaming silver of his suit like scales in the sunlight. His suitcase was maroon and gold leather, custom-made, with his Chinese ideogram monogrammed upon it. It was hot already. The planes coming in made streaks against the brown, smoggy haze. Victor's chest hurt briefly. He thought of taking a few puffs off the portable oxygen unit he carried at the club, just so he would be able to sing well tonight. It was a Friday night and the Jade Pheasant would be packed. He liked anticipating the crowd.

Tam entered the terminal and strode to the check-out counter, parting the crowd neatly like a blade through grass. Without really seeing him, people moved and obliquely filled in the gaps behind him. Tam would be a hard man to tail, Victor thought, as he struggled to catch up.

Tam stood with his tickets and passport out. He tilted his sharp chin at Victor.

"I'll be all right. And," he added in a flat imitation of Arnold Schwarzenegger, "I'll be back."

The messenger made it before noon and caught him on his lunch break. Harper swung around at his desk, pleasantly surprised. He fished out an extra twenty for the messenger. "Can you do another delivery?"

The young man's eyes glittered. "Off the books?"

"If you want. I just don't have time to phone the company and schedule this." El spread his hand over the neat, brown-papered package he'd just finished taping.

"I don't do drugs."

"This is nothing of the sort."

"If you say so." The long-haired youth looked at him with a brittle expression.

"I say so," El answered, using his corporate voice.

The twenty was snatched from his fingers. "Whatever you want."

El held up the package containing the second part of the clay tablet. "The Jade Pheasant, on Broadway, in Chinatown. See that Victor Jue gets it." The address was black-inked neatly across the brown paper wrapping, but he repeated it nonetheless.

The messenger flipped a wrist and the twenty disappeared. "He'll have it before two."

"Fine. And thanks." El watched the young man wend his way through the museum and leave. His delivery vehicle was double-parked New York style out on the street, but no one had ticketed it. El pocketed his tickets for the Greek. Amber had penned a note saying that Cal had been upset but walked through the company headquarters with an ear to ear grin all that morning anyway. El felt a faint twinge of guilt. He assuaged it by thinking of the delight Susan would feel over a picnic dinner in the open amphitheater, good music, cannons, and fireworks.

And it would do him good, too.

Harper looked outside at the picnic grounds and saw the children beginning to wander. He left his desk and walked outside, waiting for the teachers to let their students know it was time to continue the tour. A young lady approached him and stood on one foot, her brown sack clutched in her hand.

"Where's the other guy?" she asked.

Harper guessed her age at around nine or ten. Her hair had been streaked professionally and she wore Koala blue shirts and shorts. Her Nikes looked two sizes too big for her feet. Even expensive shoes, he reflected, had to be bought big enough to grow into. She puzzled him. He was the only male docent here today and she'd not met the doctors. "What other guy?"

She considered him with gray-blue eyes. "The one who eats our lunches if we don't want them."

"Ah." She meant Digger. His glance flicked involuntarily across the street to the pillared lot where he'd met his terrible end. "He's gone now."

"Oh. He was kinda neat. He told stories for the lunches, ya know? He was homeless, wasn't he?"

El smiled gently. "I think so. I didn't know him well."

She sighed. Without another word, she slam-dunked her bulging lunch sack into the nearby steel barrel and skipped off to join her classmates. El watched her go. He felt a sense of loss. With a last look at the site of Digger's demise which neither the police or the newspaper had been able to divine the cause of, Harper turned to go in, a new wave of young scholars at his heels.

Susan was bent over her grid pads, sketching out placement for a living room, when she heard the rear door squeak open. The scent of roses flooded the small room. She did not look up, knowing Angelo brought an apology, and not wishing to give in to him again.

The intruder stopped at the other side of her desk. He smelled of roses and an unfamiliar cologne. The actor's, she thought, and gave a slight, disapproving sniff.

"*Cara,*" he said.

Without glancing up, Susan bit off, "You're no more Italian than I am. And if I ever, ever put you in a position like that, you'd never work with me again. How dare you do that to me? You always call before you go to an appointment—you *knew* he had a snootful! You knew what Dimitri was expecting, and it wasn't *me*."

Smoothly, Angelo said, "We do what we have to."

"You didn't have to do that."

The bouquet of flowers bounced off the desk in front of her. "What do you want me to do, beg? We have to have business to pay bills, Susie, and if you think that stack is high—" Here Angelo took a deep, gulping breath, "Wait until you see what's coming in the mail."

"That's your concern. We agreed going in that your gambling debts are *not* chargeable against Il Mode."

"Sometimes one has no choice."

She looked up angrily, feeling the heat rise from the pit of her stomach and spread. "You're a good designer. I'm a good designer. Our talent speaks for us. That's all we need. Stunts like this. . . ." Her words trailed off and she waved a hand, unable to express her contempt.

Angelo held a defiant pose. "He liked the work overs for the formal dining room and the solarium. He wants you to come back with me."

"As if I'd ever set foot there again."

Angelo perched a rounded hip on her desk corner. "You know he's not like that. How could he fool millions of people around the country weekly if he let himself go like that? It was the coke talking."

"It was an asshole talking!"

"Ah, but a rich one. And we have the job. He starts filming the new season again in a week or two. We haven't much time for consultations. He will treat you like a princess." Angelo spread his hands and smiled engagingly at her.

Susan went limp and knew disgust at herself for giving in, but the thought of juggling invoices made her queasy. Reluctantly, she said, "You had better get the money up front before it goes up his front. And if either of you stiff me, I swear I'll go to the *National Enquirer* and get my money for an exclusive."

Angelo waggled a finger at her. "Nasty, nasty."

"But a threat."

He sighed. "And a good one. All right, *cara*. Whatever you want." He stood up, saying, "I have a luncheon appointment." He retrieved the roses with a languid hand and was halfway to the door when she protested.

"Hey! My flowers."

He shrugged eloquently. "You did not claim them. And my luncheon partner will be most impressed." He swept out the door.

Warm piss evacuated from Tembo, soaking his trousers and sinking into the dirt with its acrid smell before he realized he was still alive. His heart thumped heavily and began beating again. He took a shuddering breath. Digging his elbows into the dirt, he began to crawl out of the hole once more, the taloned paw which curled about his ankle tightening its hold, but not dragging him back.

Rather, it was Tembo who dragged the demon out, birthing him from the slime and clay from under the rim of the terra-cotta flooring. It grew as it issued forth as though the seal Tembo had broken was a narrow canal exit to the womb of its existence.

As Tembo reached the top and stumbled back, catching his sleeve on his hot lantern, the beast lay for a moment, half-birthed, outstretched in the dirt, its slit eyes glowing yellow. A massive head raised and looked up at him. Tembo shuddered. His foot had gone icy cold within the curled paw.

The demon's hide shone like rich stone, slate and purple within gray depths, the slime quivering over it and breaking away like an obscene placenta. It struggled now to free its hindquarters, kicking away, never releasing Tembo, and then it was through, as big as the hut in which Tembo had lived and which he now wished he had never left.

It breathed and shone like an elaborately carved temple dog, neither dog nor lion but both, curls at the back of its head, nostrils wide with its gusty breath, talons sharp as saber teeth. And it laughed at Tembo. It spoke, in a deep bass, booming voice, a Chinese dialect which he did not recognize.

The demon's paw pinched closer about his ankle, bringing a freshet of pain to flesh and nerve he'd thought dead forever. Tembo let out a yelp and began to beg for his life. The beast quirked its head and listened, eyes gleaming with amusement.

Then it spoke again, its voice buffeting the very air, drumming in Tembo's ears, and though he heard the words, it took him a moment to realize he could understand.

"Where is the emperor?"

He grappled for reality, hearing without comprehension though he knew the words. He gasped out, "Nothing—no—no emperor."

The demon crouched on the ground beside him, and even crouched it was as large as the earth movers which had been clearing the road only yesterday—ah, gods, was it only yesterday?—and its breath scorched him.

"You released me, therefore I owe you mercy. But do not think I will give mercy to an idiot!"

Tembo clutched his head as his skull reverberated with the other's voice. Tears squeezed out of his eyes. He would have voided again in his panic, but his bladder was empty. "Wh— What emperor?"

The demon looked back over its massive shoulder and opened its doggy-lion jaws in amusement. Its eyes sent out beams flashing across the terra-cotta figurines. "*That* emperor."

"Huang?" Tembo's voice went high. "Dead. Dead nearly two thousand years."

The demon released him abruptly. Blood burned back into his foot and he screamed with the flooding pain. The demon rose and looked over the archaeological site, its eyes glowing like two massive moons. Then it began to laugh again, louder and louder.

"Free," it said. "To do what I will. And what I will do is find the other. Nothing will stand before me!"

Chapter 14

Irving paced his apartment. It was cloyingly hot, and yellow light streamed in patchily through the old, drawn blinds which had been crisped by years of summer heat and could no longer withstand it. His pate was covered with perspiration and he ran his roughened palm over it again and again. The remains of both his breakfast and his lunch littered the tiny wooden kitchen table. He had not gone in to work and it was the first time, save for Sylvie's death, when he had not opened the store on a weekday.

He still wore his pajamas and scuffs and he had managed to sleep a little in the morning before the heat and smog began to creep in. He was exhausted now, he could feel it in his bones, but he could not sleep again and he could not go to work. He did not think he could walk the distance as he usually did, and knew his hands and arms trembled too much for him to drive.

But he did not reach for the phone. Irving circled his apartment restlessly instead, sometimes slouching in his old armchair and watching TV, but unable to concentrate on anything for more than five minutes. Then he was up again, pacing, circling the apartment, his palm itching to grab up the phone.

But he dare not call Susan. His dreams were branded on his retinas, so that whenever he blinked or closed his eyes for more than a second, the image flared up—flames gouting, Susan surrounded, terrified, *burning*. There was no fool like an old fool, he thought to himself. He had worried about himself and his shop, clinging to Susan like a lifeline only to know now that it was her danger as well, and he'd brought her to this.

He had to protect her, but he no longer knew if his fear was rational or irrational. The insane don't worry about being insane, he thought, therefore he must still be sane ... but he remembered old Louie who'd worried for years about being insane and *he had been*.

Like those who did what they were most afraid of ... the man terrified of falling who jumped because of his compulsion ... he found himself obsessed with fire. He'd turned on the gas burners every time he'd gone through the kitchen, watching the orange-blue ring of fire before twisting the knob off again. How could he protect her? Irving found no thought that comforted him and plunged once more into his armchair.

He only knew that he would not call. Not today. Not for his life would he call Susan. He picked up his worn leather tome resting against the side of the armchair. He stroked it lightly before opening it. There were not many in Judaica who studied the *Cabala* the way he did. The trouble with opening a door to the mysteries of Yahweh is that it sometimes left an opening for other, darker things. He wondered what the new, eager young rabbi at the temple would think of him and his studies. He wondered what the young man would think of his dreams, and of the faintly whispering, almost heard voices which haunted him? One light, clear, pure, the other deep, rumbling, tainted. They would think him *meshuga,* for certain. He set his mind on staying awake and reading, and attempting to understand the ancient mysteries. His head nodded despite his efforts.

But when he closed his eyes and drifted off to weary sleep in the sultry heat of the apartment, he dreamed of fires. He dreamed of shuffling through the tired and littered streets of the city, great chasms opening in the asphalt and the smell of gas before flames burst into being, torches spouting into the air. Like a storm inundating the city, waves of sparks beat down, meeting the gas geysering from below, and the subsequent explosions gutted the city. The brown hills of Hollywood and Griffith Park were swept with orange blazes. People walked like grotesque, animated spirits, their hair adrift on the hot wind, comet-trailing heat sparks behind them, their arms and legs and torsos wrapped in curling flames. He sprinted between them shouting for Susan and sometimes Sylvie and always for water, for rain, for help, until his throat was too seared to utter any sound. The dream kept him captive. It would not let him go. He sobbed in weariness and knew that he would not wake until he found Susan.

Tears ran down his seamed face, drying quickly in the late June heat, and his hands twitched restlessly, telegraphing the futility of his dreams, but the old man did not wake.

Susan looked up from her work. The thought that she had not yet heard from Poppa crossed her mind. She reached out to call him, then drew her hand back. Sid wasn't entirely wrong in that they fed each other's problems. She knew that she filled her loneliness with Poppa's needs. If he didn't call her, she would have to call him later, to let him know she'd be out that night. A pang twinged her. Should she explain it was El Harper? Or should she tell him it was a client? Uneasiness at the thought of lying made her mouth dry. Putting off the decision of what to say, she drew her purse over and examined her checkbook.

July was just a few days away and she hadn't enough balance to cover her mortgage. Billing was down at Il Mode as neither she nor Angelo liked to chase their customers for past dues. All in all, they had few problems in collectibles despite that. Susan chewed on her lip. The Drexlers hadn't paid the balance yet for their new master bedroom. She had no choice. She'd have to call for it and hope Fran Drexler wouldn't be upset with her. The Drexlers were friends of David and Terry and Geoff's brother had recommended her highly. David was so unlike Geoff that Susan did not think of him as Geoff's brother. Just . . . David. He was too like Maida.

Susan pulled up the Drexlers' record and dialed. Fran Drexler answered, crisp, efficient, more like a CEO's secretary than a society homemaker. "May I help you?"

Susan identified herself. The efficiency gave way to welcome.

"Susan! How are you! Leo and I just love what you've done for us."

"I'm glad," she answered. "This is difficult for me to ask. . . ."

"Then don't hesitate, dear. What can I do for you?"

"Well, the billing came due at the first of the month and—"

Fran Drexler stopped her in her tracks. "Didn't you get my check? Angelo called for it two weeks ago. I sent it right out."

Susan felt out of step, as if she were being spoken to in a foreign language. She couldn't respond.

Eager to be helpful, Mrs. Drexler added, "Do you want me to call my bank and see if it went through?"

Susan grasped for words. "No. No, that's fine, that's quite all right. I'm sure it's just a matter of paperwork. Neither of us has a head for business."

"Well, you just let me know if you need me

to check. It only takes a moment. Everything's all computerized."

Still taken aback, Susan thanked her and hung up. She stared at her check register. That had been her commission, solely and completely. Angelo had stolen from her as well as from the business.

Angry tears stung the corners of her eyes. She didn't know what to do, didn't know what she could do. He'd flung it away gambling, she knew that much, and she'd never see it again. As for her bills, they would have to lag until she could make up the income. And, if she had to, she could borrow the mortgage payment from Poppa Irving.

Susan blinked hard. It was overwhelming, this constant juggling of funds and bills. She wanted to be able to sit back and take a deep breath, to be taken care of, not to worry. She wanted to be shed of all this.

She closed her eyes. It would not happen. She took a deep breath. One step at a time. One day at a time. One bill at a time. She opened her eyes. She would float a loan from Poppa and then take care of business. She reached for the phone.

Irving struggled to wake from a dreamless sleep as the phone jangled and jangled. His arm had gone to sleep and it needled him as he reached for the instrument. The receiver dropped from numbed fingers with a crash. He picked it up, mumbling an apology.

"Poppa! Are you all right? I called the shop first. What's happened?"

"Ah, Susie, Susie, *shayna*, don't yell at me. I'm an old man." Poppa rubbed at his bedewed pate. His mouth felt like cotton. It was too hot to sleep in the afternoon. He felt old and dull.

"I'll be right over."

"No. No, no!" The thought of her coming near frightened him into alert wakefulness. He thought he could smell the decaying, rank scent of methane. He sat up in the armchair, his cramped body protesting. "I'm fine. I was up all night with eye-talian heartburn. I told you. So I stayed home to sleep a little. If a man can't take a day off his own business, what can a man do?"

"You're sure it's just indigestion, Poppa?"

"I grew up with pastrami and corned beef and salami. I know a good heartburn when I feel it." He gave a short laugh. When Susan echoed it, he knew he'd eased her mind.

"All right." Her voice hesitated. "I won't be home tonight, but I'll take my beeper. You page me if you need me."

He hated the pager, but he felt better knowing she was within reach. "All right, all right. Now you go on and let me rest." He cleared his throat. "I've got some magazines here I want to read."

"Going to play hooky for the whole day, eh?" Her soft voice laughed again. "Call me if you need me."

"Good-bye already," Poppa answered. The line went dead, but he held the receiver for a moment as if he could bring her back. Then he hung up slowly. He checked his watch. What was an old man to do?

It was still early afternoon. The rabbi would be at temple readying for Friday night services. He sighed. He needed to talk to someone, someone who understood more than he did, someone who knew the secret name of God and who had studied the *Cabala*. He reached out his hand again.

Angelo pushed in the front doors of the Pantry, ignoring the glares from the line of people snaking along the street side of the building. The Pantry was basic, historic Los Angeles, stucco and plain, its mismatched wooden chairs filled with middle-class customers and tables covered, on good days, with red plaid plastic tableclothes which could be wiped down quickly as customers were ushered in and out. The right-hand side of the wall was a grill and there were swinging doors to another kitchen through which waiters hurried, and the smell of sourdough permeated the air. The high windows to the left side were covered with heavy wire grille and the glass was parchment colored, clean but waxed by years.

Angelo ran his glance over the chalkboard menu. He really wanted some cold salmon and a salad, but this was chili-side and pork chop heaven. The best he could do was a brisket sandwich with a small dinner salad. He sidled past the wall-mounted proclamation from the

Mayor of Los Angeles, citing the Pantry as a historical landmark, a café which ran twenty-four hours a day and had never closed since its opening decades ago. And all its waiters had served time. They were just as basic and crusty as the restaurant, hardworking and unassuming.

Angelo's luncheon partner raised two immense rusty colored eyebrows as he set the roses on the table between them. He slid his platter of sourdough aside. "Well, well," he said. "I do not often get flowers." His voice held a touch of New York's Little Italy.

"I'm certain you know someone who will appreciate them."

A thick, square hand reached out and pulled the roses across the table, claiming them. Angelo knew he could not touch them again, even if his luncheon partner got up and walked off without them. He sat down and eased off his white jacket, wishing he'd left it in the car.

The Pantry stood in the shadow of immense office buildings, a Gibraltar of a building whose time had come and gone and which stoutly refused to surrender its position. Angelo had left his Jag in the bank building's parking lot across the street, not trusting the Pantry's own littered, asphalt lot. He picked up the menu with its thick red bordered plastic cover and scanned it, hoping against hope for cold poached salmon with dill sauce and an endive salad on the side. He found none. Their waiter squeezed briskly through the myriad of tables and Angelo placed his order while Tony waited patiently for his attention.

Angelo felt the brown-eyed stare upon him and turned to face it uncomfortably. Tony Galado was a big man, florid of complexion, his auburn eyebrows at odds with his dark hair and complexion. He sat in suspenders, his gray and navy pinstriped shirt a little rumpled about his torso, his long sleeves rolled back to accommodate the weather and heat. Tony tapped the brown-glazed tabletop with a blunt nail. "You are not doing what we discussed, Angelo."

He lost his appetite completely. He came up with a smile which seemed to slide off his lips even as it curved. "I needed a vacation."

"You do not need to increase your indebtedness, to me or anyone else," Galado said. "I spend this time with you because I like you and I have an investment in you."

"I've made good," Angelo said defensively.

Tony paused in mid-movement, his large hands deftly tearing a huge hunk of sourdough in two. He looked over the white mountain of bread. "Perhaps you're not as smart as I thought you were."

Angelo fought the impulse to squirm in the ladder-back chair. His side salad was slid across the table, followed by his own platter of bread and cold butter patties as the waiter shadowed past. He reached for his knife and a crust of his own. "I'm making arrangements," he said, "to branch out. My partner holds me back. Her style," and he shrugged eloquently, a Latin shrug, indicating her lack.

Tony beetled his thick brows. "She pays her bills," he said, before filling his mouth with the snowy bread. Angelo thought of communion and the Eucharist. He put his aside.

"Susan's a great girl," he explained, "but she has a very plebian sense of style. I need someone who can expand with me . . . someone not afraid to experiment, someone who breathes with the same creativity I do. . . ."

"You have someone in mind?"

"I do. Susan has to be bought out first."

"So these additional monies you ask me for is not to pay off recent debts, but to finance your move."

"Yes." Angelo plucked at his green salad. "I won't deny I lost my ass in Vegas. But I can handle that, if I know I can spread my wings here. This is strictly a business loan."

Tony paid attention to his thick pork chop, dissecting it with the somewhat bent knife given to him. "I have to consider this," Galado said. He proceeded to eat in silence.

Angelo plucked another chopped leaf from his salad. He could not read Galado and did not like that. He was accomplished in reading most people. People gave him exactly what he needed to maneuver them into doing what he wanted them to. But Galado was different. Perhaps it was his East Coast demeanor. Perhaps it was his natural predator's style, although Angelo had dealt with predators of all kinds in L.A. He decided to nudge the man a little. *"Caro,"* he began.

In a flash, Tony was leaning across the table, face in his, Angelo's right hand pinned to the table. The man said lowly, harshly, "Don't speak Italian to me, you freaked-out spic. Don't ever speak Italian to me!"

He let go of Angelo and dropped back in his chair before anyone in the restaurant had even noticed. Angelo drew his hand and wrist back into his lap, where he massaged his hurt gently. "Yes," he said. "I'm sorry."

"Let's move on," Tony said. He skinned the last of the meat from his pork chop bone. "I'll give you the money when you can show me you've bought Susan out and brought in this new partner."

Angelo felt his nostrils flare. He couldn't bring Tajah in without the money. "Tony," he said, and stopped. The other was being munificent and knew it. Any more pleading and the loan might well be off entirely. He took a short, tight breath of desperation. "Thank you." He thought of Tajah with the brunette hair extensions and the kohl-lined eyes, and the promise of contacts within a vast strata of L.A. he'd never been privy to before. He might be safe with Susan, but with Tajah he could soar. He never gave crashing and burning a second thought.

Tony stood. He swept up the check. "My treat," he said. "For the roses."

Angelo nodded again.

Galado looked at Angelo's full plate. "Eat," he

added. "I wouldn't want my colleagues to think you sick or anything. Terminal illnesses make them nervous."

Angelo flushed. "I'm healthy," he muttered.

"One nevers knows, does one," countered Galado. "And somebody in your position has to be extra careful." He picked up the roses in one crushing hand and then left, cruising his chunky body across the crowded restaurant floor with a fluid grace.

Angelo stared at his plate. It would be nice when he was successful enough to crush people like Galado under his thumb like a picnic ant. It would be very nice. He took a steadying breath and began eating his lunch.

Tembo gathered himself to run. He could feel the heat of the demon's body in the darkness although he could not see until the great lamplight eyes were beamed in his direction. His own lantern had burned out, and the batteries of the flashlight had given way to the night, and he sat in a miserable, stinking heap, hugging his knees to his chest.

It occurred to Tembo that this might all be a nightmare—he *had* hit his head after all—and that he might still be lying next to Rose Wine in sleep, her bare legs entangled with his ... but the stink of his clothes and their damp chill upon his legs instead of her sweetness convinced him otherwise.

It also occurred to him that the demon appeared to be resting, content to lie outstretched upon the ground next to the crevice which had birthed it. It might be weakened from its struggle to emerge and, if so, now was the time for Tembo to run.

He wanted to run. He wished for the strength and ability with all his heart, but his body did not obey him. He straightened his legs and then drew them under him. His sinews trembled with the strain. Did the beast keep him near? Did it command his very bones?

Tembo gathered himself slowly.

The demon's head moved slightly. Its beam of sight glanced across Tembo's feet. "Go ahead," it rumbled. "Run. I would like the chase."

"And what would you do with me?"

"Eat you when I catch you." The voice drummed at Tembo's ears, its pressure nigh unbearable.

"And if I don't run?" His chest hurt and his feet tingled. He got off the ground and into a squat.

"I will eat you anyway." The demon looked squarely at him, blinding him. "But you have more of a chance if you run. I have not blooded yet. I have not regained my full power. And their influence," the demon looked away, across the terra-cotta army, his look illuminating them in fire, "weighs upon me."

Without further thought, for fear the demon could read his mind, Tembo launched himself. He flung himself toward the rear of the site where the remaining catwalks could swallow him up while the girders and stanchions might entangle the demon.

The beast erupted with a roar that made the earth pound and the building whine with vibrations. Tembo lost his hearing shortly after that, his senses muffled as though drowning in deep, dark water. He could almost hear himself breathe, gasping, as he raced through the night over uneven, earthquake plowed ground. Fear for his life spurred him.

The demon's hot, foul breath blasted him. He churned desperately faster, and knew that he had lost as the night lit up in front of him, eyes like boiling moons staring down at him.

Tembo's last thought was that he had been a fool. He should have run *amongst* the army instead of away from it. After all, they had kept the demon down for hundreds of years. Too late the thought struck him for his head was already rolling, tumbling, along the ground, separate from his body.

Chapter 15

Domino protested loudly at being left behind, after sniffing suspiciously at the wicker picnic basket in El Harper's hands, and being rebuffed firmly but gently when he tried to lift the latch with his cat's paw and open the hamper. Susan, changing her clothes in a furious hurry in the bedroom, came out in time to see the last of her pet's embarrassing behavior. She tied her white silk blouse in a knot at her naval and straightened out the front crease in her navy trousers. She picked up her muslin-colored blazer. "Okay?"

El looked her up and down. She wore espadrilles with a moderate heel and he didn't think the sometimes hike from overflowing Griffith Park parking lots would bother her too much. He rather liked the effect of the rest of it. The silk blouse spilled open to show a lightly freckled neck and throat curving into a hint of full breasts hidden below. "I think," he appraised slowly, "Nearly perfect."

She plunked down a pert red straw hat on her head and he laughed. "Now you're perfect."

She turned an ankle. "A patriot all the way. Besides, we kind of match."

He wore white summer trousers with a blue jacket and blazing red suspenders over a comfortable white shirt. They hooked elbows and did a pose in front of her lobby mirror. Its antique English surface reflected them back. Susan suddenly unhooked her arm. She pushed Domino away from the picnic basket.

"Whatever have you got in there? Domino's ready to make a raid."

Harper rescued the hamper. Domino clung to the wicker with all four paws, but his ample Himalayan body weighed him down and he had to drop off as El swung the picnic basket. Susan snatched him up and exiled him to his bathroom and hallway.

"I'm sorry. I've never seen him behave like this."

"I'll give the chef his compliments."

Domino cat-howled from the hallway. Susan grabbed her purse. "Ready?"

The cat's voice rose louder. Harper tilted his chin toward the captive. "Will the neighbors complain?"

"It's likely, but he's got a rescuer on the way. The girl next door likes to come in and feed him. She's got a key."

"Then I'm ready. We'll just have time for dinner before the concert starts." He started to put his arm out again, but Susan dodged past him and through the open door.

Heavy traffic did not seem to bother Harper

as he threaded the car through the streets en route to the theater. He hung an elbow out the window, and with the radio on low, hummed off tune to a Mariah Carey song and let Susan relax. After long moments of comfortable silence, he turned toward her slightly.

"How's your grandfather?"

"I don't know. He stayed home from work today and that's not like him."

El seemed to deflate a little. "I'm sorry. I thought I helped."

"Oh, it's not that. I think you did. I haven't had any calls from him ... he's just getting older."

"And you worry."

"Yes."

"I would, too." Harper frowned thoughtfully. "My grandparents are gone. So is my father. My mother's too busy for me to worry about, but I think about her a lot."

Susan thought of the parents who refused to talk to her, who hung the phone up silently whenever they heard her voice at the other end of the line. No rudeness, no, they were the epitome of polite society. They simply refused to acknowledge her existence.

Harper didn't seem to notice her lapse. He leaned forward and turned up the radio, catching part of the news.

". . . .Authorities today say there is still no break on the mysterious death of a Los Angeles transient known as Digger who was mutilated and then torched to death, his disembodied hand and pack the only clues to his murderer. LAPD hopes that anyone who might have seen the before dawn incident three days ago will come forward. . . . In sports today, the struggling Dodgers try to hold onto first place as they begin a three game away series in San Francisco. . . ."

The sound faded out again. Harper said flatly, "I knew him."

"Really? How?"

"He lived by the museums. He used to cadge lunches from the schoolkids. Sometimes we'd get complaints from a parent that some dirty old bagman had scared their child, but generally everyone liked him. He'd tell stories while he finished off whatever they didn't want in their lunches. Pretty harmless."

Susan shuddered. "Who do you think killed him?"

"I don't know. I was there when the police found the remains."

"Oh, God."

"No . . . I mean . . . it wasn't that bad. Just clean ash. No carcass, just ashes." El paused thoughtfully. "I don't think he was torched. Cremated, maybe, except it was done right there, on the spot. It would take one hell of a lot of heat to do that. Eerie . . . just like he spontaneously combusted."

Susan looked at El, his strong profile, the melancholy lines etched naturally in his face, offset by his natural humor. "That can happen to people. I read about it once. Just—poof—ashes."

Harper looked briefly at her. "The kids are going to miss him," he said simply.

Susan shuddered again.

To make amends over the somber mood he'd created, El began to tell her funny stories of the kids he chaperoned through the museum. It pleased him when he could see her visibly relax and begin to laugh.

On the opposite side of the hillside acreage from the immense park and stables and riding area, near the observatory, the Greek Theater nestled in the open. Its high thicket walls hid the paraphernalia of the fireworks display but El pointed it out to Susan as they entered the bowl. The *1812 Overture* concert traditionally included fireworks and even cannon fire, but its conductor varied from year to year. John Williams was returning that summer to conduct some of his infamous movie theme music, along with other selections, and the crowd jostled one another to get into the bowl and picnic before the sun set at eight and the concert began in earnest.

The orchestra section was the best area for picnicking, the seats arranged and fenced off charmingly, with gateleg drop-leaf tabletops to be pulled up for eating and dropped back down at the box's side for the performance. Most boxes sat four, occasionally there were larger boxes, and then the rest of the theater simply held seats, but that didn't stop picnickers. They sat with their box lunches or picnic baskets atop their knees, thermos or wine bottles clenched between their feet.

Outside, snack bars sold gourmet baskets as well as simpler fare, and buckets of fried chicken could be seen riding the shoulders of theater goers everywhere. Susan stopped inside the bowl to catch her breath. The Greek columned stage was festooned for the Fourth of July and she felt happy, truly happy, for the first time in a long time. She flashed a smile at El.

"Which way?"

"Down in front," he answered, "third row back."

She made an "ooh" and said, "I'm impressed." Boxes that good were normally willed between families. She wended her way to the indicated row and aisle.

The box which El held tickets to sat four but, as he handed her in, he said only, "We'll be alone tonight."

She perched on the white lawn chair and set up the table so El could put down the basket. He sat it next to his feet, opened the lid so it hid the contents from her view and when he looked up, the sparkle in his eyes told her he'd done it on purpose.

A blue checked tablecloth came out first. He brandished it like a magician, snapping it neatly over the tabletop. Matching napkins followed, as did blue plates. The plastic ware was in white and red pieces, heavy duty utensils. El said, "I hate plastic forks when the tines snap off."

Then he brought out a clay insulator and slipped out a bottle of champagne. "Moet," he said. "Good but not overly pretentious."

Susan stifled her laughter as he presented it over his arm. He opened it carefully, saying, "It wouldn't do to shoot someone in this crowd."

Of course, the basket offered up champagne fluted glasses, crab tarts (no wonder Domino had been interested), and water crackers with a sampler of pates. Susan sipped at the chilled champagne, dry and not too sweet, and savored for a moment the feeling of being pampered. "I needed this," she said.

"Oh?" El snapped his crab tart into his mouth quickly and tried to look intelligently interested over too full a mouthful.

Susan laughed at him. He put a napkin to the corner of his mouth while chewing and swallowing quickly and said, "I don't want to miss my share."

For the next few minutes, like opposing toy soldiers, they lined up their sides of appetizers. El tried to cheat, hiding extra tarts in his overly large hands, but she caught him at it and then fined him a tart for trying. But he looked so remorseful she gave it back.

He brought out melon balls marinated in sweet wine. "Second course."

Susan had never tasted anything quite so heavenly. El watched in amusement as she downed every piece of melon flesh in her portion and then drank the sweet wine.

"I've brought a hedonist with me," he observed.

"Oh, you have no idea," Susan answered. She slipped her feet out of her shoes and curled up on the lawn chair. "To think that people really live like this."

"Ah, but do they appreciate it?" El leaned forward conspiratorially. He refilled her champagne glass.

"No. They couldn't possibly." Susan took a sip and felt a bubbly comfort. "You should see what I deal with. Furniture thrown out just because the owners buy super trendy designs or fabrics and get sick of them in a year. I could stock a store with barely used furniture."

"Why don't you?"

She shook her head. "I channel the goods to charity stores. They get a write-off and the charity stores get quality goods to sell for more than reasonable prices to people who aren't so fickle and I've done my good deed for the day." She downed her glass. "What else have you buried in that basket?"

"Ah." El bent over. "Baguettes filled with lobster salad." He produced the main course with a flourish and Susan said, "I've died and gone to heaven."

Heavy summer rains swept across China. The plane carrying Rose Wine bore the brunt of the monsoon front, dipping and trembling as wind and storm beat at it. She sat frozen in her seat, belt tightened across her lap, afraid to move, as if her slight weight could propel the plane in one direction or another and send it sliding to its death. She had not wanted to fly, she had never flown before, but her benefactor and guide had insisted. He had trucked her through the night to the airport and had taken her through, ignoring the many groups of armed soldiers searching the passenger lines.

His fingers like wire cables upon her arm, he had steered her between them, saying, "They're searching for male students. You have nothing to fear."

And although she quailed when her ticket was presented, the officials had not even looked at her when stamping it and passing her through the gate to the great field where the planes rested.

Now she was flying, and her guts clenched like a soldier's fist inside her stomach. The graceful young women who served the passengers whispered among themselves. There had been an accident in the cargo hold while loading. Someone had been mortally hurt. Their faces paled by their makeup, they paled even more when they talked about it. She had heard only snatches of the talk. It sickened her to hear of limbs torn off and blood splashed upon the freight and suitcases. She shut her eyes, hoping to also shut out their quiet voices.

The plane would take her south to Canton and there, closest to Hong Kong, she would face the most dangerous leg of her journey. The border would be guarded heavily and the concentration of the search for fleeing students intensified so close to freedom. She would have to be most careful finding her new guide and benefactor ... it might even be that her contact would not be able to help her, and she would be alone.

Keeping her eyes closed, she tried to think only of Tembo. His fingers had stroked her face most gently and yet his passion had been fiery. • For him she must be strong and serene, for him she must make it across the border. It would be Saturday night when they landed. On Saturday nights as students, they had gathered to drink a little beer and talk long, long hours into the night. She would never see most of those faces again. Rose Wine drifted into sleep.

The dinner rush hour ran well into nine o'clock on Fridays. Victor enjoyed playing the host, singing special requests for anniversaries and birthdays, promising more songs later in the cocktail hour. When he finally retired, Ling Lee, who stood in for Tam Chen, had left the day's mail and a package on his desk. He picked the package up and recognized Harper's printing.

He opened the parcel carefully and found a second clay shard in his hands.

Victor sat down suddenly, looking at it, stunned. He fumbled open his desk drawer and took out the original piece and fitted them together.

There was some damage. Ideograms all along the fracture would have to be guessed at, but, remarkably, the tablet was whole. It was no longer than a dinner plate and no wider than the length of his hand. At last he would know the story behind the Great Hope and Great Evil he had previously deciphered. He set his watch alarm and stole a little bit of time to begin working on the mystery.

They ate four alarm lemon tea cakes in the dark at intermission, the lemon zing cleaning her palate and the sweetness sinking comfortably into her senses. Susan felt sated with good music, good food, and good company. She helped El repack the basket quietly, lower the drop-leaf table and swing it back into position along the box side, and opened the chair beside her so he could sit down. She tossed her hat onto the top of the hamper and let her hair cascade down. She didn't see the expression on his face in the dark, but his warm flank brushed up against hers and she leaned back, finding him a sturdy support.

"Ah," murmured El in contentment, echoing hers. "I should have tried the champagne sooner."

She gave him a knuckle in the ribs, felt him flinch, and laughed softly, adding, "Don't get too comfortable."

"Not yet," he answered.

She quieted as the music began again and realized that, although the amphitheater filled
with the strains of adventurous music from favorite movies, she could still hear the steady,
even beat of his heart and the flow of his breathing.

It was a masculine sound she had never really
even known she'd missed before, and now it
seemed to fill some aching void. She shut her
eyes and listened closer.

The jumble of noise from the Jade Pheasant's
kitchen jarred Victor as Lee Ling came in and
bowed deferentially. "Will you be singing tonight?"

Victor's alarm chimed softly in conjunction.
He put a hand to his stiff neck and rubbed it.
"How's business?"

"Good."

Jue looked over the tablets and the papers he
had strewn over the desk. "I have something to
finish here, unless I'm being asked for outside."

Lee inclined his chin. "I think," the older man
said, "you will not be missed. It is a busy night."

"Good." Victor's gaze fell back to his work
and he pencil sketched an ideogram carefully.
Ling's shadow fell across his papers. Victor
glanced up and met his gaze. The older man
cleared his throat, saying only, "I'll take care of
it."

There was a pause during which he hesitated.
Then Victor said, "Do you read classical Chinese?"

Ling's eyelids stretched, showing his embarrassment, although he did not color the way a Caucasian would. "A little," he said. "Although mostly I read the I Ching and play mah-jongg." He pointed at the ideogram. "That is sometimes interpreted merely as 'fire,' but those extra brush strokes intensify the interpretation. Today it might be called 'dragonfire,' particularly if combined with a dragon tile."

"No," Victor said, eying the ideogram uncomfortably. "This is not a tile. But it is a potent sign."

Lee Ling nodded confidently, before turning and heading back the way he'd come.

Victor sat back in his chair. He looked at his scholarship. "I don't know what you found, old friend," he said to the absent Harper. "But you're playing with hellfire, wherever you are."

Harper turned his chin very slightly. "Are you sleeping?" he whispered softly, not wanting to wake her if she was.

"No," Susan answered quietly. She roused slightly. "How long before the fireworks?"

"Maybe another twenty minutes or so."

She said, "I should find the bathrooms." She retrieved her purse.

"I'll come with you."

"No need. I've my good luck talisman." She opened her purse, found the feathered amulet he'd made for her, and slipped the cord over her head. "See?"

Someone behind them shushed them lightly.

Susan made a face at El and slipped out of the box. There was no moon to light the evening sky, and the amphitheater had been dimmed in anticipation of the fireworks, so she picked her way carefully along the aisle, the white fencing of the boxes a dull gleam in the darkness. Once to the side, she quickly found her way out and to the restrooms.

The bathrooms were nothing fancy. She examined her makeup in the broad mirrors before leaving. "You've had too much champagne, girl," she reproached herself. "It makes your eyes shiny and your face light up."

A big, comfortable woman next to her overheard and laughed. "And what, child, is wrong with that?"

Susan smiled. "Nothing, I guess." She put her purse under her arm and made her way outside.

Big pines feathered the outside hedges like tall sentinels. Up on the hillside to the rear of the seats and technically outside the theater, she could see a blink of light from a flashlight. Someone lay on a blanket outside the theater preparing to watch the festivities. Then she saw, in the illumination from the snack bars and restrooms, that two someones shared the blanket and a kiss as well. Susan looked away, feeling guilty for having stolen a moment of their happiness. She went back into the theater at the front entrance, quite close to the stage.

She stood in the darkness again and blinked her eyes to accustom herself before trying to move along the aisles. The talisman feather tickled the hollow of her throat and she put a hand to it, tucking the necklace outside her blouse.

The music swelled with romance and adventure, reaching a crescendo. Susan put her hand to her cheek, suddenly feeling very warm. Then, as she looked back across the bowl and up the rows of boxes and seats, she could clearly see the skyline of the park through the trees at the rear.

Something launched itself, gliding, sailing across the bowl. It gave a hoot which the music swallowed up and Susan barely heard it. She froze, watching the wild bird come in on a silent wing glide, the predator of the night, its wide owl eyes on her.

A flashlight beam from an usher swung up, pinning the bird in the night, and it was an owl, its wings outflung, skimming over the bowl. Susan caught her breath at its beauty and then caught it again, as she realized it had begun to plunge downward, at her and the stage.

It was so strange, she could not move. The champagne dulled her senses enough so that she did not know what to think, except that the owl came at her, barely visible in the velvet darkness, and that she was warm, so terribly warm, from the drink. Something in the hedge behind her thrashed.

Susan caught herself at the last moment and flung herself aside as the owl dove at her face, claws out, eyes glowing bright yellow. As she went to her knees on the rough cement steps, the bird grazed her. She felt the fan of its wings across the back of her head.

A screeching whistle split the night. Pink and white gold blazed about her as the darkness exploded.

Chapter 16

Sound and fury erupted around her. Wrapping her hands over her head, she landed chin first and felt the grit bury into her skin. Sparks showered all around her. She could smell burned hair and feel the heat. She was burning! Then there were hands on her, tugging her out of the way, pulling her out of sizzling light and into the shaded darkness. She blinked fiercely. El's blurred visage swam into her view.

The shrieking and sparkling continued. Thick smoke filled her throat. She coughed and flinched, looking over her shoulder, to see one of the tall hedges spouting forth fireworks. With a muffled sound, El yanked her to her feet. He hauled her out of the cascade of light and sound and into darkness. Another pair of hands were on her, helping. Harper patted her all over, saying to one of the young ushers, "She's smoldering."

Dazed, Susan let them rip off her blazer and El stomped it into oblivion on the ground. She shivered. "What happened?"

"Damn fireworks display fell over and caught

on fire. If you hadn't been ducking that bird, you've have gone up like a torch." Harper breathed hard, as though he'd been running. "I couldn't get to you in time."

"But you did." Susan spread her hands, dazed, and looked at them. "I'm all right."

The usher said, "Are you all right, ma'am?" as if disbelieving her.

"No, she's not. She's in shock." Harper put an arm protectively about her waist.

She realized they'd pulled her back outside. The errant display fizzled out and the John Williams' conducted music swelled up again. Her chin hurt. She shivered. "I'm okay."

A navy-blazered usher joined them, seniority printed like age upon his brow. He repeated the question, then added smoothly, "We'll be happy to pay for any damages."

"My jacket . . ." Susan said dazedly, looking at the trampled heap at her feet.

"And a bandage," added El. "She'll be fine."

"First aid is that way," said the supervisor. He led the way. El took her arm.

"Do you want to go home?"

"No." Susan caught herself, finally. She was all right. She took a deep breath. "But I think we'll have to sneak back in after the commotion we caused."

El laughed softly. His hand squeezed comfortingly about her arm. "That's my girl," he said.

She looked up at him. Despite the laugh, unhappiness had etched deeply into his face. "It was almost worth it," she said, in wonderment. "I haven't seen an owl in the wild for years. All I could think of was that it was coming for me."

"I saw it," El said. "And I couldn't get to you in time."

She shook her head. "But it wasn't the bird that got me. It was the fireworks display. What set it off?"

"Who knows? It probably sparked itself when it hit the shrubs. There's really no such thing as safe and sane." His grip about her tightened imperceptibly as the senior usher slowed in front of them.

The usher opened a nondescript door behind the snack bar. It led into a room in the concrete bunker which had a desk and phone and a few cots. An older woman looked up from a book and got to her feet as they walked in. The usher consulted with her in low tones and then left them alone. Susan didn't say much when the nurse checked her over for bruises or sprains.

"Anything hurt?"

"Nothing seriously."

El said mildly, "We don't want to miss the fireworks."

"From what Gil told me, you were in them headfirst." The woman smiled. She Mercurochromed Susan's chin and slapped a Band-Aid over it. She handed over a form, saying, "Just fill this out for management. We've never had this happen before, although sometimes ash from the explosions will burn car paint down in the lots."

El watched with the air of one listening to something distant. He was listening to the concert, Susan realized. When she was ready, he was true to his word and sneaked her back in through the rear aisles. They'd just made their seats when the first strains of the *1812 Overture* began. It was a typical late June night, and the air began to cool and dampen. Susan shivered and El quickly took off his jacket and draped it around her. They listened to the music with their feet propped on the picnic basket and "oohed" and "ahhed" with everyone else when the cannon fire and actual fireworks began to boom.

She leaned her head on his shoulder and something drifted out of her hair. She plucked it out of the air as it wafted down. A silken brown owl's feather lay across her fingers. "This one's for Domino," she said. "Now he can't complain he doesn't have one of his own."

El chuckled deep in his chest and she heard it rumbling, and thought of a sleeping lion. She tucked the feather away in the pocket of her slacks.

The demon emerged into the night, feeling his new skin crackle and stretch as it attempted to expand into his new form, that of Tembo, but he fought to keep himself compressed, coiled like a spring before an attack. He knew what Tembo knew, a cacophony of tumbling knowledge and emotion, bursting throughout his body, disrupting his own demon senses. Having absorbed Tembo, he knew instantly that the world had changed greatly. He also knew that many things had changed not at all. The mighty still reigned. With stealth and cunning, he would find a place for himself. With stealth and cunning and power such as he would gain when he found and defeated the other.

His minor demon quested to the south, but he was not constrained to waiting for the blood demon's reports before he began to move again. He wanted to be away from ancient Xian. The emperor's army tugged at him still, magic latent and deep in their simple clay bodies. He would be sealed within the earth yet if the diggers had not forgotten what lay below the shield and awakened him and then the earth had shrugged as if weary of its burden.

Mankind defeated itself, as always, and he could rely on that. Once outside, he let his form go and drifted into a massive dark storm cloud and shaded the moon while he tasted the different scents of the trade winds. He could not ride the wind long, for his essence was of earth and water. It was the sultriness which kept him aloft. For fun he loosed the rain and listened to the screams of those who drowned in the deluge as the night wore on.

Rose Wine came awake with a jolt and a cry, to find the stewardess' hand on her shoulder and an unsmiling face above her.

"It is time," the stern woman told her, "to fasten your seat belt. We are landing." Behind her plain visage, dawn's light streaked through the plane's windows. It was morning, early morning, and Rose Wine had made it to Canton.

She apologized and the stewardess left. She uncurled her legs, pins and needles spiking her feet, and buckled her belt solidly, tightly, fearful of breaking any more rules. To call attention to herself could be fatal. She looked toward the window where a passenger had yanked up the screen and bright light flooded in. She thought of sanctuary, a day and twelve hours behind in time, an ocean away, and wondered if she dared hope to reach it. She had to. Not only her hopes rested upon it, but those of many others. They had chosen her, a poetess, with her ability to memorize and recite for hours, to remember the benefactors and hiding places of the students now being hunted. When she reached sanctuary, she would be free to give out that information so that they all could be rescued. Even Tembo would not have suspected it of her. She had not told him for fear of endangering him as well.

The plane swooped down, leaving Rose Wine gulping in her seat, both afraid and glad she had not eaten much before boarding, her hands gripping her seat belt tightly for extra security.

As the great swinging weight of the airplane skidded and slowed, pressing her back into her seat, and then came to a halt, she scarcely dared to breathe. She let the others push past her, into the aisle and away, and left among the last. The plane's great metal body shook and clanged as the cargo handlers below seemed to attack it.

She paused at the top of the stairway, one hand on the rail. The air stank of oil and smoke and tarmac already heated by the sun. She stepped down and hurried to catch up with the flow of passengers ahead of her, crossing into the terminal. The bustle and confinement confused her. Without seeming to, she put her chin down and followed, blending into the hordes in the suddenly noisy buildings, aware that the army was everywhere, looking, watching, their hard dark eyes scanning the crowd.

A silver-haired grandmother in old style coat and trousers cupped her hand about her elbow. "Daughter-in-law," the woman chirped. "It is good to have you home."

Rose Wine felt her dinnerless stomach clench and bobble in fear. "Honorable Mother," she stammered. How to persuade this elderly woman she had accosted the wrong person?

The old lady gave her a harsh stare. "Rose Wine," she said. "Are you well?"

The sweat that had begun to spring up on her forehead ran down into her eyes, but the fear began to ebb. This was yet another of her benefactors. Rose Wine gave a pallid smile. "I am well," she answered. "But I may be with child," she lied so that others overhearing might understand her pale face and hesitation.

The grandmotherly benefactor stopped and made a motion of pleasure. The army surrounding them looked away, frowning, and did not look back as they linked elbows.

The benefactress lowered her voice. "Bags?"

"Nothing," Rose Wine said. She carried her roll of belongings, meager as they were, with her.

"Good. Let us leave here then." The grandmother stretched her tiny steps into a brisk pace, leading Rose Wine through the crowded building into a vast symphony of noise outside.

A battered truck awaited them. Its interior was redolent with the smell of garlic and chicken. The gap-toothed driver was of an age with the woman, battered brown hat pulled down to his eyebrows. He smiled until his eyes disappeared into his wrinkles and she felt instantly reassured. Rose Wine got in and slid across the seat. The silver-haired elder hopped in and slammed the door shut.

"Hurry," was all she said, with a thinning of her lips, and she looked back at the milling army troops that filled the sidewalks of the terminal.

Rose Wine watched, too, with a kind of horrified fascination that did not fade as the troops suddenly scattered and then began to club their rifles down as something massive charged among them . . . a dog, she thought . . . which escaped their punishment and plunged back and forth among the crowd, creating havoc. She watched until the truck had jolted away from the airport and into busy Canton traffic. The style of the city was far different than what she was used to, and she found her stomach tighten as if she still had the airplane seat belt buckled about it.

The elder put out a lined hand and patted her knee. "You have made it this far," she said. "We will do what we can to see your journey has a successful ending."

"Thank you," Rose Wine said in her still, small voice. "Thank you very much."

Victor came awake with a jolt as the phone rang. His head was resting on a corner of the tablet. Numbing pains stabbed through his forehead as he grabbed for the receiver. Tam Chen's brisk tones rang clearly though he was an ocean away.

"Boss. I'm in and settled."

Victor's mouth felt like cotton. He wet his lips and took down the hotel information Tam recited dutifully. When Chen paused, Victor said, "I suppose you've already been measured for a suit."

"Two, actually. My tailor's moved to Vancouver, but his son is still working here."

Victor's fuzzy mind began to clear at Tam's subtle reminder of the metamorphosis Hong Kong was undergoing. Communist China might well find a completely deserted island when it took over in three years, with the exception of those businesses it had already begun to infiltrate. *Orchestrated insanity,* Victor thought. His fingers crabbed about his pencil.

"And your vacation?"

"Well planned," Tam said confidently. "I meet my tour guide tomorrow morning."

"I'll talk to you after," Victor answered.

"Okay, boss. Any problems there?"

"None at all." Victor put down his pencil and rubbed out the numb spot on his forehead where the clay tablet had imprinted its corner. "Give me a call when you get back."

"Sure thing."

Victor hung up slowly after Chen had gone, listening to see if he could perceive any tap or interference on the line, though he knew electronic surveillance was far too sophisticated in many quarters to give itself away. But still, he listened and, hearing nothing, he hung up.

His desk was strewn with paper. He looked at the cryptic notes he had been making to himself. Little of it made sense.

Great evl and great hope was still all that he truly understood. He checked his watch. It was after midnight. The kitchen would be closed and the bar quieting down. Morning, he thought. Morning brings great hope with it. He gave a sigh and stood.

Susan stood hesitantly on her front step. She took off his jacket and held it wrapped about her hands. "I'd like to ask you in," she said finally, awkwardly, "but I don't think this is the night."

"I understand," El said, and he sounded as if he really did. He gently took the jacket from her hands. "I only hope this wasn't a mercy date."

"A mercy date?"

"To pay me back for talking to your grandfather last night."

"Oh." Susan felt her neck grow warm. She shook her head. "No. I mean—you were wonderful with him—but tonight sounded like fun. And it was."

"Minus the singe marks."

"Hey, what's a little singe?" She began to smile, saw his face moving closer to hers, and shut her lips quickly, preparing for the kiss he intended. Their mouths bumped tentatively. She thought, *Shades of junior high;* and then his lips sought hers more assertively and she moved into the circle of his arms. He was tall enough that kissing tilted her head back, stretching her throat, and she could feel her pulse jump in it. Guilt surged in her and then thankfulness ... thankfulness that someone still wished to kiss her in this passionate way, thankfulness that she was still alive and wanted.

El released her abruptly and stepped back. He put a finger on her still pursed mouth. Her lips felt full and pulsing beneath his touch. "Stop now," he said, "or I'm going to be very unhappy about not being invited in."

Susan gave a shaky laugh. "We can't have that."

"No." He took another step or two away, turned half around and said, "What are you doing tomorrow night?" He caught himself. "Actually, tonight. Saturday, that is."

"Nothing."

"Dinner, then. And a movie. We can argue about which one we want to see and then go see a foreign film with subtitles in a theater so dimly lit they can't be read."

"Sounds wonderful."

"I'll call."

With that he was gone, out of line of sight of the juxtaposed condos. She would have to go to her front window to see him walk to the parking lot, so she backed up quickly through her door, leapt over Domino, and parted the slats just enough to see between them.

Harper walked with a lean, canted stride that made it looked as if he walked into a high wind, formidable but not unconquerable. She watched him as he reached his car and disappeared into it. The slats snapped back into place about her fingers.

She looked down to see Domino encircling her ankle, sniffing with delight at the cuff of her pants where a bit of lobster salad had dropped. He delicately fished it out with one chocolate paw, made a sound of contentment, and swallowed the tidbit.

"What I went through tonight," she said to the cat, "so you could have that snack, you wouldn't believe."

Unrepentant and ungrateful, he rolled over and presented his considerable stomach for a rub. Susan bent down and tickled him for a moment while he squirmed about on his back.

Chapter 17

From the corner of her eye, Susan caught a shadowy movement on the patio. It straightened and the sliding door moved under its volition. She jumped with a gasp, kicking Domino away, her shoulders bumping into the wall. A window frame rattled, but the picture stayed on its hook. It was the closest thing to hand and Susan thought of tearing it down and pitching it.

Then the figure moved into the dim light.

"Poppa!" She caught her breath. "What are you doing here?"

"I thought to make use of that key you gave me. It's been hot, so I took a nap outdoors." Irving gave her a crooked smile, his face sunken with weariness. He wore his pajama tops tucked into his shiny black pants and both were wrinkled and sour smelling as if he'd been in them all day.

"Oh, Poppa." Susan moved to the air conditioner thermostat. She kept it on eighty for the cat and turned it down now to sixty-eight. "You need something cold to drink. Iced tea?"

"I had some." He waved a hand. "Any more and I'll be up all night." He eyed her. The rims of his lids were red and crusted and his eyes looked like flakes of coal, hopeless, tired. "You been out?"

Susan felt the crush of guilt, which she'd let go of when El kissed her, come flooding back. "You should have paged me."

"What for? You need a life." He pulled out a dinette chair and sat on it, and she saw for the first time that even the slight chair dwarfed his slender frame. His shoulders were bowed as he leaned forward onto the tabletop. "Did I do wrong, Susie? Am I an old cocker for barging in here like this?"

She hugged him gently. "Never. I would have felt much, much better if I'd known you were here. Stay as long as you like."

"Then I'll come more often." He patted her arm before she ended her embrace. "You sent your boyfriend home."

Susan crossed to the kitchen, found the orange juice, and poured him a glass, saying, "It's acid-free, so drink it." As she watched him take the juice, she added, "He's not my boyfriend."

"But he's a maybe?" She sat down and kicked off her shoes. Domino came back, his fur rumpled, and lay across her shoes, fastidiously ignoring her for his hasty departure earlier. "It's scary, Poppa. Do I have room for both of them?"

Irving wiped his lips with a knobby, well-callused finger. "One's living and one's dead.

Take my advice. If you need room, kick the dead one out."

"But it's Geoff!"

"I know who it is. You think I don't know? But you're young. You got all of life ahead of you."

"You wouldn't do that to Sylvie," she said softly.

Irving shrugged. "I don't need to. I'm an old man. I need another wife like I need another hole in my head. You, on the other hand—" and he gestured eloquently. He finished his juice. "So you've dated before. How come you're asking questions now?"

"I don't know." Susan drew rings on the table with the dew off the glass. "It seemed like it was time to."

"Ah." Irving stood up, padded into in the kitchen, and refilled his drink. He came back. "Then I'd say this Harper fellow is a definite maybe." He brightened. "I'll call Maida and let her know where I am."

Shocked, Susan said, "But it's after one!"

"So? At least she'll know where I am. I'll tell her not to worry." With an impish expression over his hollow features, Irving went to the phone. He dialed and stood waiting a moment. Then, "Hello? Mai? This is Poppa. I know, I know. I'm at Susie's. I'm gonna be here a day or two. She's got air-conditioning and a big screen television, that's why. Okay? Talk to you later. Go back to sleep." He hung up triumphantly.

Susan laughed in spite of herself. She got up and stepped over Domino. "I'll fix the bed up for you."

"Don't bother. I did it myself, already. You got a nice place." He sighed, barely audibly, as he glanced around it. He had rarely intruded on her life. When she was with him, it was either at Sid and Maida's, or the tailor shop, or the ancient apartment he'd lived in for forty some years.

Susan tracked with him. "It's hard to imagine Geoff here, isn't it? He never was, really. Just a couple of months." Just long enough to buy that big screen television Poppa had just sounded inordinately fond of. "So where have you been all evening?"

"At *shul*," Poppa answered. "At the temple, talking to the rabbi."

"Oh?" Susan paused, watching the older man.

"He's the one who told me to take care of the living. He said they needed more help than the dead." Irving passed by her en route to the guest room. "I told him that was some education he got to pass out advice like that."

"Poppa!"

` He winked at her from the doorway. "Aw, *shiksa*. What good is a rabbi if you can't argue with him a little? Anyway, it's late. I'm tired. You need your sleep." He disappeared into the bedroom, then popped back out. "Oh, and a Mrs. Lerner called. She wants you to have breakfast with her in the morning. She saw something divine she absolutely must have and she wants to show it to you." His mimicry was obscured by his own heavy accent. With a wiggle of his eyebrows, Poppa disappeared again as Susan let out a groan. Morning seemed unbearably close.

Once inside the room, Irving clutched the door frame behind him as he closed the door, his entire body trembling. He could smell the smoke on her, smell it as if she had already stood the trial and walked away whole from the pyre, and what would she have thought of him if he'd told her that? He would not let her go as he'd had to let go of Sylvie and Geoff and all the others, a parade of them passed his old tired eyes whenever he shut them, and the rabbi had sat and talked with him and told him, "Give the living your help. The dead don't need it."

And so he had to stay with Susan, to protect her from his vision.

He crossed the darkened rooms, unknowing and unheeding of the overhead light, because his inner vision of fire, ever burning and leaping, cast its own light and that was all he needed to see by. He fell upon the bed and into sleep, too old and too weary to stand guard anymore that night.

They fed Rose Wine and gave her a change of clothes, so that she might look as if she belonged in their southern district. She thanked them profusely, for the weather was hotter and stickier than she was used to. When the curtain of darkness fell, they all rode in the battered truck and made their way further south and east, toward the island of freedom known as Hong Kong. The roads were busy even at night, lorries of soldiers being carried back and forth.

The grandmother watched with her aged lips thinly pursed as though she sucked a lemon. "It will be difficult to get the others out," she commented.

"They're in hiding," Rose Wine said. "They will stay until they know there is safety."

The old man laughed, his brown hat bobbing up and down on his forehead. "There is safety in nothing," he said. "But we will try."

The grandmother said only, "Hush, old one." She patted Rose Wine on the knee. "Now remember what I tell you."

And she recited to Rose Wine the directions from the road down through the tangled grove to the shore, where she was to wait until a boat came for her. From under the seat she fished out an old machete knife, its handle rewrapped with hemp, its rusty blade sharpened. "You will have to cut your way down. Do not leave much of a path or it will catch the soldiers' eyes."

Rose Wine gingerly took the machete. "I understand." She looked out the window at the night, where bamboo and other growth hugged the coast road. It would hide her as well or better than the darkness, she thought. She shivered in spite of herself.

The old woman's shoulder bumped hers.

"Rest," she said. "I will tell you when it is time."

Rose Wine obediently closed her eyes. She thought of Tembo and the others to give her strength. If she were caught, she would be raped and battered, perhaps even tortured, but the captors would never think to seek the answers her frail body held. That was her only hope. If captured, they would never know what they had.

If and when she made it to freedom, she would write another poem. Composing it against the still backdrop of her closed eyes, Rose Wine drifted into a light sleep.

She awoke abruptly when the old truck jolted off the road, wheels bouncing desperately over monsoon flooded and summer sun baked ruts. Her knees braced her from sliding into the dashboard, and the elderly woman had her arms thrown about Rose Wine as well.

They bumped foreheads. "Go now," the woman said. "Quickly."

Rose Wine grabbed her roll and her machete and leapt from the cab, leaving the two elders to close the door after her. She caught the shadow of herself imprisoned in their headlights for the barest of moments and then she plunged into the undergrowth, headed toward the trees, the beach, and the landmarks she'd been given. The boat, when it came, would be narrow, sleek, fast, and modern. Its driver would be her final benefactor.

Rose Wine bit the corner of her lip in determination, hoisted her roll onto her back, and gripped the machete firmly. As the coiling grass and thick bamboo closed behind her, she could hear the drone of more lorries upon the road. More soldiers, never ceasing. She hoped the grandfather and grandmother would get their truck out of the ruts before there could be any trouble. She hurried, using the machete only to chop herself clear when she could move no other way, always keeping her eyes focused on the shore and the groves marking it, bent over the water and the rocky edge. The smell of the sea was sharp and clear, the strongest sense in the night. A single white eye turned itself upon her, a patrol boat cruising slowly along the coast. Like a cyclops, it beamed upon the shore. She dipped to the ground and hugged it. The chug-chugging faded away. She did not stand up until all she could hear was the faint beating of the surf upon the shore.

As she stood, she could see the small bay and outcropping whose landmarks the grandmother had pressed into her mind. There was little beach—the bamboo and trees pressed hard upon the cliffs here—but Rose Wine's heart leapt at its sight. She shrugged into her roll and picked up the machete. Her destiny was in view.

As she looked back once, she thought she saw a movement. Bamboos leaned and wavered. A darker shadow flowed among the shadows. Rose Wine chewed her lip in hesitation. Did she see or did she imagine? She tightened her hand upon the machete grip. What chance did she have against armed soldiers?

Grasses whispered. A sharp crack split the air, the sound of a branch popping under a heavy step. But she saw nothing. Then the noise came to her, the high-pitched whine of a fast engine. Another boat on the water. Without looking, she knew it could be the boat come for her. Sucking in her breath as if it alone could fuel her, Rose Wine turned and plunged toward the cove.

"Halt!" The sharp command tore through the air like summer lightning.

Rose Wine went to her knees, her heart in her throat, afraid to move. She could hear bodies thrashing behind her. Two, maybe three at the most. She pushed the machete blade under the grasses to hide it and twisted around.

If she talked much, they would catch her northern dialect and know she was suspicious. So instead she let out a tiny cry, a cry she'd heard often in the peasant village of her youth, a sound of dismay the pig girls made when the stubborn swine broke through their pens and led them running through the mud and muck. Her cry sing-songed across the soldiers' approach as they drew near.

A flashlight beam played across her face. Rose Wine winced at its intensity. Behind it, three uniformed soldiers watched her.

"What are you doing here, girl? Answer me," the one to the fore of the other two barked. The bamboo shadowed his round face. His heavy rifle stayed slung across his chest, but the other two had theirs trained on her.

Her fear rushed in her ears like a mountain stream. She closed her eyes in a faint rush and felt herself swaying.

"Girl!" the officer snapped. "Answer me. What are you doing here? Are you lost?"

Rose Wine caught herself. She put her hand to the neck of her jacket, ripped and hanging loose from her plunge to the ground. She fingered the torn fabric. "Raped," she answered the soldiers.

The two in the rear eyed each other. She read the thoughts on their faces as clearly as if they'd spoken them. A peasant girl, walking to Canton. What else did she expect? And she would get little better from them. Rose Wine added a sniffle to convince them of her plight.

The officer in front looked unswayed. "Get up and let me look at your hands."

She pulled her legs under her, mind racing. Her hands would betray her. She'd no marks of daily farm work, no calluses at all except that used to guide her pen strokes. She squeezed her fingers about the hemp-wrapped handle of the machete.

"Come on! Get up, I said. Let me have a look at your hands, girl."

No marks at all except a writer's callus and the staining of ink along the cuticle. Rose Wine licked her lips. "Raped," she whimpered again.

The soldier's face tightened in determination.

He looked over his shoulder at his men. "Bring her to me."

The two looked at one another and then stepped around him. Rose Wine prepared to fight.

A snarl split the night. Something dark and massive jumped the officer from the road at his back. The flashlight went flying. He screamed and tumbled to his knees. Crimson flowered in the darkness as he sprawled under something huge that mauled at his neck and scalp.

The nearest man let out a burst from his rifle. The beast snarled again, flesh unhurt by the bullets, shook his prey then leapt into the muzzle of the firing weapon. Its momentum brought both soldiers down.

The sharp scent of gunfire and the blare of orange bursts and the heavy, musky and foul scent of the beast filled the night. The soldiers screamed as it attacked them. Hot blood, coppery smelling and thick, filled her nostrils. Rose Wine froze. Her heart hammered in her throat. What was it that so savagely tore human flesh?

The flashlight had landed close by, its beam searing the dark. In and out of its illumination, she saw the beast moving as it ripped and tore. A dog's shoulder, no, a lion's haunch, no . . . the massive jaws of a bear . . . no. . . .

Rose Wine forced a shuddering breath down her throat. An oily rankness covered the inside of her mouth, as if the beast's scent coated it. She must run while it fed. She caught up the machete, lurched to her feet, and sprinted toward the beach.

It bounded with her, knowing her mind. Bamboo and brush flattened under it. Rose Wine staggered and fell back. Its glowing eyes held her as it plunged to a halt. They stood, considering one another.

As big as a water buffalo, it was, swelled like a tick from the blooding of the three soldiers. She blinked. Its statuesque form was that of the lion dogs which guarded temples from demons—but it was a demon itself, mane curled thickly about heavily muscled neck and shoulders. Its eyes smoldered. In the ancient days, in the poems and classical tales, such a thing would have been sent by the gods to defend her. But the glitter and blood lust in its eyes told her differently.

"Go away," Rose Wine whispered desperately. She clutched the machete. Why wasn't she dead already? Why did the monster hesitate?

It trod a heavy paw in her direction. She backed up a step. Its jowls opened in a doggish grin, amused. It came a step closer.

The heavy rifle fire had damaged it a little, she saw in the moonlight, rather like darts thudding into wet clay. She could scarcely hope to scratch it. Her curved blade wavered in her hand.

Along the water, a thin droning caught her attention. She could hear it above the pounding of her own heart and the thick breathing of the demon. For a beat she did not recognize the sound, and then she did. It was the boat, the boat coming to pick her up. So near and yet so hopelessly far. . . .

Rose Wine lunged. She chopped at the thing's thick neck with the full weight of her leap. The blade sang in the night air as it swooshed downward and the demon gave before her onslaught.

Tam eased the throttle back and checked his watch. He had only minutes before the patrol boat would turn round at the point and head back. The air hung heavy and sticky. It would rain again soon, not that that would ease the humidity or temperature any. He took a handkerchief from his pocket and wiped his face, then the palms of both hands. Something dark showed on the linen. Frowning, Tam held it to the instrument panel's dim lights.

Somehow he'd gotten back the handkerchief he'd given Victor, the one with the ideogram branded into its cloth. Tam stared momentarily at the oddity seared into the fabric, then folded it over and tucked it away. The happening seemed a lifetime away. He would have to check the tong rumors when he returned. The loss of a neighborhood gang of young toughs did not assure safety for Victor. He did not like leaving Victor and the Jade Pheasant unprotected for so long.

The pocket tape recorder pressed into his sternum. He had brought a rendering with him, so that the student might understand, as his American Chinese might be too foreign. He'd recorded it locally and sealed it in plastic against the monsoon rains and the ocean. It rested in his shirt pocket, oddly enough, over his heart. Tam touched it to make sure it was secure as the rendezvous landmark came into focus. Tam eased the boat across the tide breakers, headed for the tiny spit of beach below rugged sand and stone cliffs and breaks of bamboo. He thought he saw a movement along the cliff, furtive and quick, headed in his direction.

Tam beached the cigarette boat as well as he could, shut the engine off, jumped out into the water, containing a gasp as it rose icily to his chest. He pushed the boat farther ashore, beaching only its needlelike hull. The tide came with him as he strode out, foaming as if it birthed him, under the splinter of a moon and the wine dark night.

The student pitched headfirst down the cliff, gorse and bamboo breaking the fall. Tam watched the slender body tumbling down. A girl, he'd been told, though he could not see the difference now, and she turned a pale face toward him even as she fell.

"Run!" she pleaded in Chinese he barely understood.

Adrenaline surged. He reached back into the boat for his automatic rifle as the girl somersaulted onto the sand. Something curved and cruel glinted in her hand.

He expected soldiers. What he saw barreling down from the clifftops froze his blood for a second. Tam felt his jaw drop in surprise. "Holy shit."

A great, blood-red beast, almost hidden in the night, save for the glow of its yellow orb eyes. A dog—a bear—a lion? His thoughts raced even as he leveled the rifle and let it burst. The thing growled as it surged toward them. A nightmare put together . . . had it been set on her scent? Were there soldiers behind it? He squeezed his hand tightly upon the trigger.

Gunfire shattered the calm. Tam staggered back a step into the surf as the rifle bucked in his arms. But he missed the creature bounding downward at the girl and it never missed a step. Tam sighted more carefully, to miss the girl, and squeezed off another round.

The bullets spit into the night. He could hear the thud as they hit, and yet the massive dog did not stop or even sway. He could hear himself cursing. "Shit, shit, shit." There was nothing stopping that beast short of a tank.

Tam ran forward, grabbed the girl, and hefted her to her feet. They had a chance to outrun it. Maybe the ocean would slow it down. They ran backward across the strand to the boat. She carried a machete in one limp wrist.

She pawed desperately at him, chattering. The only word of the dialect which he could recognize in her fear and haste was "demon."

Holy shit indeed. The hair rose on the back of Tam's neck. He rested the rifle butt on his thigh and let out a third burst as the beast came roaring onto the sand, less than two man-lengths away.

What in the hell is it?

The girl made a faint sound in his arms. The beast came to a stop and opened its jaws. Tam could see now, in the very, very dim moonlight, that chunks of it were gone, torn from it, and yellow light seeped out like blood from its wounds.

It gnashed its teeth and put one feathered paw closer. Tam had another round left. He raised the muzzle of the rifle. The creature's white-yellow eyes blinked and followed the movement.

It knows. Tam thought. A cold chill ran up his spine. The ocean surf foamed and dragged at their ankles. The cigarette boat bobbed restlessly, pulling from its mooring, ready to drift away. *It's not natural and yet it knows this is a weapon.* He wet his lips and tried to shift the girl from his front to his flank.

His heart drummed in his chest. The girl panted, her breast heaving within the embrace of his arm. She half-raised the machete. Blood as thick as clay dripped from it. Tam realized she'd already faced down the beast once. He gathered his courage to do the same.

The beast opened its gaping maw, spilling light out onto the sand. It reared up and leapt. Tam saw it all as if in slow motion. He steadied the automatic rifle. He fired a burst at its mid-section, enough power to cut a mortal creature in half, muzzle spitting red-orange.

Chunks of the beast spit away, but it did not falter. The force of the firepower ought to have knocked it back on its haunches, but the arc of its leap continued forward, unaltered. Tam braced himself for the contact.

They hit like bighorn rams smashing into one another. He felt teeth gouge deeply into the meat of his thigh. He jammed the rifle muzzle into the beast's throat and it let go, snarling. Pain shimmied through Tam's body.

Rose Wine cried out and tore away from his hold, machete up. They clashed and the girl went down, sprawling at Tam's feet. The machete clove into the creature's shoulder and when it landed, that leg caved under it.

Tam shoved the butt of the rifle into its snapping maw. The beast tore it from his hands with a toss of its head. He heard the weapon crunch as if it were a piece of cellophane and knew it was gone. He kneed the weeping girl aside and reached for the machete.

The thing spit out his rifle, metal pieces raining from its jaws like broken teeth. It grinned with amusement at Tam. He was looking down the gullet of his own death. He tightened his grip on the machete and swung.

Like a matador, the beast dodged him. Its jaw slashed him, catching the fatty underside of his forearm. The wound opened up, stinging like hell, and his hand was instantly drenched in his own blood. The machete twisted in his fingers. With a gasp, Tam pivoted in a *tae kwon do* move and kicked out, catching the monster in the throat. Teeth snapped at empty air.

With a samurai slice, he came about with the short blade.

It descended through the beast as though he tried to carve quicksand. Tam wrapped both palms tightly about the grip and hacked again. It swiped a paw at him, mewling deeply in anger and pain. His shirt tore under the slice of claws the length of his hand. The tape recorder tumbled to the sands, along with his handkerchief with the branded insignia. The beast charged him, stumbled upon the handkerchief and went to its knees. It howled and he saw with surprise that its flesh smoked where the handkerchief touched. He drew his breath tight and cocked the machete. Tam axed it, cutting deep into the shoulder muscles which held its head. The demon-thing growled and swam to get up, out of the sand and tide, its blood flowing darkly into the water, staining the foam.

Tam raised the machete for one last blow and cleaved the beast's head from its body. It spat out the remains of his rifle and died, still biting, upon the sand.

Yellow light poured like butter out of its cavernous body. The handkerchief lay in its path, blazing silver white until immersed, and then the thing simply collapsed. Tam stood, panting in disbelief.

A whirlwind rose from the sands, smelling of hot brass and iron and carrion. Tam braced himself as the devil wind tore round and round, the limp carcass of the beast rising within it. It soared skyward and then, against the night, Tam saw a massive darkness, an immense beast, whole, its bulk purple-black against the velvet. The whirlwind was sucked into its gullet and then, just as suddenly, there was silence. Tam swore that the night wind beast turned smoldering red eyes on him and *saw* him. His bladder felt weak, but he held his water and his ground and stared back at the creature.

The night went empty in a blink of crimson.

The girl moved feebly, bringing him back to his senses. Rose Wine struggled to get to her feet. She sprawled into his arms as he dropped the machete and caught her. His arm screamed with pain as he tried to hold her, and his leg threatened to give out under him. His pants leg darkened with blood.

Her tunic was blood-slick. He saw the massive stomach wound gaping. How could she have even run with that gut wound? She must have been something, petal soft on the outside and steel on the inside. He touched her cheek in admiration and consolation. He could do nothing. She smiled weakly at him.

"Benefactor," she said in English.

He nodded.

She clawed at his shirt. In Chinese, "Listen." Or perhaps it was, "Hear me." He wasn't sure. He bent close. It mattered not that the boat moved restlessly and the water had begun to rise, inexorably swallowing the spit of sand upon which he knelt and held her.

She began to recite. A poem. He could tell by its pacing. He hushed her. Tam retrieved his tape recorder, pulling it free of its wrapping and held it to her lips. She began again. His fingers against her chin felt her face growing cold, her lips already like ice. The only thing he understood readily was the word "Tiananmen." The only thing he could do for her would be to record her legacy.

The boat pulled mulishly at its beaching, rising and bucking when her voice stilled. He held her for a long moment, counting the empty minutes that she did not breathe, then lowered her. Tam left her, knowing the tide would swiftly take her body. He pushed the cigarette boat off the sand spit easily—another second or two and he would have been marooned—one hand holding the tape recorder dry. It had not been enough that the hard iron fist of the government had chased her down. Something unnatural had come after her as well.

He ripped the sleeve off his jacket and bound his forearm, then his leg. He did not know what had killed her. He knew only that it had succumbed to the base iron of the machete and perhaps, just perhaps, to the ideogram emblazoned on his handkerchief. Old magic, he thought, long thought to have gone its way in this world. Demons and iron.

He wondered what he would tell Victor in the

morning. His mouth tasted of bitter defeat and death. His arm needed stitching and discreet medical attention. He pocketed his recorder and piloted the boat toward sanctuary.

Chapter 18

The demon felt his youngling come back to him. It came howling on the back of the south wind and thudded into him with the force of a thunderclap. Its death had been sudden and unexpected. The demon felt no remorse, only anger at the incomplete mission. As he reabsorbed his essence, he came across a bit of material at the core, that which was not clay and water and which stung and slapped at his senses.

The sign of his nemesis, burned into this square of cloth. The demon let it drop away, flutter to the ground far below, and hovered among the storm clouds a little longer, pondering. It now had a direction. The cloth had come from sanctuary and the flesh the blood demon had been tracking had expected to find sanctuary across the sea and then the ocean, far and away to a shore the demon itself had only suspected lay across the horizon. *California.* The word lay across the demon's tongue and mind like a hot iron bit.

It would travel East, in the path of the sun, as far as earth and water could take it. The demon gathered itself from the storm front and began to move in the only way that it could, in the shaking and trembling of the earth and in the rain from the heavens.

Under its touch, China heaved and suffered.

Susan patted one last bit of hair into place. She eyed herself critically in the mirror. Half a night's sleep hadn't done her much good, she decided. She made a face and left the bathroom. She picked up her purse and keys. Poppa sat, with Domino at his elbow, watching the birds gather upon the patio. There were not as many as there had been, but the phenomenon was still startling.

She paused. "I've left you money for lunch. Call the pizza man, okay?"

Poppa Irving craned his neck to look at her. His hawklike nose seemed even more prominent as his face retained its hollow look. He had not rested well, either, no matter what he'd said to her. "Of course," he said. "You'll be with Mrs. Lerner?"

"All morning. Then I'll come back and rest and we'll go out tonight."

"This Harper won't mind an extra person along for the movie?"

She wrinkled her nose. "If he does, then he's not in line for the boyfriend position. It'll be okay. Just don't let Domino eat too much pizza. He'll get sick if he does."

"All right, all right." Irving shifted impatiently in his chair. She'd laid some of Geoff's old sports clothes out for him and he looked rather like a ten-year-old wearing big brother's jeans and polo shirt. "We'll be fine." He chucked the cat under the chin.

Domino had been looking a bit puzzled at the company but now seemed to enjoy the attention. His tail whisked across the tabletop.

Susan hesitated at the doorway, but Poppa flapped his hand at her without looking back.

"Go on, go on," he said. "Before you make me feel like an old man."

At that, she smiled slightly and left, locking the door behind her. The sight awaiting her in the parking lot daunted her momentarily. Her car was splattered with bird droppings, a handful of them lofting and winging away even as she approached. Susan wrinkled her nose a second time, from the odor.

"God," she said. "What did you do, wait in line for this privilege?" Water laws or no, she grabbed up the gardener's hose lying along the shrubs and hosed down her streaked car as well as she could. She'd have to run it through a wash to get it really clean. She got into it gingerly and eased it out of the condo lot. A few birds winged with her, heralding the passage of the car through the still morning air.

Tajah stretched across Angelo's black leather sofa like a leopardess. He admired the taut line of her skin and form. She stirred him in a way that most women could not. He would not be faithful to her, of course, and she had told him that, excusing his infidelity before it even happened. His taste for men would draw him from her eventually. They were a handsome couple together, he thought, admiring their reflections in the gold-veined mirror across the room, he just a silhouette behind the sofa and tawny Tajah. They were not sexed, he thought, male and female, but energy, raw and sensual and unconfined. Energy which burned and which would leave its brand upon whatever it touched.

Sizzling. He liked that thought and held it for a moment.

Tajah made pouty lips. "When?" she said.

"Soon," Angelo soothed. "She can't hold out much longer. She's on her own, she'll need the money."

Tajah put out her arm, curling it backward, so she could stroke his neck. "Soon?"

"Very soon." He had made arrangements with Galado. Galado was the essence of a discreet businessman. He expected to hear sometime this weekend of a tragedy befalling Il Mode. Bad wiring perhaps. Something combustible. Anthony smiled at himself in the mirror. Something *sizzling*.

A sluggish, sultry breeze stirred the knee-deep ash as Dano waded through the blasted area below Mt. Pinatubo. The mud and ash awash like a tsunami down the Arakan River had flooded everything. It looked like the end of the world, but the skinny, intense ten-year-old did not mind it. It smelled far better than the garbage dump ghetto to which he'd been consigned by life. He and his mother had hitched here, hoping to find some salvage, something of value in the villages destroyed and abandoned by the eruptions. The mount was unstable. No one had moved back into these areas. No one knew when the volcano would belch again, to combine with rain and flood the lands below with mud and lava and death.

The ground was hard and packed as he picked his way across it. It dug at his shell-like calloused feet, cutting despite the hardness of his skin. His mother had gone on, a torn and patched sheet slung across her back like an enormous, if sunken, pack, but Dano lingered behind. He paused at the corner of an adobe shack. The roof had gone, torn or burned away, the threshold sunk in a three foot sea of mud which now lay like concrete. But inside, something glittered on the wall.

He paused before entering the abode, then ducked inside the leaning walls which, although seemingly about to collapse, were firmly footed in the hardened mud. A small picture frame glowed where a stray beam of sunlight struck it. Dano pulled it down and examined it. Elvis Presley. It was not of much value, except that his mother liked American rock and roll. He tucked it inside his ragged shirt. A gold-toned cross was nailed firmly next to where the picture had hung. The gold color did not excite him, he knew it was doubtless only cheap jewelry. He pried that off, breaking a nail, and tucked it away also. He was about to turn away when he saw the object lying in the corner, like a wave-rider, as if it had been washed ashore and marooned. Dano picked it up with excitement. It was an electrical appliance. For what, he didn't know, but it had small whirling blades at one end and he thought it might be used for stirring. His mother would be most pleased with him. Perhaps this year she would not abandon him when she traveled to Subic to be with the soldiers. Perhaps this year she would take him with her. He could earn his keep shining shoes and running errands.

The walls of the house shimmered, as if the heat made them sway, as he tucked the appliance in his shirt and left the ruin. Outside, he paused. The air held a strange odor. He turned on his heels. The ground seemed to tremble under his rough feet, and he could hear a deep rumble through the earth. His dark eyes shot a frightened glance at the volcano. Plumes of purple smoke wafted into the sky. As he looked, the mountain began to spew.

Dano turned to run. They were close, too close. The air would fill with ash and they would drown in the hot mud. That was how he had lost his father and uncle and aunt two years ago. Then the rains would come and flood everything again.

Something reared up from the street in front of him, growing out of the shadow and mud and ash of disaster. Its eyes glowered at him. The spirit lion sat on its haunches, its head taller than any ruin, and opened its jaws in laughter.

The hair rose on the back of Dano's neck. He fished inside his shirt, curled fingers about the cross, pulled it out, and hurled it at the beast. The demon snapped at it, snatching it out of midair, and the tiny bit of jewelry crumbled in its teeth.

The boy's heart quailed. He had faced toughs in the garbage ghetto, bullies for the salvage to be combed out of the stinking refuse, even bullied a few younger inhabitants himself. He'd gone days without food and through hot, stifling Philippine nights without water. He was used to being on his own for months at a time when his mother left to earn her yearly expenses at the American base. But he had never faced anything like this and he knew he looked death in the jaws.

Behind him, the ground heaved and readied to receive the latest deluge from volcanic disturbance. Ahead of him sat something inconceivable that smelled of new death and old blood. Dano spun around again and sprinted, off through the broken teeth of buildings and ruins, with the laughter of the beast-thing echoing in his head. He ran with all his slim-limbed speed, twisting and turning through the labyrinth of the village. He ran until his lungs seized up and cramped, burning and closing off breath, and he came to a wheezing, staggering halt at the edge of the ruins.

He closed his eyes and doubled over, the appliance and the picture frame digging into his ribs. Before he could catch his breath, something hot and carrion scented drifted over the back of his neck.

Dano looked up into the gleaming ivory tusks of the beast. The boy got out one last scream for his mother before it devoured him.

The morsel, for that was all the scrawny boy was, still filled the demon with more thought and knowledge of the world. He cared for none of it except for what he filtered out about California and Americans. He could glean a harvest of meat from the volcano's latest spewing. He could picture, as the boy had, death riding on a wave of destruction. He needed the replenishment, for traveling beneath the ocean floor taxed his abilities greatly. It was conceivable he might not make it across the expanse of ocean to the other shore if he did not feed well. He would turn north and east, to another cluster of islands before foraging east. He would eat like the fatted calf.

The demon opened himself to the earth again and delved deep beneath its surface.

Tam Chen placed a call to Victor at the Jade Pheasant warehouse, where Victor stored most of his restaurant supplies plus the modest import/export goods for a side business which they used to cover their other interests. He had shed his bloodied clothes and calmed himself over what he had witnessed. He'd sealed his forearm wound with tape and wrapped it. The deeply gouged puncture wounds in his thigh he'd poured half a bottle of good hotel bourbon over, even as he thought about rabies. His hands still felt unclean and he wiped them constantly, first one and then the other. He was picking it up, he realized, from the pocket recorder as he handled it once more, waiting for the satellite connection to bring in Victor's voice. He took a bathroom towel and wiped it as well. It came away faintly crimson.

Jue answered.

"Boss," said Chen, identifying himself immediately.

"Tam! How are you? How was the tour?"

"Disastrous. Boss, I think you've got problems. Are you still working on that project for El Harper?" How to warn him, how to tell him what he'd seen without being thought insane. Tam juggled possibilities, came upon nothing solid.

A pause, lengthened by the distance between them. Then, "Yes."

"It's bad *joss*. It has to be." Bad fortune did not serve to describe all that had happened that night.

Victor responded carefully, "Was your tour rained out?"

That was part of their code, reasonable in the monsoon season. Reasonable to be rained out. Reasonable to have rescue operations aborted by military presence. Not reasonable to have deadly beasts pursuing and slaughtering them, only to be swallowed by immensely larger and more formidable deadly beasts. Beasts that ignored gunfire and defied gravity but succumbed to cast iron.

"Worse than that, boss," Chen said. He picked his words carefully, muffling the panic that had begun to creep back. He sipped at the remainder of the hotel bourbon. "I was nearly hit by lightning."

Death almost, for him. Death, certainly, for those they were trying to bring to safety. There was a mild buzz on the line. Chen reacted fearfully, thinking of surveillance, until he realized it was a long, drawn out sigh from Victor.

"Can the tour be rescheduled?"

"Not at this time." Chen said sadly. Without the information the girl was purported to carry, he could do nothing about retrieving the others. Word would have to be filtered through to them, new connections established, new bribes laid. "I'm getting my suits and coming home first flight out this morning."

"I'm sorry to see you cutting your vacation short."

"Never mind about me, boss. You watch out for yourself. We have bad *joss*." Chen absently turned the recorder deck over and over in his hard, dry palm.

Another pause. Then Victor said, "Will you be there a while?"

"For the moment. My flight's at mid-morning."

"Have a good trip home."

The line went dead.

Chen hung up the receiver. He sat back on the bunch of pillows he'd stacked up. His body felt bruised and sore all over. The phone toned softly and he snatched it up.

Victor said, "I think the line is clean. It should be anyway. What the hell happened?"

"You wouldn't believe me if I told you, boss. But she's dead. She didn't make it."

"How could she be dead? Was she followed?"

"Not by the army. My old grandmother could tell you better than I what we saw out there— as big as a water buffalo, with fangs—it sliced her up pretty good. She didn't have a chance. I tried."

"Are you all right?"

"I'm beat up some, but I'm fine. It's my mind that's messed up." Tam reached out and took a long drink from the long-neck bottle sitting next to his bed. "Boss, I've never seen anything like it, except maybe carved in stone and plaster . . . biggest and ugliest dog I've ever seen and meaner than a pit bull."

Victor asked, "Have you been sick?"

"Hell, no!" Tam sputtered a little, then calmed. Jue had the right to ask. Tam had caught malaria a couple of years ago. You never recovered from malaria, just put it into remission. "I'm fine, boss. But the girl. . . ."

"Damn. I was told she might be carrying information about the others on her. Did she say anything? Pass you anything?"

"She started reciting. I got part of a poem on

tape. She was out of her head with pain. I don't even think she knew she was dying."

Victor said slowly, "She was a poet. I was told she would probably be a Pulitzer candidate if we could get her out and keep her free. Guard that tape with your life. Don't get it translated there, it's not safe. Bring it back. Just maybe she told what she had to tell anyway. And Tam—"

"Yes, boss?"

"If it was anybody but you. . . ."

"I know," Tam said, and he did. "I'm sorry, boss. Go to Harper. Maybe he knows what's going on. These things didn't start happening until he brought you that tablet. And be careful. An AK-47 barely slowed this thing in its tracks. I had to use a machete on it."

"Damn," muttered Victor and the line went dead again.

Tam hung it up, picked up his bourbon and took a very serious drink.

Power breakfasting with Mrs. Lerner meant Blood Marys at the crack of nine o'clock, croissants with smoked salmon and herbed cream cheese, and fresh raspberries. Susan felt slightly cross-eyed when they had finished. Mrs. Lerner—"Call me Ava, Susan—" insisted on driving. They cruised down Wilshire and as they approached Hancock Park, the Page Museum with the condos stylishly a block behind, the older woman wheeled into the parking lot of the art museum sharing the acreage. Susan blinked.

"Is this where you saw it?"

"Yes. It caught my eye immediately." Ava Lerner flashed a wrist encircled by both a Rolex and a tennis bracelet. "Oh, good. It's after ten. They're open." She slid out, her Claiborne skirt rising up her knees. She leaned back into the car, faint worry in her light brown eyes. "Are you feeling all right, Susan? You don't drink much, do you?"

"Not . . . normally," Susan got out. Her head went light for a moment like a balloon wafting away and then she got a grip on it.

Mrs. Lerner smiled. "Then, dear, you really shouldn't drink so early in the morning. Do like I did—order it virgin."

Susan narrowed her eyes against the early morning glare and tottered after Ava Lerner, who was charging up the art museum walkway.

Great murals decorated the front lawn. Their primary color brightness reminded Susan of fast moving subways, the murals painted with graffiti artist quality. Only in California would artwork be shown outside without regard for inclement weather, she thought, as she determinedly followed after Ava Lerner. At least Mrs. Lerner, clad in a teal blue skirt and creamy white blouse, was easier on the eyes.

Inside, the glass and cement building offered a measure of dignity. The various immense rooms held artwork of all styles except Old Master, but Mrs. Lerner was on a pilgrimage of her own and veered off into a side wing where patrons were already gathering.

The exhibit could have been seen from the east wall window, and, indeed, the three solemn Chinese gentlemen faced the La Brea pits as if bowing to all that was buried there, she thought, as she and Ava Lerner came to a halt. There were antique silk tapestry screens, vases, water brush paintings, a Tang horse whose glaze was crackled with the patina of age, and these three terra-cotta statues.

Mrs. Lerner clasped her hands and sighed. "Aren't they marvelous? On loan, of course, and only here three more weeks."

Susan took a closer look. They were nearly her height, and the placard at their feet said they had been made life-sized over two thousand years ago, and each gentleman had been individualized to represent an actual member of Emperor Huang's army. "They are unique," she agreed. "But, Mrs. Lerner, they're not for sale. These are priceless treasures. From what I've heard, we're fortunate the current government will even let them tour. You can't expect me to call the embassy and try to buy one."

"I suppose not." Ava Lerner's lower lip puffed a little in a cursory pout. "But you'd think they'd have reproductions. Wouldn't you?"

Susan eyed the workmanship. "I doubt it. It would take a lot to duplicate this. The Tang horse, now, has been done. Perhaps you'd care for that?"

Ava turned her spoiled expression toward the

magnificent porcelain horse. She considered it. Then she turned back. "But the statues are so . . . different."

"That they are." Susan leaned closer to the glass case. The coin necklace about her neck came loose from her open-throated blouse and fell forward, clipping the glass with a sharp ring.

Susan let out a startled yelp and stepped back hastily, grabbing thin air for balance. Ava Lerner caught up her hands.

"What is it?"

Susan stared at the statues, saw nothing, and took a deep breath. "Nothing, I . . . I thought I was going to set off the alarm." She gave a shaky laugh and tucked her talisman back inside her blouse.

Ava laughed. "Dear Susan. No wonder we get along so well. You're a ditz just like me. Well, come along to the gift shop and let's just see if they're offering reproductions of these gentlemen or not."

Susan let Mrs. Lerner enfold her hands and escort her down the wing. She quickly looked back once over her shoulder and saw nothing amiss.

But for a moment, just a moment, she could have sworn the statues moved, hands and eyes turning to her, their clay attention captured by her as the necklace had struck the glass.

Tiny beads of perspiration dotted her upper lip. She leaned on Mrs. Lerner and chalked it

up to Bloody Marys in the early morning. It
could be nothing else . . . could it?

Mrs. Lerner compromised, settling for heavily glazed "mud" figurines of elegant Chinese
poets and scholars available through the museum. The statuary looked nothing like mud,
porcelain figures painted and enameled and
gilded, but they pleased the fickle woman's
taste. Susan placed an order as her thoughts
cleared, already planning what fabrics to use
for the living room which would coordinate
with Ava's new passion for things Chinese.

Mrs. Lerner drove her back to the high-priced
condo so she could measure and they could
plan. Her husband Carl mumbled a hello and
farewell, golf bag over his shoulders, as they
entered. Susan only hoped they would be finished before Mr. Lerner made the 19th hole.

It was late afternoon before she got free. She
went to Il Mode and sat down with a sigh, her
light-headedness now reduced to a dull throb.
The mail had come. She sorted through it
quickly, pleased to see two checks. She hated to
short-circuit Angelo, but she decided to deposit
them in her account first, and then write a check
to Il Mode for the balance after her commission
and partnership fees were taken out. If she ran
the checks through the business, Angelo would
suck them dry, vampirelike, before she ever saw
a cent. At least she had her mortgage covered.

She called Poppa. "Any pizza left?" The

feather from the talisman tickled her neck and she took the necklace off, dropping it onto the table. Her hoop earrings followed.

"A slice or two. This cat of yours has gas."

"I'm not surprised. Pizza isn't on his recommended diet. I'll be home soon. Did Harper call?"

"Not yet. Maybe there's no date tonight."

Susan smiled at the wistful hopefulness in Poppa Irving's voice. "Maybe. Wonder where I can get a backup date?"

"Just the two of us'll go out, Susie."

"That sounds good, Poppa. Make Domino walk around a little bit if he's bloated."

"Walk? I should make the cat walk? Now I know why he's called a Himalayan. He's been him-a-layin' here and him-a-layin' there ever since you left."

Susan laughed in spite of herself. Poppa made a growl of contentment. "Hurry up, *shayna*."

"I will. Just a few more minutes." Susan hung up. She pulled down her appointment book. Working with Ava Lerner was exhausting, but fruitful. And she'd pulled in a neighbor who'd then insisted Susan measure her living room for work. The job might not come through, but she'd be in the woman's thoughts for future work. She sketched in the notes and dimensions she'd taken down, and added a few more observances of the condo's present decor and lighting problems. It would be a challenge if she were hired.

The minutes had stretched into an hour when

she looked up. Poppa would be worried. She closed her appointment book, grabbed up her purse, and left. She'd made it to her car in the alley lot when she remembered she'd forgotten the necklace and earrings.

Susan dropped her purse and book on the car seat with a sigh, and turned back to the shop. Keys in hand, she opened up the back door.

Halfway through the back room, she heard something in the showroom. She plucked up her jewelry and listened. It was indefinable, like the muffled roar of a train coming through the night, or the tide gathering for a crash onto the shoreline. Susan paused.

The air inside the shop felt still and heavy. She reached for the showroom door and pulled it open even as the searing heat of the knob registered in her hand.

Flame leapt through, knocking her back and onto the floor. Someone screamed with pain and fear. The raw tearing of her throat told Susan it was herself. She lay helpless. The world became an inferno. She watched the fire lick over her, a tongue tasting and seeking her out.

Chapter 19

El struggled awake to the drone of the air conditioning and the anvil-like pounding of someone's fist on his front door. He kicked his feet free of the tangled sheets and staggered out toward the entrance. He customarily wore only pajama bottoms and the surgery scar on his chest stood out lividly. He thought of throwing on a robe, decided that anyone coming to visit him was a friend and would not be offended, and went to the door bare-chested.

He was wrong on both counts. His brother Cal filled the threshold, an early morning scowl encrusted on his lean face, and his eyes narrowed at the sight of his brother's chest. Cal looked like him, only with gray at the temples despite the fact the he was the younger brother, which was to say that they both looked like Raymond Massey in his young Lincolnesque prime. Looking at Cal reminded El of how difficult it was to portray Lincoln as a yuppie.

"Have a nice night?" his brother said without preamble. "Was it a good show?" He brushed past El into the foyer, smelling of Ralph Lauren's latest men's cologne and a goodly dose of L.A. smog. He must have driven his convertible that morning.

"Good morning," El said dryly to the empty stoop. "Won't you come in?" He closed the door to save on energy as his air conditioner began to labor, endeavoring to cool the entire L.A. basin. He faced his brother. "Yes, actually, it was an excellent show."

"Good." Cal dropped into the Scandinavian leather chair which was also El's favorite. "Put a shirt on or something. I hate looking at that."

El dropped his chin and ran his finger from bottom to sternum as he said, "From stem to stern, eh? Bothers you? Think you might have the same defective ticker?"

"Oh, shut up, El," his brother said wearily, refusing to look at him until Harper pulled a shirt out of his closet and put it on.

Out of brotherly orneriness, El picked the T-shirt he'd gotten from the American Heart Association. It showed the organ in graphic reds and blues and read "Have a Heart" across its emblem. As he reappeared from the bedroom, a faint tinge of gray flickered across his brother's face, but Cal refused to give him the touché and merely tightened his lips. Cal had not visited him in the hospital. Their mutual mother's excuse was that it distressed him too much. El was certain of the distress but thought the excuse too convenient. *Only one of the many things between them not to forgive him for*, El thought.

He sat down, too, draping his long legs over the arm of the chair. "You didn't come for tea."

"No. You know, the place seems much bigger without Debbie cluttering it up." Cal had not liked Debbie. He claimed she'd come on to him once or twice. El was still not sure whether to believe it. "I'd like to have come for my tickets back, but you've used them already."

"They were my tickets," answered El mildly.

Something flashed in Cal's eyes and restored a little color to his pale face. "You forfeited them. Silence is consent."

"Not always. I had a need for them last night and you might as well know that I will have a continuing need for them. You'll have to make do with your own box. It holds six, as I recall. You'll simply have to pare down your entertaining budget."

Cal responded, "You returned your company car and credit cards."

"I didn't need them."

His brother stood and began to pace, back and forth, energy recoiling. El watched, remembering that he used to have that kind of edginess, like a teakettle always ready to boil over. He didn't miss it. He didn't need to have "the edge" to enjoy life.

"So are you giving up the firm or coming back?"

"I don't know yet."

"Haven't you read any of my letters? You have to make a decision, you can't put it off indefinitely."

El raised a finger. It was something their father used to do when he wanted to be listened to. "I took a year's sabbatical, asked for a six months' extension to that, and was given it. Those six months have barely begun. I have plenty of time."

"You might, but the company doesn't. The Pacific Rim market is growing by leaps and bounds and we have to stay competitive. I can't make moves without your vote and *you won't answer my fucking letters!*" Cal came to a furious halt in front of Harper.

"I sent in my proxies," El said.

"It wasn't enough!"

"What does Donovan say about all this?"

Cal made a move as if to pull out a cigarette, aborted it in mid-gesture (he must have given up smoking), and answered, "Don doesn't take sides, you know that. But he's not like you and me. He doesn't have the instinct for the kill."

"And that's what you want from me, the kill?"

Cal's eyes flickered an expression through them, unreadable in their hazel depths. "I have that," he said.

"Then you need nothing from me."

"I need to know if I'm right!"

El said nothing. He let the moment stretch until Cal's face calmed and his brother repeated, "I need you."

To which El only replied, "But I'm not sure if I need you."

Cal hesitated. Then, "So we have to let it stand this way."

"For a while longer," El put his hand to his scar. The bone ached a bit. His heart beat firmly underneath his palm.

"I don't have to wait for you. I can force you out."

"You gave me disability leave," El pointed out. "If you renege on it, I'll haul you up before the Labor board. Or our own board. Either way I'll get a healthy settlement and you'll get your hand slapped. Cal, you can't afford to earn the mistrust of your own board of directors."

There was a harsh pride in Cal's face as he said, "You think you've given up the kill, but you're still a ruthless son of a bitch. You've got me over the barrel on this and you won't give an inch."

El shrugged. "It could be worse. I could be in the office every day telling you you're wrong and butting heads with you."

"Even that," his brother answered ruefully, en route to the door, "would be better than nothing." He left without saying good-bye, just as he'd come in without a greeting.

El lifted his other hand and held both of them to his chest, cupping the feeling of his beating heart. He took several deep breaths and when he finally moved his hands away, they were trembling. He thought of calling Susan but decided not to, not until he could keep the emotion out of his voice. Damn Cal for stomping all over his life once again.

* * *

Tam wiped his hands on his knees for the twentieth time since entering the plane. He did not like flying, but he refused to anesthetize himself for it. He valued his wits too much. He could not book a flight directly to L.A. from Hong Kong. Instead, he was going to Tokyo and then to Anchorage, where he hoped he would be able to take a flight straight down to L.A. without very much of a layover. He'd told Victor his plans. The thought of another leg made his mouth drier and his palms wetter. He wiped them yet again.

The business class on this plane was subdued, scarcely lit for those who wished to sleep en route, and the only audible sounds other than the soft whisper of the stewardesses were the clicks of lap-top keys as other passengers worked. The plane shimmied as it caught the outer edge of a massive tropical storm system working its way up the mainland coast of China, and whenever Tam looked out the window, he could see a vast, boiling curtain of storm clouds.

Sometimes he thought he saw an even vaster, darker shape among them, chasing him eastward, with eyes that glowed an unholy color. He would look until the phenomena faded, but he knew he could not ask if anyone else noticed it.

Tam put his hand in his pocket, checking on the security of his tape recorder. He'd taken it through the security systems by hand, not wanting to subject it to X-ray and electronic scrutiny. He had only listened to the tape once. He still understood very little of what the girl had said, but even dying she had had a strength and poise to her verse that had shaken him.

He felt asleep without knowing it, thinking of the girl, and he awoke as the plane hit a deep pocket and dropped suddenly enough that someone back in coach let out a startled scream and the stews moved quickly to calm the passengers.

Outside his window, he could see the dark turmoil surrounding the plane. They were no longer riding on the edge of the storm system. It had caught up with them. Tam leaned forward to look, trying to pierce the chaos, and a single, glowing eye rose before his face.

He jerked back in fear. The eye considered him. He saw his own reflection in it and knew the being saw him. Yet the beast was as insubstantial as the storm clouds.

The beast gave a slow and deliberate blink. His wounds twinged, burned, and twisted as though the beast were a puppeteer and his limbs strung to the other's desire. Tam sucked in a gasp, fingers coiled about the arms of the plane seat, the buckle digging into his stomach. He fought not to cry out in pain. His mind burned with the impossibility that the beast knew him, marked him. He stared back into the lambent eye. *You won't have me. I'll die first.* Cold laughter echoed inside his thoughts. *That is a possibility,* a hollow, booming voice answered him.

Tam threw it off with a shudder and a sound-less cry. His thoughts were abandoned. The plane jerked and bucked, and Tam felt an icy cold move through him, through the plane it-self, passing eastward. He gasped with the shock of the cold. His guts felt turned inside out. He could see others react as well, like a jolt had run through them. He thought he saw a nearly imperceptible dark form range through the fuselage and then disappear.

The plane suddenly plunged downward. The overheads popped and oxygen masks dropped with the rapidity of descent. His stomach ele-vated into his throat at the same time and he swallowed hard, grabbing for the mask. Thin screams tore through the airplane. The implacable Japanese stewardesses ran to their charges, putting oxygen masks on and quieting the fearful as the plane continued to dive.

He could feel the pilot wrestling to pull the nose up as if he sat in the cockpit. His arms ached, his jaws ground, sweat beaded on his forehead. Tam Chen blinked rapidly as his ears popped painfully again and again.

Then the plane responded. It shook as it an-swered and began to level again. Tam Chen gasped into his mask with gratitude.

A trill of Japanese flooded the cabin, then, in stilted but nearly precise English, the captain informed them that because of mechanical dif-ficulties, the flight would ground in Tokyo and they would not continue to Anchorage. Other arrangements would be made for them.

Son of a bitch, Tam thought. What *was* that? His bound arm and thigh had gone numb, a throbbing ache just below the surface of the bandaging. His stiff black hair practically stood on end. He held his breath, trying to remain calm when the announcement to ready for landing came. He checked his seat belt twice to make sure it was secure.

They'd been attacked; the certainty made him both cautious and helpless, for no one would believe him. Where was his proof? The ten-thousand-foot plunge was not without precedence. The beast had tried to stop him . . . and failed. When would the next attack come?

Hot, dry raindrops were smattering the runways when they landed. Tam hurried through the tunnel. He tried to concern himself with getting a hotel room when he had no reservations, but the skin at the back of his neck stayed up like a dog's hackle. He slowed at a bar just outside the passenger arrival terminal. The set was on and he could not translate the announcer's emphatic narration, but something of newsworthy import was happening. He thought the picture showed Mt. Fuji, but a storm centered over it. People hurried through the picture and there were rescue personnel.

He tapped a gray-suited businessman on the shoulder. The young man looked at him somberly over a pink umbrellaed drink.

"I'm sorry," said Tam. "I don't understand. What's happening?"

"Volcano," the young man said quickly. "Mt.

Unzen. After two years, erupting again. Very unexpected. Very dangerous. Several people killed."

"I see," said Tam, although he didn't. His informer repeated, "No warning. Very unexpected."

The hairs prickled at the back of Tam Chen's neck. He smoothed them down unsuccessfully. The two of them watched for a moment in companionable silence as the narrator, his back to the offending mountain, stood assessing the situation in front of a dramatic scene of fire engines and helicopters.

Tam stared at the ash and plume issuing from the newly awakened volcano and told himself he did not see the body of a massive lion-dog leaping through it. Eastward bound, heading across the Pacific. He did not, *could not*, see it.

The young businessman sucked his drink down and retrieved the pink umbrella. He used it as a toothpick. "Very unexpected," he said a third time. "And the other one, in the Philippines, Pinatubo, erupt as well. Lots of mud and ash. More deaths."

The stilted English spurred Tam. He turned away without another word, even as the surprised businessman said, "Buy you a drink? Hey!"

He ran through the tide of humans walking the airport corridors. Tam had wasted enough time. It was critical to get hold of Victor. The beast *was* moving east, bringing death and destruction with it. He knew its destination. He did not know why or understand how he knew, but he *knew*. The beast had invaded his mind and left its tracks behind in his own thoughts.

It sought Los Angeles.

Victor pushed the pile of invoices aside, the writing in both English and Chinese, and turned his weary eyes to the notes and tablet. His desk in the warehouse was more of a tabletop, the overhead lighting a dreary fluorescent that occasionally blinked low and then brightened again, fixtures swinging trapeze high amid the open beams of the warehouse roof. Only Tam had the guts to shinny up those beams to change the bulbs in the light fixtures. Consequently the bulbs went a long time between changing.

The warehouse was just now feeling the afternoon heat and in another hour or so it would be stifling. But it was quieter here than in the restaurant and solitude suited Victor at the moment.

He hated losing Rose Wine. He hated the untimely and perhaps critical disruption in the lifeline he and Tam had been setting up to draw the students out of China. Every day was of the essence and now they'd lost many. He refused to reconcile himself to defeat.

Nor would he let the tablet defeat him. Although the two parts comprise a whole, it was not the whole of the story, he thought. Perhaps there had been a second tablet. If so, where might it be? In a private collection, hidden from covetous eyes? Or maybe even in New York or

Chicago at one of the cities' famous Chinese collections. And if it was there, where had this one come from and how had Harper gotten ahold of it?

And why would Tam insist it was bad *joss*, the Chinese equivalent of fate, luck, and destiny, all rolled into one? What had it to do with Tam and Rose Wine and the creature he claimed he faced?

He had never before doubted Tam's veracity. He did not like doubting it now, but he could not accept what Tam had reported to him. That there had been a dog, a guard dog, tracking, seemed possible. That it could have been on a par with the Hound of the Baskervilles, he doubted. At night, on a near moonless evening, with the enemy at your back and rushing you from the fore as well, doubtless one could see many odd and unnatural things.

Victor pulled down one of his massive reference books with a sigh. His exhalation puffed a cloud of dust from the leather cover and more wafted up as he opened it and began thumbing through vigorously. He had identified the first emperor Huang and a triumphant battle and even some vague references to handmaidens, or perhaps that had been priestesses, but nothing came together. He began to search for the ideograms which had defied his scholarship and stopped dead when he found one that coincided.

The warehouse lighting seemed to flicker. Victor felt his eyelids blink several times rapidly, but the translation under his fingernail did not waver. *Demon,* he read.

He pulled his papers over carefully and skeptically laid the thin white paper over the yellowed pages of the book.

The outlines roughly matched.

Victor sat back in his chair with a woof of disbelief. He began to shuffle through his notes, papers flying, and one by one began to run down the errant ideograms. He did not lean back again until the perspiration streamed down his face like tears and sweat plastered his expensive shirt to his chest.

He picked up his phone and called El. There was no answer. Gathering up his papers and the book and the artifacts, he headed out of the warehouse at a lope, determined to have final answers. The fireproof steel doors thudded shut behind him with a ringing that obscured the sound of his phone, though it continued to ring loud and long in determination.

Victor never heard it. He got in his car and tore out of the parking lot, headed for El Harper's home.

El shook off the paralysis that the fight with his brother seemed to leave him with. It was after noon. He looked around his place and realized that if he hoped to bring Susan back, he needed to clean. So he showered and dressed and went to work, carefully, deliberately, stopping now and then to take his pulse. Damn Cal for reminding him of his weaknesses and none of his strengths. Just damn Cal for everything.

El stopped late, realized Susan hadn't called, and called her. The phone rang until the answering machine picked it up. He didn't want an answering machine, he wanted her. So he hung up and turned on the TV instead, while he fixed a cold lunch.

It was near five and the heat of the day had begun breaking at last. He watched the local channel casters chat among themselves, discuss the golf championship game that day with a near fatal lightning mishap on the course, and then tease the viewers with "mysterious doings at the La Brea tar pits."

El sat up at that. He flipped channels, heard nothing more, and finally returned to the happy news channel. After more inconsequential chatter and a report on the local weather, they went live to their feature reporter. She looked a little wilted by the sun and heat but found a happy smile just as the cameras focused on her.

"Hancock Park and the George C. Page Museum, popularly known as the La Brea tar pits, have had more than their share of notoriety this summer with the mysterious death of one of the homeless residents who regularly slept here in the park, but nothing to match with today's mystery. This is Shannen Fowler with Exceptional Newscasts, live on the scene. Every year when the sun heats the tar to a consistency not unlike mud, amateur archaeologists are invited to join in a dig. The asphalt which is brought up is rich with bones and fossils and skulls by the drumfull, providing plenty of work until the next summer's dig. The excitement of finding the skull of a dire wolf or a saber-toothed tiger or perhaps a woolly mammoth keeps these amateurs coming back year after year." The reporter paused dramatically. "But nothing compares with what the diggers found today."

El sat up with a whoop as the newscaster finished her report. He dialed Susan again and determindedly stayed on the line through the machine's answer. She had to be home, maybe showering, but if they were going out tonight, she had to be there.

The message went blank with a clatter and a curse. El recognized Irving's rich New Yorkese patois as he interrupted. "Susie! Susie, is that you?"

"No, Mr. Aronson, it's me, El Harper."

"Oh. The guy." It sounded like *goy*, El thought. He responded, "I take it Susan's not home."

"No. She should be, but she's not. We're going to the movies with you tonight, eh? So she should be here putting on her face. That girl works too hard."

"Is she at her shop, then?"

A puff and a half-growl. "Where else should she be working? I worry about her. She's not safe alone. I'm here to protect her, but there—"

"Where is her shop?" nudged El gently.

"On Robertson." Irving rattled off the address, adding, "she parks in the back." His voice faded, then came back with an odd clarity, almost devoid of accent. "She's burning. I see it. She's burning."

"Mr. Aronson?"

There was a muffled sound, like a sob. Then, "Hurry."

El dropped the phone in his haste. Excitement over the pits fled his mind as he grabbed the car keys, vaulted the vacuum cleaner in the living room, and left.

Chapter 20

The hot air and flames roaring over her sucked the breath out of her lungs. Stunned, Susan lay there and watched the blaze curl over her, diminish, and then roar back. She put her arm over her face, talisman necklace still entwined in her hand, her poor burnt hand. In seconds the open doorway had become an inferno and yet . . . and yet the flames seemed to be repelled from her. She put her hand up and the blaze retreated yet again, gray curls of smoke trailing in its wake. She fought to breathe. *Smoke,* she thought. *The smoke is worse than the fire.* She started to scoot on her back.

As the upholstered furniture in the showroom caught , the fire retardant foam in the cushions would begin to smolder, its toxic smoke and fumes just as dangerous as the active flames. But there would be other fuel for the fire. The draperies, the carpet swatches, the wood furniture . . . she blinked. Her eyes felt hot and sooty. She wondered if she had eyelashes left. She wondered if she would make it out alive. *Poor Poppa, alone again. Poor Domino. And El. . . .*

With a gasp, she got her elbows under her and flipped over, facedown. Every bone in her body hurt. The back of her head felt as though it had a lump as large as a goose egg.

Smoke curled all around her. It was like crawling in fog, but worse. The heat stifled her and the smoke made her cough, achingly, her lungs starved. Her eyes watered in protest until she could barely see. The back door had to be this way, had to.

She thumped into a chair leg, looked up, saw an ornate cherry wood turning. No! She was crawling to the side. Susan took a shivery breath, shallow, trying to filter out the smoke, and she coughed again, coughed and choked until spit ran out of her mouth and nose, and her head ached unbearably. She writhed about on the floor like some blind, primordial worm vainly seeking a way out.

Her arms gave out from under her and she collapsed, strung out, eyes stinging and watering, gasping for air like a dying, beached fish. Seconds. It had only been seconds since she'd reached for the door and the backdraft blew in. How could she survive until someone could get to her? She thought of El and their last kiss. It had been so good to be alive again, even if only for a few hours. She heard glass shatter behind her and the fireproof door to the rear boom like a drum.

* * *

Harper was out of the car door even as he threw the gear into park. A flock of sparrows took to the air, disturbed, but hovering over the building, circling and cheeping in distress. Birds again. He thought of the owl and Susan's story of birds on her patio. There were people standing in the alleyway and Susan's car was there. He heard glass shattering, but could not see it. The smell of burning was ripe in the air and he could see gray strings of smoke from the front of the building.

"Fire" they said, and he stumbled to a halt. "Is she out?" he said, accosting the crowd. "Is Susan out?"

Heads shook. Someone said, "What do you mean?"

El stopped and faced the man, older, suited, fastidious. "Is Susan Aronson out of the building?"

"I didn't see her," he said. He twisted his hands. "My gallery is next door. My paintings. The sculptures. I called the fire department."

El twisted back. There was no time. He took his shirt off, wrapped it bandana style across his face and ran for the bright green back door that said with florid style, *Il Mode delivery* across the archway.

With every step his heart drummed louder, its pump laboring to meet the demands he was putting on it. He breathed a prayer for it to keep beating, solidly, soundly, before he opened the door and crashed inside.

He emerged into a maelstrom of smoke and

ash, thick as soup and hotter than anything he could have imagined. The blaze leapt at him, spouting, dragonfire, as the fresh air sucked in from the door fanned it. He kicked a desk chair in front of the door anyway, its beam of light the only beacon, cutting the smoke knifelike.

"Susan! Susan!" he yelled, pausing before getting ready to pierce the fog himself. He could see orange flame as the backdrop, the front of the building, the thin wall facade that had separated showroom from back offices and storage disintegrating into smoldering ash and tumbling downward. "Susan!"

Her voice answered, "El?" The noise smothered with choking. Head down, he plunged in the direction of the noise. He took three great bounds, his lungs protesting, needing air, and thrust his hands downward in search of the coughing, praying.

He met flesh. Without caring what he gripped, he latched onto it and pulled, sliding it after him as he set his heels and inched backward.

Like dredging through the tar, he thought, and heaved again, and then Susan came up in his hands, one about her arm and the other pinching her waistline. She got to her knees, doubled-over, coughing and retching, too weak to move. El licked his lips, feeling his heart swell to bursting inside of him.

There was no help for it. He bent down, put his shoulder under her rib cage, and hefted her up across his back. He kept hold of her wrist, trying to balance her dead weight, and stumbled toward the door even as the air roared and a whirlwind of heat burst into the office. His feet went white-hot, he could feel the searing heat of the linoleum flooring, and then he was outside, going to his own knees on the asphalt.

He got back up like a bent and broken carriage horse. He took three more steps away from the inferno at his back. Susan coughed again, weakly, and someone met him, saying, "Let her down. We've got her."

He would never have surrendered her body, but he recognized the slick coat and professional gear and let the fireman/paramedic take her and lay her gently on the ground.

Another man gripped him by the elbow, steering him across the lot and sitting him down, braced by the wheel of the smaller fire engine which now blocked the alleyway. El watched, bemused, as muslin hoses snaked across the lot and began to swell with water, as the fireman deployed their weapons. The paramedic at his side slipped a mask over his face and said, "Breathe."

El looked at his shoes, thinking wearily that they must be melted, he'd felt the fire through them, but they looked normal to him. He put his head back and listened as they coaxed Susan into breathing, and he tried not to let it matter, tried only to calm his thundering heart.

A paramedic dropped a heavy hand on his shoulder. "She'll be fine," he said. "A little smoke inhalation. A couple of minutes under the mask. We won't even need to send her in for observation."

El nodded wearily.

The fireman dropped into a squat next to him, putting their eyes on a level. "I'm supposed to say, let us do the rescuing, we're the professionals ... but she might not have made it if you hadn't pulled her out."

El nodded again. The fireman patted his shoulder a second time and then left to join his fellow workers. A shadow fell across Harper. He looked up. It was the heavyset, fastidious gentleman. His face was pale.

"She all right?"

"They think so." Harper's voice rasped a little. He cleared his throat.

"They said they're going to save my place, but there might be some smoke and water damage. Her shop, though," and the gentleman gave a fluid shrug.

"Bad luck," said El, his voice muffled by the oxygen mask.

The man nodded. He walked away and joined the crowd, watching as the firemen fought to save the other segments of the stucco building.

He took about three more breaths and when his lungs stopped stabbing, he removed the oxygen mask and made his way to where they had Susan lying down, a light blanket over her. The necklace he'd given her was entwined in her fingers. Her right palm was swathed with bandages and rested across her stomach. She looked up at him.

"How do I look without eyebrows?" she husked.

She was disheveled and pale, but looked fine. He lowered himself to the pavement beside her. He took her bandaged hand delicately between his two. "You look pretty good," he said. He touched one half-gone eyebrow. "Most of it's still there."

"How—" Susan ended abruptly.

"Poppa Irving sent me. He said . . . he was worried." The memory took El aback for a moment. The old man had known. How could he have known? Was this the culmination of his worries?

"Poppa! I have to call." She flinched under the blankets.

"I'll call." El said, patting her hand comfortingly. "I'm fine."

The paramedic who'd treated Susan came back. He took the oxygen paraphernalia from around Harper's neck, checked Susan, and said, "You don't need to be hospitalized, but I'd suggest you see your own physician when convenient. Keep the dressing dry on that burn."

Susan nodded. Harper said, "I need to make a call."

The fireman shook his head. "Phone bank for the whole building is out. We'll need you here for our reports. Then you can go."

Her eyes were red and brimming. She nodded again. El recaptured her bandaged hand and did not feel like letting go.

* * *

There is a current across the vast Pacific which connects the rim to the mainland. Beachcombers on southern Alaskan and Canadian shores upon occasion find glass balls and cork floats torn loose from Japanese nets that come drifting up on their sands after a long journey. The tide is a long slow one, along a deep trench, a water current which affects weather as well. As it nears Alaska, it begins to curve downward, imitating the shelf off the mainland. Gray whales sound the shelf and follow it south, all the way to the bays of Baja California in tepid Mexican waters, where they court their mates and birth their calves.

It also draws illegal whalers. The orange and black *Matsoya* bobbed in the cold northern waters of the upper Pacific, its hull cutting through peaking waves, its watch sharp-eyed for prey. Its holds were already half-full, its decks being sluiced down to rid it of gore and despair, its sailors in the chest-high rubberized suits and boots to protect them from their wet work. The pressurized hoses washed a crimson tide of death from the surfaces. Hoists and nets prepared to pull in the next living carcass for butchering. The harpoons were loaded and readied.

The blood on the water drew the demon like chum drew sharks. It shivered out of the ocean floor, rising quickly through the water lest its earthly substance be overcome, and rose in the spray, smelling the coppery essence of the blood. The chore of traveling within the earth had weakened it and although it had fed upon the islands, fed on fear as well as flesh, it hungered again.

To kill, it must be more substance than element. It gathered its resources carefully and began to solidify. Upon the waters as the ship surged toward it, it began to resemble the dark gray and barnacled flesh of the whaler's prey.

The spotters shouted. The crew reacted with frenzied, coordinated action.

The demon took a dark pleasure in leading them on as it caught their thrill of the chase. It skimmed the waters, letting its bulk sleeken like that of the old leviathan, leading them on. The illusion of whale brought the crew to the harpoon guns. The *Matsoya* was a strange mixture of old technology and new. Of its three harpoon cannons, one contained an old but well sharpened cast-iron spear, the other two were of the finest steel alloys. The sailors manning them looked down their sights and hollered for the captain to bring the ship around so they could get off their shots.

The cannons fired, two at once and the third a little after, cables snaking through the air, barely visible through the exhaust and spray. The demon felt their piercing as a minor irritation, but the third, the old iron spear, took it below the water with a surge of pain. It bellowed below the surface where none could hear it and its demon flesh quivered and ichor ran from it, staining the waters.

With a soundless howl of fury, the demon turned round on its hunter and made it the prey.

The demon and the hull of the ship slammed together. The crew cried aloud in surprise, two among them slipping and falling overboard at the impact. The demon snapped at them. Their flesh was chewy but blood sweet inside and the creature savored their screams as it swallowed them. The hull of the *Matsoya* shuddered as the demon charged it again, slewing it about in the churning ocean waters, and then the fishermen screamed in panic as they saw what overtook them.

The helmsman did his best to swing the ship out of harm's way, but nothing could be done. The demon shed its harpoons and cables like harmless quills and then shredded the nets which a few quick-thinking whalers had dropped on it. Its eyes glowed lambent as it picked and fed at will, then sounded and came up beneath the foundering ship and turned it over.

Four of the crew remained to cling to its hull as it went down and the frigid waters of the northern Pacific took them. The demon, not interested in these last human sacrifices, went down again, to the earth fathoms below, blood sated, a single harpoon in its side like a thorn which melted from its flesh as it dispersed and sounded one final time before melding into the earth.

* * *

Despite good intentions, the sun had sunk low in the hazy sky and the fire had been reduced to wet char before the firemen were done, all their questions asked of Susan, and reports filed, and Susan and El were at last free to go. Harper drove her car. It was the better vehicle and he didn't care if he left his own in the lot.

Onlookers shuffled away as he steered between them.

"I was lucky," Susan said. She looked back at the darkened hulk which had been Il Mode. The firemen had shored up the interior walls. She wondered what the overall damage assessment would be. She fingered the blue and gold feather in her lap, playing with the tiny riblets which composed it, ruffling and smoothing them. "How did you know?" she picked up the thread of the conversation that had been interrupted by the firemen.

"Poppa told me." El cleared his throat. "Do you think he's psychic?"

"He must be." Susan put her head back on the headrest with a sigh. "And now that it's all over, he can get back to normal."

"Over?"

She shifted her head to look at him. "It has to be. This has to be what he saw."

He felt uneasy, but he did not argue with her, skillfully winding through the Saturday night traffic which had begun to collect as the night came on. Susan didn't say much either, but she did not pull her free hand away when he covered it with his.

When he got her home, she stood on the sidewalk while he got out her keys.

"The lights aren't on." she said softly. Her voice was still hoarse from the smoke, giving her a sexy, throaty tone. He rather liked it, except for what she'd gone through to get it.

He looked up toward the windows. The condo was indeed dark. "Maybe he's in the back. He has to be waiting for us. He doesn't know what happened." They hadn't had a chance to call because the fire had knocked out the phones in the entire building. He hurried up the walkway and put the key in the door.

An adjacent threshold opened a crack and a pretty face looked out at him, an old-fashioned, oval shaped face, with light brown hair. The girl said, "Susan! They've come to get him. They're taking your grandpa away."

"Away?" Susan repeated sharply. "What happened, Nina?"

"I came over to help him feed Domino and hear some more stories. People came. He told me I should go home. He was crying," the girl said soberly. "I think they hurt him!"

"Are they still here?"

Nina gave a shaky yes.

Susan put a hand around her shoulders, but Nina would not come out of her house. She squeezed the girl affectionately. "It's all right. He was scared something had happened to me."

Nine shied away from Susan's bandaged hand. "What is it?"

"A small fire. I got a little burn. But Poppa

didn't know how small it was. We couldn't call." Susan kissed the girl on her fluffy bangs. "I'll tell you more tomorrow."

Nina gave a solemn nod. As she retreated into the safety of her home, she said, "Wednesday is the Fourth. I'd like to have my salary so I can buy a ticket for the fireworks and baseball game."

"All right. You've earned it." Susan let her go and shut the door. She joined El.

"Who's here?"

Her face looked drawn. "Probably my in-laws." She pushed past him into the condo.

As lamplight flooded the house, the cat on the dinette table got out of his curl and stretched. Loud voices in the living room at the back didn't seem to disturb him. He gave El a cross-eyed blue look, rearranged himself, and flopped back down.

Susan noticed the cat's inattention. "He knows them or he'd be under the bed." She took a deep breath. To El, she said, "You don't have to stay. This is my family, my problem."

"You've been through a lot today and I don't feel like leaving you alone."

She looked at him for a long second, then let herself smile. "I don't feel like being alone. Okay, just remember you asked for this." She pushed her hair off her shoulders, smelled the smoke on herself, and marched forward.

Sid stood with his back to them, overshadowing Poppa, who sat slumped on the edge of a wingback chair, his face in his hands. Sid looked like Poppa, but younger and stronger, and he stood a good eight inches taller. It was in the eyes and proud nose, and Sid's hair had begun to thin off his freckled pate. But she had never seen Poppa in Sid's mannerisms. Sid could bully, and did, and had done so to Geoff, and now to Poppa himself. Mai looked up as she entered the room. Mai was elegantly dressed in a jumpsuit with a glittering gold belt that showed off her small waist. Her tennis bracelet glittered on one wrist, and her Chai symbol gold and diamond pendant rested at her throat, where the jumpsuit artfully plunged just a little. Her hair was blonde, lighter than it used to be, because it took the hairdresser longer to strip out the gray and put the blonde color back in. Her eyebrows rose.

"Here she is, Sid." To Susan, worried and yet reprimanding, she said, "You shouldn't go off and leave an old man alone."

Susan curled her fingers into a tight fist in her unbandaged hand. "There was an accident. The phones were out. Poppa, I'm okay. El took care of me."

Irving's dark gaze flew to her, then to her hand. "How bad is it?"

"A little burn. Something caught fire in the showroom. Something with the wiring, they think. Nothing much." She couldn't bear to tell him the truth. "What's happening?" His stricken gaze told her he didn't believe much of what she said. He had been crying. There were dry streaks on his face. She thought that whatever had happened to pierce his bravery, his defiance, might overwhelm her was well. She drew strength from El standing behind her and even as she thought of him, he put a hand on her shoulder. Comfort spread like a small blaze from his touch.

"He called up in a panic. He said there'd been a fire. Susan, we can't take any more of this." Sid's voice dropped a little, into stern calmness. "He called Mai at one the other night. We're taking him. We've made arrangements for him. The Hebrew Home for the Aged, near the Miracle Mile."

"That's on the edge of the Fairfax district. It's pretty near his old stomping grounds. Maybe that's best—" Mai stopped as Poppa let out a single groan of anguish.

"My own children."

Sid looked at his father. "I was never a child. I was always a little old man, just like you. I went to school wondering why God had let me live, why I couldn't have prevented the Holocaust. Pop, I wasn't even born then. I had no control over it."

Irving blinked. He put his chin up so he could meet his son's accusing gaze. "All I wanted was that you should never forget. Instead I have children who are afraid to remember."

"Sid, let him stay with me for a few days. It's my fault. I couldn't let him know I was all right. He was just . . . frightened." Susan put her hand to her singed eyebrow. "I let him down."

"No, you didn't. Not if you're well and safe."

Poppa regained some of the strength in his voice. "Not if you're safe."

Mai looked El over hesitantly, as if distastefully airing dirty laundry in front of a stranger. Her lips pursed as she chose words. "This is not really your decision. It's Sid's and Naomi's and mine. And we think this is best."

"Don't tell me I'm not really an Aronson!" Susan's temper flared up. She felt her skin warm. Sid took her measure.

"Now, now," he said. "You look like you've had a bad time of it. Let me take Poppa . . . and you get some rest. You need a life of your own, Susan. Poppa's my responsibility. Let me shoulder it."

"So I'm such a burden," said Poppa bitterly, to the air. He paid no attention as the cat slunk in and wrapped his pudgy body about Poppa's thin ankles and sagging socks and comfortable slippers.

Sid nudged the cat away. He put out his hand and caught Poppa by the elbow, bringing the old man to his feet. Irving looked more shrunken than ever next to his middle-aged American son. "Let me take care of my duty."

She had no legal right to stop them. She opened her mouth to argue one more time, but Poppa Irving flapped a hand her way and said, "Shush, little one. It'll be all right."

Mai said, "Come and visit him. You'll see."

They led Irving from the apartment, each braced on a side.

She sat down suddenly in a chair, her face

caving in. Her throat let out a tiny squeak of noise. El solemnly paced through the condo and closed the door. He came back to her and massaged her neck and shoulders as she bowed her own face into her hands.

When she was quiet and still, calmed, though her heart beat like a frightened bird in a cage of ribs, Harper leaned close. "We'll go see him tonight, let him know. And then we'll do what we can to get him out. Once he's calmed down, once he's rational, they can't keep him if he doesn't want to stay. Your in-laws aren't his executors, are they?"

"Nooo, I don't think so."

"Then that's what we'll do. You change clothes, and then we'll pay Poppa a visit. All right?"

Susan wiped her eyes dry. "All right."

He had slept in smaller places, and filthier places, but never had he been forced to sleep in a place where his soul quailed more. More because now, in his age and wisdom, he knew what faced him. Youth and ignorance he had no chance of reclaiming. So he moaned as he fell into sleep and dreamed again, of himself and the gas erupting into flame, and of Susan walking among these torches, oblivious of her danger. Buildings toppled into glowing ash at her feet and she did not seem to sense her peril. But he relished the dream, because the vision of her having been saved was false, and now he knew it, and now the terror had not only invaded his sight, but his hearing. He could hear it calling, both voices, calling to him. Irving lay on the hospital bed, his head elevated, his blue-veined hands lying across his scrawny chest, his face twitching in disturbed sleep. He could not awaken himself, could not save himself, could not warn Susan.

And worse, he slept in a house of strangers, in a sterile and yet pungent building, pungent with age and urine and disinfectant, and with the misery of others who were similarly lost and imprisoned. His own son and daughter had brought him there and abandoned him. Without waking, tears streaked down his seamed face.

The orderly in crisp whites at the front desk gave her a hard stare. "It's after visiting hours and, according to my information, Mr. Aronson needed sedation before he could sleep. It would be very disruptive to wake him now."

"I understand that," Susan said softly. "But I was in an accident—nothing major—and he knew of it. That's why he was so distraught. It would just be a very small visit. Sid and Maida should have left instructions as to who can visit. I'm family. We'll be quiet. I don't want to wake any of your other charges."

The woman chewed on the request. She was older, Hispanic, though she'd worked hard to lose her accent, her eyebrows shaved off and repainted on in a perpetual arch. She wore her hair pulled tightly back off her face, and the style accented the Indian heritage in her Latino features. She shifted her weight on the typing chair, a pile of charts in front of her. Her uniform pulled tight across her bustline.

The lobby was worn and there was activity in the bingo parlor to the left, but they had no chance of finding Poppa in the care wing without directions and permission from this woman.

"Please," said Susan. She rested her bandaged hand on the counter and the orderly's eyes flickered to it and away. "He'll give you less trouble if he knows I'm all right."

The woman sighed. "Our director is out for the evening. I don't have orders concerning Mr. Aronson yet. So I'll let you go back. We have him in soft restraints. Please don't loosen them. It's for his own good."

"I understand." Susan swallowed tightly past a sudden knot in her throat. She looked to El for strength. He gave her a very slight nod.

The woman pulled out a mimeographed map of the home's grounds. She inked an X on a room number. "Take the wing to the right, through the double doors, and up to the second floor. Remember, you promised me you'd be quiet."

Harper took the map from her. "We will."

"Okay." She turned her attention back to the pile of work in front of her. Behind them, someone shouted "Bingo!" in an ancient, yet jubilant voice.

The care wing smelled like a hospital. Susan put her hand up, shielding her mouth and nose from it without knowing why. She crept to the door marked as Poppa's room and paused. Her nerve failed her. Understandingly, Harper put his hand around her waist.

"He's all right," the man whispered in her ear. "Just see if you can wake him."

She nudged the door open. The room was made up hospital style for care-giving and it was bare except for dresser, bed, and wall-mounted TV. The knot in her throat swelled as she saw the cloth restraints tied to the rails, though Poppa had fallen asleep with his hands over his chest. She stepped quickly to his side and, after a second's hesitation, laid her hand over his.

"Poppa. Poppa, it's me, Susan."

The blue veins stood out like cords on the backs of his hands. His eyes, though shut tightly, had tiny crusts about them as if he'd been crying. She remembered what Nina had told her and carefully, with tissue from the nightstand, wiped them clean. She repeated herself, a little louder, trying to wake him.

His eyes moved under the fine tracings of his lids. El had dimmed the room's lighting so it would not be too harsh, and when Poppa opened his eyes, he stared into Susan's.

"Susie." He caught his breath. The old man looked from Susan to Harper. "What are you doing here? She needs her rest."

"I couldn't let you be alone. I'd stay all night if I could, but they're going to kick us out." She sighed. "You saw the fire, but I'm fine. You sent Harper."

Harper nodded, adding, "In time."

"I saw it right? Susie, tomorrow, you must fetch me the rest of my clothes and my book, the old book, you know the one?"

"All right. But I don't intend to leave you here. I just haven't thought of a way to fight Sid and Mai yet."

The old man took another deep, redeeming breath. "Thank God," he said. "Thank God." His face twisted. He pulled at the restraints. "My own flesh and blood."

Susan stroked his hands. "And we'll undo it. You just rest tonight. Tomorrow, when the doctor sees you calm and happy, they'll know they can't keep you."

"Tomorrow?"

Harper said, "Maybe a day or two longer, if I have to rope in my lawyer."

"A good Jewish lawyer, I hope," commented Irving.

"I think so." Harper laughed in spite of himself.

"Good. I'll wait for you, Susie."

She leaned over and kissed his brow. It tasted of salt and night sweat. "I'll be back tomorrow."

"You do that." He put his head back onto his pillow.

"You'll be all right?"

He looked at her fiercely. "I've been through worse."

"I know you have." She joined El at the door. "Tomorrow."

Irving nodded. "And bring my pajamas!! I've had enough of these gowns with the breeze in the back."

Chapter 21

Victor paced the entryway to Harper's door, determined to sit on his friend's doorstep until the man came home. Every now and then he patted the bulk in his shimmery jacket pocket as if checking that the bundle remained. He did not understand Harper's absence and, on his way here, he'd heard some very disturbing news over the radio.

One of the adjacent doorway lights went on, with a brilliant orange glow. A stout woman in a wrapper came out and looked at him.

"Are you going to stand there all night?" she asked, in a voice firm with purpose.

"Not unless I have to." Victor moved squarely into the illumination to let her have a good look at him.

Her lips pursed as she did so.

"Do you know where he went?" Victor asked, while she apparently thought over what to do about him.

Behind her, in one of the upper windows of her condo, a placard read: NEIGHBORHOOD

WATCH. And it was obvious she took her sentry duty seriously.

"He's gone out," she said finally. "It's date night, you know. Good to see him out and about. Know who she is?"

"Uh, no." Victor replied. "Must be someone new." New enough, Victor hoped, that El would not be spending the night in another bed. "It's important that I talk to him."

Her lips pursed tighter. "All right, then. Wait a minute." She disappeared for a moment, reappeared with a mug of coffee and the latest edition of *People* Magazine. "Here. And if you have to use the facilities, don't go in the bushes. Just ring my bell and I'll get up and let you in. Mind you," and she gave him her coldest look. "I wouldn't be doing this but I've seen you around before. A nice man like Elmore ought to have nice friends."

Feeling both grateful and intimidated, Victor promised to be no trouble. She snapped her light off and disappeared back inside her home.

He sat down on El's stoop with his booty in his hands. The coffee was fresh, hot, and creamy, the way he liked it, though it was a little over-sweet. But he couldn't read. His thoughts were too full of what he'd learned and what he needed to know.

Dusk passed and Victor fell victim to the lure of the magazine. Somewhere in the depths of its pages, he put his head back against the stucco archway and fell asleep.

* * *

Getting his keys out of his pocket, Harper paused in surprise at the view of his front threshold. A harvest moon had fallen and come to rest on his steps. It was Victor Jue, curled up like a stray cat on his doormat, brilliant gold lamé jacket boldly reflecting the porch light. And he'd come prepared to stay the night, too, from the looks of the coffee mug next to him and the magazine spread over his knees.

"Heavens," said Susan, coming to a halt beside him. "Is that someone you know? He has a lot of style for a street person."

"That," El said with faint irritation, "is not one of the homeless. That is one of Chinatown's premiere restaurateurs." He approached Victor Jue and nudged him. "Victor. Victor, what are you doing here?" The irritation at his unexpected guest grew. It had taken no end of persuasion to bring Susan back with him and now she was ready to bolt off at the sight of Victor.

She took a step back. "Maybe I'd better just go home. It's been a long day all the way around."

He caught her hand. "No. Stay. I'll take care of this." He leaned over and hoisted Victor to his feet as the man began to come awake, mumbling.

"Do you think his wife—" Susan halted in mid-sentence.

"He's not married," El answered. He palmed his house key to her. "Get the door open, will you?" His chest hurt as he bore the strain of Victor's loose-jointed weight. This was getting to be a habit. The man was barely conscious. He must sleep like the dead, El thought. He hoisted Victor's trailing feet over the door frame and followed Susan in.

Victor began to awaken in his arms. By the time he got him to a chair, his friend had shaken his raven-wing hair from his eyes and was blinking with owlish awareness. "Harper? God, I thought you'd never get in—"

Jue evidently spotted Susan as she rounded the room, turning on lights. He looked up at Harper. "You're going to kill me."

"Not just yet," Harper said, sitting down. "Susan, this is Victor Jue. Victor, this is Susan Aronson." His sternum ached and he rubbed it where the bone had knit back together but still worried him. "I'm curious. I like take out Chinese, but this is ridiculous."

"Very funny." Victor swept the table clean with an arm and took a bundle from his jacket, spreading it out across the expanse. "I got the second half of the tablet."

"I know. I messengered it to you."

Victor leaned over earnestly. "It's still not complete. There must be a second tablet somewhere. Something that tells the rest of the story. Or history." His white ruffled shirt fell open at the throat under his shimmering gold jacket. "El, wake up. I said it only completed the first tablet."

In the background, Susan said awkwardly, "Maybe I should make some more coffee for everybody." No one responded immediately. Victor noticed the bandage across her chin and her one swathed hand. She looked as if she'd been in a minor scuffle.

She stared back and he wondered if he was the intruder here . . . or she was. Then he saw the talisman hanging from her neck. The feather he recognized. The amulet he did not. He put a hand out eagerly. "Give it to me."

Her hand covered it defensively.

Harper said, "What the hell is this, Victor?"

"I don't know—I have no way of knowing—if what I translated is fiction or fact . . . but if it's fact, Hell is just what you're facing." The restaurateur looked at him keenly. "Did you give that to her? Can I have a look at it?"

Harper protested. "I don't like this. I think maybe this should wait."

Without taking his eyes off the necklace, Victor answered, "I've been your friend for a long time, El. You've come and gone from the Jade Pheasant for years while I watched and listened to you. You talked a lot more during your business lunches than you thought. I saw you and Debbie have awkward lover's spats, then fight for real. I probably know far more about you than you know about me."

Victor had said aloud what bothered Harper at that moment. He hesitated.

Susan made a decision and drew the talisman off over her head. "Only if you tell us what's going on."

Victor took an elegant magnifying glass from the bundle he had spread out on Harper's table and examined the amulet. "This is a coin," he said. "It'll help date the tablet unless someone is in the habit of affixing ancient coins to porcelain before he throws it away." He gave El a keen look. "*If* he threw it away."

Harper pulled a chair out for Susan, who perched there, gingerly staying close to him. Victor hummed tunelessly while he looked both sides of the coin over and then unwrapped the tablet fragments and found where El had broken the seal away.

He stopped humming and looked up. "How much do you know about China?"

"Very little," Harper said. He cleared his throat, trying to break the edge away from his tone. "That's why I brought it to you."

"How old is the coin?" asked Susan faintly.

"It goes back to the Ch'in dynasty. Emperor Huang, who is sometimes known as the first emperor of China. Ch'in ... China. That's how the nation got its name. He also standardized Chinese writing and brought together the Great Wall against the Mongols."

"And left a clay army guarding his tomb," Susan added.

Victor's even brown gaze flicked to her. "You know it?"

She smiled slightly. "There's a brace of statues on loan to the Hancock Park Museum, next to El's tar pits. I had a client who wanted me to buy one for her foyer." She spread her hands. "They're priceless. I couldn't do anything but bring her with me to the art museum and admire them. Each one is similar, nearly life-sized yet individualized. It was a great commission. It must have taken the artisans decades to create the army."

Harper put his shoulders back. "Do you mean that tablet dates back to Huang?"

"It might well. The coin does, anyway, and it was affixed with wax like a seal."

Harper's memory skipped backward. "You shied away from that tablet the first time I showed it to you."

"Unconscious reaction. I needed to brush up on my ideograms, but I must have known . . . great evil and great hope," Victor said. "That's what this says here and here." He spread his tracing paper out on the table and anchored it with the two pieces of clay. "An ideogram is one of these stylized symbols. Written classical Chinese is not phonetic. Each symbol expresses a concept, which may be a word or a sentence, an idea. Today it gets complicated. Telephone, for example, is often expressed with the lightning and talk symbols. Lightning-wire-talk, it becomes. There's been a lot of movement for a new written language, but so far it's not been too successful."

Susan looked over the paper. "How many symbols are there?"

"Thousands. To be a scribe in China meant vast education and intelligence. Our written language is nearly five thousand years old."

"And I asked you to translate," Harper said dryly.

Victor shrugged. "I wanted to be up to the task. It took a few days. When I got the second piece, it started to come together. The only thing I don't know is . . . did I translate a story or a history." Victor leaned on an elbow. "Where did you get this, Harper?"

"You'll never believe it."

"I have to know. I don't want to think you stole this from a museum or private collection."

Harper made a slightly strangled noise in his throat. Then, "It came out of one of the smaller pits."

"From La Brea?"

"Yes. It makes no sense. What would an ancient Chinese artifact be doing buried there?"

"On the contrary," Victor said smoothly as he dipped his head down and traced another ideogram lightly. "It makes a lot of sense. Listen here. This tells that Huang and his magician commissioned the building of an army to celebrate his victory. In uniting Ch'in, he faced a lot of opposition, from the gods as well as the various peoples."

"From the gods?" echoed Susan.

Victor moistened his lips. "I don't write 'em, I just read 'em."

She smiled in apology.

"The story is not complete . . . there's something about a battle with a demon which had been sent to destroy him. A second demon, I don't know about this, I'm guessing, helped

Huang. It got rewarded, was given handmaidens, and was exiled."

A stunned look dawned on El's face. "It came *here?*"

"That's what the tablet suggests, if this is where we found it."

"I think," El said slowly, "if there were a Chinese demon in Los Angeles, we'd have heard about it."

"Maybe not. Even demons probably die sometime."

"Then, if it's dead, we don't need to worry about it. If this is history," Susan said.

"Again," Victor countered, "I'm not so sure. The first demon was an earth and water elemental. This one is fire and air—or so I think. El, have you listened to the news tonight?"

"No. We were busy."

"Well, I did. On the way over. Someone tried to Molotov the Hollywood sign, missed, but set a pretty good brushfire they just got under control. And there was a backstage fire at the Greek Theater yesterday—"

"That one we're familiar with," Harper said.

"Okay. In Compton, an apartment complex garage went up, taking twelve cars with it. Arson is suspected, but no one saw anything. In Pasadena, another transient was found dead." Victor grimaced. "She didn't burn cleanly like Digger. Police are trying to determine if it's related. This is in addition to the normal fires a big county deals with. Like the arson job at a place called Il Mode. They're looking for someone called Angelo for questioning. It appears he had connections with New York racketeers and they got even."

Susan made a faint noise, but no one looked at her. She cradled her injured hand in her good one.

"What," interrupted Harper grimly, "do you take me for? Coin or no coin?"

"I hope not a thief. And I don't know what I'm thinking." Victor ran his blunt fingers through his raven hair. "Tam Chen ran into something wild in Hong Kong. He called me raving about bad *joss* and ugly critters. I need the second tablet to know if this is fact, but the fires worry me. What if Huang exiled something across the Pacific *and it's still here.*"

Susan stammered, "The necklace protected me. It kept the fire from me."

Harper's jaw tensed. "We don't know that. Maybe I just hung something of 'great evil' around your neck." To Victor, he snapped out, "I got it out of the pits. I didn't steal it, and if it came from a museum, they're the ones who threw it in there. But I don't think so. . . . You didn't hear all the news tonight, Victor. I can't find you a second tablet, but I can go you one better. I was phoning Susan to tell her what I'd heard when circumstances distracted me." He looked at the two of them before adding, solemnly, "A skeleton was found in the La Brea tar pits earlier this afternoon on the annual dig. The bone fragments have to be examined thoroughly, but they appear to be that of a young woman. Possibly Asian. They can tell because of the feet and bone structure."

"We've only found one human previously," El added slowly, rocking back in his chair. "An Indian woman. She was either murdered or ritually sacrificed—the back of her skull was bashed in—there's never been another found. And that find was thousands and thousands of years old."

"Well," Victor said and his almond-eyed gaze locked with El's. The extravagant eyebrows he brushed like furry caterpillars arched. "I came over to make sure. I didn't know you'd be . . . ah. . . ."

"On a date," Susan supplied. She rubbed her temple. "Or, more precisely, he rescued me from a fire this afternoon."

"Some date, playing Sir Galahad." Victor grinned. "I can't even get him to spring for Chinese beer. And it's cheap."

"Nothing at the Jade Pheasant is cheap," Harper said. He was flushed around the collar. He looked over the sheets of paper where Victor had enlarged the ideograms, sketching them out painstakingly. "What's this?"

"I'm not sure yet. I think it's a pheasant."

Susan's eyes widened. "A bird?"

"Maybe. It might be the ideogram for the second demon. I just haven't translated it yet."

She leaned over and grabbed the sheet of paper from him. "An elemental of fire and air . . . a bird . . . my God, you've described the Phoenix."

Harper said stiffly, "The Phoenix is mythological."

"So were dragons, but you've got a lot of skeletons hanging in your place that could have started the stories."

"We don't have dinosaurs."

Victor waved a hand. "Then the Museum of Natural History has 'em. Look, my friend, the Phoenix originated in Arabia, but Chinese folklore honors it and so do a few others. Hell, I knew I knew that sign. We have a Phoenix and lobster dish on my menu! The ideogram is slightly different. Anyhow, we have stories about it. Then it disappears from native folklore. Where did it go? What happened to it? It was immortal, remember. It rose from its own bed of ashes, reborn, eternally young."

Susan leaned on her elbows, tracing the symbols Victor had sketched with one fingertip. "If it's the Phoenix . . . El, this explains the birds. The owl. My patio. And maybe even the fires."

"I don't believe it," Harper said stubbornly.

Victor said, "But you've got more proof than anyone." He snatched up the talisman, setting the bright gold and cobalt feather twirling in midair. "I've never seen a bird with plumage like this."

Dreamily, Harper responded, "That came out of the pits. Nothing survives the pits but rock and stone and bone . . . the tar sinks in, it's like a preserving resin, but fur and hide and flesh don't survive." He put a finger under the feather. "But this did."

Defeated, Susan sank back into her chair. She rubbed the bandage across her chin. "Why doesn't it burn itself inside the tar? Tar's got a fairly low melting point."

"Too much water trapped as well. Remember, most animals were lured into the pits because of the lake and river water covering them. And, like most fires, it probably needs oxygen."

Her eyes widened. "You think it's alive down there?"

Harper, still entranced by the feather, said, "I don't know. Maybe it's in a kind of a half-life, neither dead nor renewed."

"And it's waking up," said Victor. "We've had a lot of earthquake activity the last seven years. San Andreas, Whittier, Upland, Sierra Madre—all major faults that have done some shaking locally. I'm no geologist, but I'd say there've been some changes underground."

"And if it's waking . . . and it's out of control . . . it must be trying to complete its death ritual. Total immolation, no matter what it takes with it," Susan said. "And heaven help anything that gets in its way."

She locked eyes with Harper, who, suddenly thought of old Digger.

"Heaven help all of us," he murmured.

Chapter 22

Tam Chen found himself looking apprehensively out the airplane window. His night had not been a good one. Tokyo had suffered a series of minor earthquakes precipitated by Mt. Unzen's untimely eruption and though the highrises of Japan were built to take the punishment, the sway of the buildings set off adrenaline alarms inside him. Across his lap lay an English newspaper he'd bought at the airport before his flight. He'd folded it to the international news section and now brought his eyes back to the page once more. A whaler had gone down, most of its crew unaccounted for, only three life-jacketed bodies found near the capsized vessel. He had little sympathy for a vessel poaching in waters just outside of Alaskan territory. That alone did not frighten Tam Chen as much as the small article next to it, with its graphic line illustration:

SERIES OF PACIFIC FLOOR QUAKES BAFFLE SCIENTISTS

Scientists have reported a series of quakes along the ocean floor of the northern Pacific. While not serious, the quakes have led to upheaval among marine life and the Alaskan and Canadian shores have been alerted to a possible tsunami effect. The quakes, measuring from 4.1 to 5.2 in intensity, are not along any known fault, though they are rumored to run parallel to the infamous San Andreas Fault.

The article continued, but it was the map which drew Tam Chen's keen interest. He'd taken a pencil and interconnected the pathway from Japan through the quakes, extrapolating the probable continuation. He no longer had any doubt, and now he had scientific proof. The demon was L.A. bound and moving faster than Tam could ever hope to. He had not been able to reach Victor to warn him. A feeling of helplessness stabbed through him, a feeling like an echo of that which had come at his elder brother's death during a tong fight. Though Victor was older than Tam, Tam had always protected him, hoping the past would never repeat itself. Now the possibility frightened him.

Tam folded the paper over so he could no longer read the inevitable. He wondered what had happened to the crew of the *Matsoya*. He wondered what would happen to Victor.

The beaches of Santa Cruz looked like gray sand pearls in the night, their driftwood-littered shore and wild cliff approach rugged. Trees on the cliff's edge, bent into bonsai shapes by the wind, sketched dark figures on the horizon. The faint phosphorescence of the foaming waves as the tide came in set the sands to glittering.

Sandy walked ahead of Kevin on the pathway, hugging her cardigan to her shoulders. Northern California air held a bitter edge to it that she was not used to, but she didn't mind it. Tonight she'd be able to sleep, instead of sweating and wanting. Summer semester at UCSC had begun, and so had her life, she thought. Complete at last. She flung a teasing look at the tall, dark boy following her. "Catch me if you can."

He frowned seriously. His T-shirt proclaimed PEACE: The World Tour and proceeded to name all the nuclear sites he'd protested at. She liked him for his seriousness of mind, his intensity. He knew more about nuclear disarmament than anybody she knew—all the threats and dangers of stockpiled weapons that were being stored and then dismantled incorrectly. He'd been in jail a couple of times for the protest movement he was involved in. She thought he would save the world if he possibly could.

But tonight she wanted his mind to herself, all of it, and his body as well. She gave a teasing laugh. She began to run down the cliffside path, her sandals tearing into the silt soft dirt, dashing through the ice plant and gorse and even poison oak, skittering, half in control and half in headlong flight to the lower beach. The young man ran after her with a shout and caught up only when they reached the sand together and he snatched up the cuff of her sweater and pulled her roughly to him.

Their lips met. She could taste the last vestiges of the wine cooler they'd shared on his mouth and kissed deeply, probing, imitating the sexual movements they would share later. He moaned and moved closer, shaping her body more tightly to his, and answered the probing with a response of his own.

Sandy closed her eyes and let herself meld into him. Every touch of his body against hers sent a shock of recognition and yearning through her. Life was sweet and good, achingly good. She felt the earth move under her feet, a tremor, and braced herself.

Kevin's body went tense and he thrust her a little away from him. "What's that?" he said, looking oceanward.

The roar of surf at her back grew louder. "What's what?"

"Holy shit. It's a whale or something, coming in to beach." Kevin released her entirely, except for her hand, as he spun her around.

Sandy let out a soft curse. He was into marine biology studies at UCSC as part two of saving the world and any phenomena coming out of the surf would come before their gentle lovemaking. She tried to draw him back, her blood still warm, her flesh still throbbing. She wanted his touch. "Let it beach."

"I'm serious, Sandy. Look."

He whirled her back, facing the black ocean

water, and she could see the massive form coming in on the tide. Kevin said, "We can't leave it here. We'll need dredges and nets and a tow boat. Maybe I can find somebody at the institute."

Sandy's blood chilled. "That's no whale," she said, eyes fixed on the monstrosity.

Kevin's mind had been racing elsewhere. "Of course it is," he said, looking cliffward toward the campus.

She tugged on his hand. "I've never seen a whale with eyes like that."

Yellow lanterns beamed over the foaming curl of the tide. "Oh, my God," Kevin said.

The massive head turned toward them, sculpted like a lion-dog of ancient China. Its jowls opened and teeth shone like sickle moons. The waves withdrew, leaving it standing on legs as thick as tree trunks.

They stood in frozen disbelief, then he yanked her hand, hard. "Let's get out of here."

They began to clamber up the cliffside, hands and feet tearing at the soft dirt which had spilled them down to the sand.

The demon rose behind them, with a roar of its own towering out of the waves and foam, light spilling from its jaws as it opened them to snap. It struck swiftly across the sands. The last thing they felt was its hot breath grazing the backs of their heads.

Their sweet hot blood spilled out of his jaws into the sand, and with it new knowledge,

knowledge that he had at last reached the shores he sought. That knowledge helped, but it was not entirely necessary. Under the shelf of the shoreline, he had begun to hear the voice of his enemy, subtle, sweet with longing, calling. Not calling to him, of course, but it did not matter. The demon would answer the call of his sundered power, of his omnipotence, as a lodestone turns north. But this song drew him south, inexorably, longingly, the day to his night. As he had with all his other kills, he would swallow and absorb it.

Then he would turn his attention to what he'd learned since he'd regained his freedom. This last morsel had been most interesting. Great weaponry, far beyond the spears and catapults and bows and arrows of the emperor's armies could now be flung after enemies. The demon thought to experiment a little before absorbing a power he was unfamiliar with. The male he'd eaten knew just where most of the weaponry could be found, in its various underground deposits. Most helpful, as well as sustaining. The demon was pleased with his meal.

Irving woke in the dead of night, his harsh breathing the only sound in the strange room. He reached for his *Cabala* and did not find it, his mind fuzzy and alarmed at its disappearance until he remembered just where he was. The night lay subdued around him. He closed his eyes again, lightly, heard the demon voices and knew where he must go. He knew where earth and water would meet fire and air, and where Susan was destined to die. He dropped into meditation, his mind awash with the mysteries of his study. Down the hall, he could hear an old man begin to groan and cry in his sleep. He reached out and soothed him. His suddenly keen hearing searched further. He found the orderly at the end of the hall, chair tilted against the wall, a book in his great, thick hands. He soothed that man's thoughts as well, until the orderly's chin dropped to his chest and he began to snore in a resonant bass.

Irving opened his eyes, thinking of the old days, when he had willed Nazi eyes to turn aside from the alleys, the catacombs, which had hidden him. He flexed, his arms bowed, pulling full strength against his restraints. He had strong arms, and even as he unclenched his jaw, one of the restraints came loose with a soft pop. Irving shook it off. He reached over and untied the second, shaking all over with the terror of his dreams as they burst through his hard-won calm.

He remembered Susan coming to him, telling him that it was all over, and she was safe. That had not been a dream, though the drugs they'd given him made it seem hazy and faraway. But she wasn't safe. Her danger was greater than ever. She was walking right into it.

He pressed his fingers to his forehead. It was drenched slick. He tried to dry it. The only way to save her would be to go himself. To answer the call of the fire-maker. He knew where to start.

He stuck his bare feet out of bed and climbed down, child-like, wavering and holding onto the bedrail for support. They had not thrown out or hidden his clothes. If they wanted to keep him prisoner, they should have planned better, Irving thought grimly, as he donned his things.

He padded into the hallway. The orderly's snore rose and fell. The care wing of the home was on the first floor, for ease of evacuation. All he had to do was go out the fire door. It would set off the alarm, but by the time they reacted to that, he would be off the grounds. There were no fences or armed guards with dogs here. They could not hold him.

Focused in his thoughts, Irving made his way down the heavily waxed hallway. Its floor reflected his image. He looked down at it and straightened shoulders years of hunching over a sewing machine had curved. The bone and muscle cracked reluctantly. Irving grimaced. The task was not beyond him, despite his age. He put a hand in his pocket. Cab fare. He could return to Susan's home and retrieve his car. Behind the wheel of the car, he would be fully empowered.

He leaned on the door-wide handle and went through. His passage, as he knew it would, set off the alarm. No one stopped him as he padded across the manicured lawn, saying, "They sent me this way." With shouts and cries, the personnel ran past him in the opposite direction, concerned about those who were not ambulatory. In a crowd of T-shirts and old plaid robes, flannel nightgowns despite the summer heat, and chintz dusters, curlers, and fluffy white hair, all looking around with curiosity and dismay, he disappeared.

He would fight fire with fire. World War II had birthed napalm, among its other atrocities, and he'd not forgotten its lessons. Some laundry detergent, some gasoline, and a few other simple items, and he could duplicate it. Yes. He would meet the fire-maker with power of his own. For Susan's sake. Once and for all. He would destroy the La Brea tar pits, like lighting an oil well fire, and let the demon voices drown in their own doom.

The seismo wing at Cal Tech is not impressive, despite its importance. Its main rooms resemble a haphazardly organized jumble of equipment and computers, shelves on erector-set brackets holding more equipment and sheaves of gridded paper. Row after row of such units are broken up only by the placements of various seismographs themselves and modems at computer and printer stations transmitting information from other units placed throughout the state and the world. Students, grad students, and scientists drift through, occasionally accompanied by a cameraman with a camcorder getting statements, but most days the rooms are empty of media presence and the only noise is that of the current jokes and coffee cups being crumpled and thrown into the trash can. A recycling basket for aluminum cans resides nearby. And always there is the faint skritch-scratch of needles on seismo recording paper as the machines capture the ever-present dance of the earth.

Becca Lipton leaned over the unit she monitored, and frowned as the needle began to swing in dark-inked lines. "Here's another one," she called across the room. "And it's closer." She wore a tan shirt tucked into sage-colored shorts and Birkenstocks for summer comfort on her feet. Her hair was cut short and layered in brown fringes about her face. She didn't care much for makeup and never used it unless the media was storming in for information. She felt most at ease in the middle of the night shift when she was the master of her own destiny.

Another night watcher answered back. "Where?"

She looked at the graph. It would take an hour or so to definitely establish the epicenter, but she had been tracking this cluster down the state and knew approximately where it might be. "Carpinteria, along the San Andreas."

The grad student across the way straightened from his machine. "I've got it, too. Santa Barbara's reporting in. Appears stronger there." His Vietnamese tanned and intense face pulled tight. "Are we predicting this one?"

Becca scratched her temple. "Tranh, I don't know. It's 2:30 in the morning or I'd call some-one."

The thin man gave her a steady look from dark eyes. "It's headed this way. This could be foreshocks of the big one."

"Don't I know it." Becca swirled the dregs of cold coffee in her paper cup. "But we've never had activity like this. Across the Pacific and now down the state." The needle stopped its violent swing and settled into a more normal pattern. She wadded the cup up carefully and tossed it across the room. "I think I'll call someone anyway. At this rate, it'll be here in an hour, an hour and a half at the most."

Tranh turned away as another machine toned softly, calling for his attention. He went to the monitor, studied it, and then let out a soft whistle. "Becca, look at this."

Reluctant to leave her machine, Becca joined his side. "What is it?"

"The forest service is tracking a series of fires down the coast . . . spontaneous, lightning type strikes. With our dryness, it's caused havoc. But look . . . it's following the quake cluster pattern. No, not following—preceeding!"

"What?" She narrowed her gaze and felt her brow beetle up. She'd have thick furrowing lines like her grandfather had in his forehead if she kept this up. Putting fingers to it, she rubbed the wrinkles out. "That can't be. There's no correlation between quakes and fire unless we're talking burst gas lines or something."

"Tell me about it. So what have we got?"

"Godzilla burrowing underground? How should I know?" Becca gave up frowning for chewing on the edge of her lower lip. The fax began to transmit more information. "There's another one coming up. Where is that?"

"Just below Carpinteria. The hills are dry in there."

Becca's machine began to skritch-scratch again, needle fluctuating. It chimed gently. She ran back to it. "Damn. Another quake. Not much of one. Probably a 3.5 or so. Tranh . . . get the mayor's office on the line. I don't know what this is, but we're headed for some major shake and bake if it keeps up.

Chapter 23

Victor stood up and shed his gold lamé jacket. "Time for a reality check," he said. "No one is going to believe us."

"No one has to. The proof is lying out at the lab at the museum."

Victor and El looked at one another. El added slowly, "And if she's there, other artifacts might be as well."

"Whose lab?"

"Probably Dr. Ellington's. It's in the back, not in the round house where the tourists can look in. The Old Tar himself might have her, but probably Ellington." The young lion would have her, if he could, all to himself. "It doesn't matter," Harper continued. "I have the key."

"Oh, no," Susan protested. "Not tonight. I've had enough today."

"You don't have to come if you don't want to, but tonight's best. They won't let me near the bones or artifacts tomorrow." Harper stood. "I don't know if they'll have extra security or not, but the regular man knows me. He knows I like to come in after hours and do paperwork."

The two men looked at Susan. She waved her bandaged hand. "As keeper of the feather, I guess I have to go." She retrieved the talisman from its place on the table and slipped it over her head. "Let's go."

Susan rested her head on the point of El's shoulder. Victor drove too fast, but the streets were nearly empty at three in the morning, though not completely, for this was L.A. and, like Vegas, it didn't have much of a time sense. For some people, who didn't like the heat, and for others, the scavengers of city society, this was the only time to be out and about.

Harper's heart beat slow and strong. She liked the sound of it. She put a hand up to his chest and held it over the hollow, feeling as well as listening.

El said quickly, "Everything all right?"

She looked up. "All right?"

"Never mind." He fumbled a moment. "Nothing." He put his hand over hers. "We're almost there."

She sensed it. With it came the overriding urgency to do it, to take care of the business they'd come for. Her mouth grew dry and she tried to swallow.

Victor took the curb instead of the parking lot slope. El bounced vigorously. "Damn! Even the schoolbus drivers can hit this one."

Victor flashed them a grin as he pulled into a lot. "I practiced driving an ambulance."

El and Susan slid out cautiously. The lights

around the pit had not been restored. Nor did they see a security guard. All was quiet, stilled by the ebb of mankind's tide that comes at three in the morning for those who sleep.

Victor carried his Walkman radio, earphones slung around his neck. He said quietly, "Cal Tech reports a fiver at Carpinteria. No damage reported yet, though they expect broken glass, that sort of thing. That was half an hour ago." He paused. "El, they've called an earthquake alarm."

"What?"

"They've issued warnings. That's one reason the streets were so clear. They're asking residents to stay calm, turn off their gas and other utilities, and brace themselves." Victor scratched a luxurious eyebrow. "We picked a bad night to be out."

Harper paused on the walkway. No guard. No lights illuminating the dig site and the observatory deck. His sternum ached. He rubbed it absently. He took the abandonment of the site for good luck and urged the others forward. "We need to hurry. We're on a lake of tar, water, and gas. That's no place to be if the ground starts to sink."

El unlocked the door, looked about, and waved Susan and Victor inside. He caught Victor by the elbow. "There're cameras on, so don't skulk about. They're going to know we were here anyway."

Susan hesitated before the turnstile gate and

the gift counter. El grinned. "Oletha's gone. I promise."

She threw him a sheepish look. "That was one formidable lady," she said.

"So are you." El reached out, took her good hand, and squeezed it gently.

Victor bumped into a dump of plastic pterodactyl kites, extricated himself gingerly, and said, "Which way do we go before I kill myself?"

Harper led the way.

"This is all they have?" Susan looked down at the lab table, a faint blue-lined grid underneath the bones. There was half a skull, a few ribs, a pelvic bone and a leg bone and a few scattered bones that must belong to one foot.

"Patience," cautioned El. "Rome wasn't built in a day." He looked the remains over. "There's probably more of her in the cleaning vats. They've worked hard to get this much of her laid out already."

"Burning the midnight oil," Victor said, but no one paid any attention to him. He touched a foot bone. "How can they tell she's not Indian?"

"Bone structure. Also, although I doubt this one had her feet bound—I can't remember when the Chinese did that to their women—she most certainly wore shoes or clogs most of her life, unlike a Native American, who probably went barefoot. The paleontologists can tell, just like they can tell from Greek and Roman remains who was a slave and who wasn't, from bone growth and thickness."

"And I always thought," Susan murmured, "that death was the great equalizer. Ashes to ashes, dust to dust."

El had moved beyond the lab to the counter, where plastic drums of tar were lined up and labeled. He pried open a lid. "This stuff came up with her."

Victor peered into the can. "We're supposed to dredge through that?"

"That's one possibility. I want to check the cleaning vats first. This is Ellington's lab. He may even have something hidden back in here. That would be like him."

Susan rubbed her temple again. The dull thrumming that had begun earlier in the evening had grown worse. It was not a headache, exactly, but more like riding in a car with the radio turned down to nearly inaudible. It was as though she could almost but not quite hear something. Just as her lungs and throat still ached, she chalked it up to an aftereffect of the fire. She thought of Angelo, fugitive, and wondered how many steps ahead of retribution and the law he was. And she worried about being caught in the museum when, and if, the quake hit. She shivered involuntarily in the chill lab air and rubbed her hands together. As the two men went to the back of the lab to the gigantic sinks, she leaned over the open drum of tar. The talisman swung forward a little from her neck, feather dipping over the black goo.

There was a tiny ripple across the surface of the pail. Susan blinked. The goo began to bubble and boil. Before she could pull back in alarm, something came to the top with a blur and floated out of the tar, as pristine and clean as if it had never been marred. It lay upon the surface as if called.

A match to the blue and gold feather upon her necklace.

"El," Susan got out, her voice a bare squeak. She tried again. "El!"

"What is it?"

"Look at this!" Susan backed away and pointed.

Harper peered back into the bucket. "What did you do? Did you drop it in?" He scooped the feather out.

"No-o. It . . . just came to the top."

Harper held it up. Victor looked to her talisman as if to reassure himself the original feather was still in place and said, "Another one. This thing must be shedding pinfeathers all over the place."

"It has to be down there." Harper turned and looked back at the fragments of skeleton. "If she could talk."

"It's history, then," Victor stated. "It has to be. She was probably one of the handmaidens sent with it."

Susan put her hand to the edge of the lab table to steady herself. She looked down at the bones. "Poor girl. That must have been a terrible voyage—how could they even have survived it?—to come to this. They must have tried to use the tar to cover the pyre, to ensure its burning. Maybe even built it there. Mounting it, the faithful handmaiden going to her death with her master as her emperor commanded, just like the Hindus used to do. Only they didn't burn. They got sucked down. Horribly. Inexorably." Susan put her hand to her mouth at the thought and couldn't stand to look any more.

"How to convince the others?"

Harper gripped the feather. "I'll go to Trenton. He has seniority over Ellington, a little influence, and he's got the most open mind. I'll have to show him the tablets, explain where they came from. He's got to know. If they keep excavating, they might run into a very nasty surprise."

"But they will keep digging," Victor said.

"Of course they will. But they'll be alot more careful. If it's there, Vic, we have to look for it." El stood at the door by the light switch, waiting for the others.

"But should we?" Victor returned. "The tablet refers to it as a demon equal to the first. L.A. is a tinderbox. It won't take many sparks to set if off."

"The Phoenix was a creature of goodness and wisdom."

"Was is the operative word," the restaurateur argued with Susan. "It's been nothing but destructive here." He stopped and then added reluctantly, "And it may be focused on you."

Susan put her hand over the feather. "No. No, it protected me this afternoon. When that backdraft hit me, it knocked me clear across the room . . . but all I got was a burned hand and a singed eyebrow. I swear the flames curled away from me."

El said softly, "They weren't when I pulled you out. You wouldn't have made it, Susan. Digger didn't."

She blinked in confusion, then came across the lab room toward the exit. Victor's face, as she passed him, was molded into a neutral expression. She half-smiled. "The inscrutable Oriental," she remarked.

He gave a half-bow. "Always."

They reached the door together. El opened it for them and turned the lights off.

A noise went off simultaneously. Victor cursed from the darkness. "Jesus! An alarm. I swear I didn't touch anything."

They eased into the outer passageway. Susan's voice was muffled. Then, she said, "It's my beeper."

"Thank God."

El turned on the light at Betsy's desk. "What is it?"

"Maida's number. My mother-in-law." She frowned.

"Call from here."

She nodded and sat down. She placed the call awkwardly, punching in the numbers with her left hand, and listened. "Hello, Mai." There was a spurt of sound which even the two men could hear, although not distinctly. Susan shook her head, protesting, "We did nothing. I came by to let him know I was all right . . . no, he's not crazy, there was a fire . . . I won't argue with you now, Mai, it's late— what? What do you mean?" Another spurt of sound. "I'll call you if I find out anything." She hung up. Her eyes looked darker, deeper than before as she faced El and Victor. "Poppa's gone. He walked out of the residence home sometime this evening. He simply vanished."

"He's an old man," El said. "How far could he have gotten?"

"Who?" asked Victor.

Susan ignored him. "Don't underestimate Poppa. He's tough and he's resourceful."

"He was also tied down last time we saw him."

"Who?" repeated Victor.

"My grandfather-in-law."

Victor's almond eyes blinked. "You're married?"

"Widowed. El, I've got to find him."

Harper shook his head. "You don't even know where to look."

"I'll start with home, his and mine. Maybe we can tell what he was thinking, what has been worrying him so much."

"Gas," said El.

Victor commented, "Old people sometimes have trouble with gas."

The two stopped talking and looked at him. He shrugged. "It happens."

"Not that kind of gas," snapped El. "Remember the methane leaks that broke through in the Fairfax district and caught on fire? *That's* what has him worried. He thinks it could happen again. He's afraid of gas leaks and fire."

"Maybe he's not so crazy," responded Victor. "If this Phoenix of ours can ignite the methane pool that lies under most of this end of town, we can make Hiroshima look small time."

"Maybe he's not so crazy," said Susan. "Maybe he *knows*."

"How?"

She took Harper's hand. "I don't know. Maybe the Phoenix sends out subliminal distress signals. It was a god, wasn't it? A demigod?"

"Stories from prehistory," answered Harper.

Victor put his hand up. "Not in China. We had literature for three thousand years before Huang. Two thousand since, remember."

Harper looked solemn. "Susan, I can't. . . ." He freed his hand and absentmindedly rubbed his chest. "Tomorrow. We all need to rest."

"I can't rest with Poppa on the streets somewhere." She pulled back. "I understand. This is a lot to ask of you, so soon. But Poppa's a part of my life."

"It's not that—"

She interrupted. "Just take me home."

* * *

The outside of the museum lay in pitch darkness. El locked the door behind them. He stood for a moment.

"This isn't right."

"What isn't?" Victor had a hand on Susan's arm to keep her from stumbling on the museum walkway.

"Earthquake warning or not, there should be a guard around here somewhere."

The sixth sense that Tam Chen had tried so hard to teach Victor prickled at him a little. "Trouble," he muttered. He looked about. "You stay here."

Harper looked inclined to obey, but Susan started forward. "We stay together."

El gave her a look.

"Well," she said defensively. "We should stay together."

Victor hung back as both stepped forward together. "What is that smell?"

"L.A. smog after a hot summer day."

The restaurateur shook his head. "No. Huh-uh. This sets my teeth on edge." His head swiveled rapidly. "If you're coming, keep close." He moved out on point, and that's when his mind realized what his body, his senses were telling him. Not since Nam had he smelled that pungent smell, and it did not come from the tar pits, though napalm was a distant cousin.

His arm ached to cradle his rifle. His palms itched. He could feel the stink sinking into his sinuses where it would take weeks, months of smelling garlic chicken cooking in the Jade Pheasant kitchen to take it out of his mind. Days to remind him he was home again.

Just behind him, El whispered, "What is it?"

And Victor told him. Susan gave a fluttering gasp, caught her breath, and said, "Napalm? Who would have napalm out here?"

And why? El reached for Susan and brought her protectively close to his side.

The silhouette that was Victor creeping up on the silent dig site motioned for the two of them to circle right. El nudged Susan in that direction. In the shadow of the building, away from the street and the high lamplights placed for safety and joggers, little could be seen.

Susan found herself imitating Victor's stealthy moves, yet, if she stood up and marched boldly half an acre away to the curbside, she would be facing the condo project, gates and all, where Ava Lerner resided. *Half an acre away from reality*, she thought. *That's all I am.*

A flare went off, so close to them that El let out a yell of startlement and flung up his arm to block his eyes. Susan stopped, blinded, afraid to take a step in any direction. Then she saw Victor flying through the air in a low tackle, and the flare-holder and the restaurateur rolled on the ground.

She recognized the "Oof" and "Oy!" of the unknown man. "Poppa!" She sprinted in rescue. "Victor! Let him up! That's my grandfather!" She batted at them to untangle them.

Victor got to his knees, panting. "He's rank with napalm. Get that street flare away from him before he sets us all on fire!"

El grabbed the flare and pitched it. Susan gathered up the groaning elder and cradled him. "Did you have to hit him so hard?"

"It's all right, Susie," the old man wheezed. "He didn't know if I was a *meshuga* or not. Me, I'm not so sure myself." He hugged her back. He looked at Harper. "Get her away from here, you hear me? She's got to leave now."

"Poppa, we're going to have all sorts of trouble now getting you out of the home for good. And what are you doing with this ... stuff?"

"You think I broke myself out of that home for my health? And this stuff, I made myself. To protect you. Of course I'm lousy with napalm. I'm going to burn the place down."

Harper said mildly, "That's not the voice of a rational man, Susan."

She shot him a look. "After what we've been talking about all evening, you would know? You can judge?" Back to Irving. "How did you get here?"

"I took a cab back to your place, got my car and keys, a few necessities, and drove over. I know what I have to do."

Victor had gotten up and was dusting himself off. In the flickering light of Irving's flashlight, he examined a torn ruffle. His demeanor reminded Susan of Domino when the cat had embarrassed himself and tried to hide it by vigorous and self-conscious grooming.

Susan helped Irving to his feet. "Are you hurt? Did you break anything?"

He squeezed her cheek. "I'm fine, *shayna*. But you take your Mr. Harper and go home."

"We're not leaving you to do this," El told him.

Irving let out an exasperated noise. "I should stand here all night and argue with you? Listen, you already think I'm crazy—but I dream. I haven't had a night's rest in months. I dream. It gets more and more vivid. And the more I dream, the more I know. I know what I have to do. If I burn, it's all right." He started to shrug, winced, and thought better of it. "But if I can save Susan. . . ."

"But you did, Poppa. This afternoon—"

"No! This is the heart of the danger. That was a little trouble, not this. This is the heart of it all." He peered at Harper. "Is it not?"

Harper hesitated a moment and then answered, "Maybe."

"See!" He crowed in triumph and shook a finger at Susan. "And he brought you here. Shame on him. Now he can take you away."

"Mr. Aronson, I would never have brought Susan if I thought there was anything that could happen."

"But you didn't think long enough, Mr. Harper," Poppa shot back. "When you're old, like me, you'll find lots of time to think long enough. When you're young, you have to learn to make time, to think things through."

Victor had circled around the perimeter of the skirmish. He called back, "Here's the guard. He's out like a light. What did you do to him?"

"That's Louis. Is he all right?" El asked sharply.

Poppa made a face. "Of course he's all right. He's sleeping like a baby. I gave him a little tap, that's all."

"Poppa!"

He raised an eyebrow at Susan. "What? Do you forget I wasn't a meek and mild tailor all my life? When we came back to America finally, I was ready for some peace and quiet." He waved a hand. "He'll be fine in the morning."

Victor began to drag Louis away from the area where the napalm stink was worse. He came back. "We've got to get this cleaned up somehow or the first spark will set it off."

El looked at him in the meager light of Poppa's old flashlight. His mouth quirked. "I'm tempted to leave it this way for Ellington. He could use a setback or two to his ego." He changed tone. "Any way we can dilute it? Or neutralize it?"

"No." Victor paced. "Think of it as a thick, gelatinous gasoline." He took the flashlight from El and shone it into the pit area. "There's standing water here. I think we can burn it off without damaging the actual dig area any. Pops here didn't have enough time to disperse it well."

Irving drew himself up rigidly. "I have more."

"We don't need more," El reprimanded. "And she doesn't need to be running around cleaning up your messes."

Susan put a hand up. Those subliminal voices running through her headache buzzed louder and louder. "Please don't fight. Let's just get out of here."

"This is not a fight," Poppa said heartily. "This is just a discussion." He looked at Victor and his dangling ruffle. "I can fix that for you," he said abruptly. "A little tack here, a little seam there."

"Good. You owe me," the round-faced man answered.

Susan thought she felt the earth dance a little under her feet, a minor tremor, an aftershock to the bigger jolt of several days ago. She looked to Victor, who looked back, and then they both looked at the ground. The quake came to a halt. With its halt, a wave seemed to rise from the ground. It made her vision waver. She felt its hot curtain expand. She put the back of her hand to her forehead as though measuring a fever. "El," she said, but Harper did not hear her.

A handful of crows rose in a flurry from their night perches in the trees along the edge of the jogging path. They circled with mournful cries, saw her, and came on the wing.

She did not flinch. She bore the feather. She wondered what they would do.

Victor exclaimed, "Holy Christ!" He dodged to one side as the v-wing came at her, sculling and crying, their yellow eyes faintly gleaming.

Both Harper and Poppa went silent.

Susan blinked as the crows came at her, swooped past her forehead, circled, and came out again, crying with distress. She felt the ground grow warm through the thin soles of her shoes.

"El, it's getting very warm."

The air was still and heavy.

The birds dove at her face, brushing her back, baffling her with their wings and their harsh CAWKs of fear.

She turned to El. "Run," she said, her voice whisper-thin. She took Poppa by the elbow. "Run!"

He hobbled with her. El and Victor waited a beat then dove after her. With the sound of ice cracking or a cannon booming, the pit gained a voice and a tremendous fireball shot up, blazing into the sky where it arced into the distance. A comet tail of sparks showered down harmlessly.

"Like a goddamn Roman candle," said El.

"Except that we were standing there." Victor cleared his throat. "And part of that blast was napalm going off."

Susan stroked her grandfather-in-law's arm. "Poppa, you'd have gone up like a torch."

He did not seem to hear her voice. Tears began to roll down either side of his strong featured nose. "Listen," he said. "Can't you hear?"

He put his tailor-callused hand lightly over her mouth and repeated, "Listen. Can't you hear?"

And Susan listened.

Chapter 24

It was a chorus, no, music . . . no, not even that described it. It washed through her, draining her of all emotions and casting them upward, until her throat tightened with pain. It continued to well up inside of her until her lips opened to let it out, all of it, and she heard nothing issue but silence and her own sobbing breath.

Poppa had dropped his work-worn hand from her mouth. His eyes shone brightly. "Do you hear?"

She nodded wordlessly.

El put his hands about her shoulders. "We've got to go, to get out of here. That fireball is going to bring a reaction."

She pulled away restlessly. "No." The sound grew faint and she moved toward the pit to recapture it. Victor was arguing with Irving, saying, "What other gear did you bring?" and she moved past them as if they did not exist.

Only the voices existed. The chorus of music for which she had no name rose in litany as she neared the blackened edge of grass which rimmed the shed and stands and pit. The smell of the fire spout hung on the air like brimstone. *One could believe in hell,* she thought, *and this is heaven singing its warning.* She wanted to answer its siren call, if only she could understand it.

"Susan!"

She flinched at the sharp voice behind her. She half-turned to answer it, but the litany, the sweet sounds of the pit, drew her back.

El stood, baffled, watching Susan drift moth-like toward the tar pit. Victor brushed past him, muttering, "This old geezer has more gear than I saw in Nam." His arms full, he nudged Irving down the walkway with him. He raised his voice to El. "Let's get out of here!"

A siren split the air. It was still faint. Harper turned his head to catch its direction. It was conceivably headed their way.

"Susan!"

The woman tilted her head. The backlights of the museum filtered warmly outward, catching her blonde-streaked hair in its illumination, giving her a halo of gold. She lifted a hand up, her bandaged hand, and held it out in entreaty, seductively, toward the pit.

The siren's wail grew closer. El broke his hesitation and joined her in three bounds.

"Let's go."

She looked at him with tearful eyes, smiling. "No."

Sleep without dreams, without motivation, without emotion or care. But not without thought. Her mind flicked from image to image, touching without sorrow, manipulating without conscience. Faces parading, watching her: Geoff, Poppa, Maida with disapproval etched into her face, Sid who would never look her in the eye, El, Angelo, her parents.

And she thought of burning. Of the showroom fire, with its tongues of heat curling over her prone body, dragonfire licking the air, scenting her, tasting her with curiosity before malice, her rescue before destruction.

She thought of El again and his sweet, tentative kiss before the probing, fuller ones of passion. It was her last conscious thought before she slipped below the waters of deeper sleep in answer to the summons. *She had been called.* She grasped the necklace tightly and dreamed of singing. The feather she touched bridged the gap between centuries in a sudden, breathtaking swoop.

A breeze stirred the mercilessly hot air along the riverbanks, singing in the treetops, and Pearl Moon paused on the bridge, her hand still curled about her brush, the fabric for the new fan she painted beginning to drift in answer to the wind. Chimes in the tree branches bending overhead gave off their soft music, but she did not feel their tranquility in her heart.

A pigeon's wingbeat rode the wind and it glided to a halt on the bridge railing. Sharp eyes peered at her as she spoke to it and the creature hopped onto her wrist. Skillfully she tweaked the bamboo cylinder from its leg and read the message inked on a shred of fabric inside.

"I AM CALLED."

It bore Jade Blossom's signet.

Pearl Moon crushed the fabric in her hand. Her brush dropped unnoticed to the bridge. It slipped through a slat and fell to the sluggish waters below. She put her hands to her heart and bent her head. The pigeon left with a soft coo.

She would not cry. A handmaiden for the great emperor of Ch'in did not cry. The great battles had been won, a court was being assembled, artisans from all over the provinces were being brought in to construct Mount Li for Ch'in and Shih Huang Ti. This would surely be the Golden Age of the world, the Shensi province and the Yalu River the center of the universe.

And she would surely be called to join Jade Blossom.

A clog sounded on the edge of the bridge. Pearl Moon looked up, her heart skipping a beat. Her headdress tinkled softly as she lifted her chin. Its tassels tickled the line of her jaw.

The emperor's herald stood awaiting her permission to approach. Pearl Moon's words froze in her mouth. She ended up saying nothing, only extending her hand.

He came forward and bowed. He said nothing either, only put a small blue and gold feather into her palm. Pearl Moon closed her hand about it tightly, lest the wind take it, and destiny, away from her.

"Tomorrow morning. You have a journey overland to the ocean. Emperor Huang has sent horsemen ahead to have a ship readied for you."

Pearl Moon gave a composed nod, composure she did not feel. She would not shed a tear in front of this courtier. She turned her back, saying only, "I will be ready." She picked up a new brush, dipped it, and continued painting. Her tears fell unbidden and flowed through the cracks of the bridge and into the stream which would carry them to the Yalu River, where they would be as nothing.

An emperor commanded her to serve a God. What good were tears before such a command? Pearl Moon would go wherever it would lead her.

Susan fell back, stumbling, her head throbbing, as Harper caught her by the elbow. She looked down at the necklace she wore. The handmaidens carried those feathers, the child-women chosen to serve the Phoenix. She felt a sudden weight upon her thoughts.

"Susie!" said Poppa sharply.

She reached out and put her hand in his. "I'm all right. But I . . . can't leave."

Victor had one hand on his earphones. His eyes shone with intensity. "El, I'm getting more about the earthquake warning. This is what Tam Chen was trying to tell me about, but he only had a piece of the puzzle. Listen . . . a pathway of cluster earthquakes from China across the Pacific floor to Northern California."

El blinked. It was late. "What's that got to do with ugly critters?"

"No, listen. Look. A massive quake at Xian. Some damage to the archaeological site—remember what Susan told you about the statues? That's where they're located. That's where our boy Huang is buried. That was six days ago. Aftershocks since. Tam runs into a demon dog. It nearly tears him limb from limb, nothing modern fazes it. He has to use a machete on it—but first, the insignia of the Phoenix stops it in its tracks. Then, this. Mt. Pinatubo in the Philippines goes up and then Mt. Unzen in Japan. Both of them have been pretty quiet in the last two years. His plane is forced down at Tokyo and he can't get a quick flight back, but he's full of dire warnings. Now this arc of quakes across the ocean floor."

El shook his head, feeling loggy. "I still don't see . . ."

"There's been a demon buried under that site," explained Victor. "According to the tablets."

"The one the Phoenix faced. Or," and El swallowed hard. "Or there *was* a demon buried there."

Poppa stated, "It isn't any longer. I've heard it coming. It brought me here. I don't care if you think I'm crazy. I have to do what I have to do."

Ed did not dispute the older man. He and Victor looked long and hard at one another.

"Well, boys," said Susan into the silence. "It

looks like we don't have any choice about waking the Phoenix, do we?"

Poppa cried, "No."

Victor's eyes were bloodshot with the lateness of the hour. He tapped the palm of his hand. "I agree with him. The demon signatures are equal. I don't see it any other way. The capacity for damage is as great with the Phoenix as it was with the vanquished foe. That's why Huang exiled it, probably. He was a strong man. He didn't intend to entertain challenges to his power."

"Then what do we do about it?"

"Nuke 'em." Victor rubbed his eyes. His black hair spiked upward from the night's activities and he sported a definite counterculture look. "How do I know? Let sleeping dogs lie."

"But it's not asleep." Harper's glance went to Susan's face and lingered. "It's reaching out, combusting at random. Are these distress signals or a supernatural power gone insane? It doesn't matter. It's destructive. It's murderous." He looked back to Victor. "What did you say Tam Chen finally used on that beast that jumped him?"

"An old cast-iron machete. Probably World War II vintage, when steel was hard to come by for ordinary tools."

"From a previous age," El murmured. "Old weapons to fight old magic."

"So you stand over the pit with a Bronze Age spear and stab the first thing that moves."

They looked at one another, and El laughed. He said, "No, I think I'll throw you in as bait. Preferably while singing, 'Feelings.' "

"What? I thought you liked my singing?" Victor made a mock face of shock.

Irving gave them all a fierce, hawk-eyed look. "Time," he said, "is not on our side."

His remark galvanized El into action.

"What are those?" Susan said in distaste as El held up the rubberized suits.

"Waders. Trout fishermen's waders, actually. We're going to be knee-deep in tar. It gets messy. Try not to destroy any bones or fragments you find. Just shovel 'em over the side. We won't make much progress at night. The tar cools down a little."

Susan said faintly, as she shrugged into the overall portion of the waders, "I don't think it's down too far now. If it is. . . ."

"We'll do what we can. That's all we can do."

Susan touched the talisman at her throat, for luck. She picked up a shovel. "I'm ready."

Poppa steadied the flashlight beam over his wrist as he sat on the grassy bank and watched. Victor's waders were meant for a man of taller stature and came up nearly to his chin. Harper made crude knots in the straps to take up slack even the buckles couldn't handle.

"Thanks, Dad," Victor said dryly. He hefted his pick and shovel. "I hope this is a good idea."

"It may not be, but it's the only one I've got

at this point," answered El. He stepped into his own gear.

It looked like a mountain tarn, a pool of bottomless depth and darkness. It reflected the sliver of a moon back at them as they paused at the sides. Strings and stakes marked territory and levels. El stepped over them and down, saying, "Stay to the side where it's reinforced and shored. Otherwise you could get sucked under, too. There's wood to make step terraces as you descend. Okay?"

Victor nodded. Susan licked lips gone dry as paper and then forced a nod as well. She stepped into the dig area, wondering if it knew she was coming.

"It's warm," she said.

"What?" El looked at her, then the tar. "It can't be."

"It is. It's like soup."

He put his shovel in and stirred about. "We'll sink like stones if anyone slips. Stay to the edges where they've sounded 'em."

Victor put up a hand for silence, but even as he did so, they could feel the ground begin to move again. Susan grabbed a spar for support. The tar stirred sluggishly.

"A big one at Sylmar," he said, listening to the radio. "A really big one. We haven't much time."

On the outskirts of the L.A. basin. Literally a hop, skip, and jump away. El began to shovel, spooning away the tar that washed onto his booted feet. He dumped the residue over the lip of the pit, uncaring. Victor joined him. Susan struggled with her equipment, but she dug determinedly at the tar.

Panting, Harper said, "Susan. You've got a feeling for it. If you think another fireball is on its way, yell so we can clear out. Okay?"

"Right." Susan bit her lip. Her fire-blistered hand hurt and tore as she shoveled with it, but she kept working. Across from her, El cut deep into the side of the site, clearing his way down at an incredible pace. He laid down two terrace board steps and kept shoveling. Victor did not seem to make progress, but his work kept Harper from being overwhelmed, as the soupy tar kept trying to flow in where it was being dug out, dirt lip of the pit or not. It was like trying to make a hole in the ocean. Irving watched impassively. Susan put her hand up and waggled her fingers at him. He gave a brusque nod.

"If we find the Phoenix," Victor huffed as he shoveled. "What'll we tell people when we bring it home?"

"You tell people we're in the Condor Relief Program," said El. "Keep shoveling. You're all that's keeping me afloat."

Susan's left hand went slick on the shovel haft. Splinters worked their way into her palm. She hit a ka-chunk with her next dig. She backed the spade head out a bit and went back in.

A good-sized skull rested in the tar as she brought it out.

"Dire wolf," said Harper, eyeing it briefly. "Go ahead and dump it. The museum's got hundreds of them."

Susan dumped it over the side. The thickish lump of resin-colored bone and tar tumbled in a heap. She took a deep breath.

El had sunk nearly half his height on his edge of the site. He stopped, resting on his tool, waiting for the two of them to shovel away excess before it began to flow down into his work.

Susan bent her sore back into it and shoveled harder, faster. She thought she heard Victor begin to hum, "I've been working on the railroad."

Voice and music swelled in her head. Not Victor's, but the call she'd come to associate with the Phoenix, gone deadly still since the Sylmar quake. "Oh, God." She put a hand to her temple. "I have him."

"What?" said El simultaneously with Poppa's, "Susie!"

She looked down to El. She held tightly onto her shovel as the tide of emotion threatened to sweep her away again. "It's singing to me. El, we've got to be close."

Victor kept shoveling, but sang out, "Cal Tech reports that was a 6.2 at Sylmar. They're predicting a bigger one here . . . any minute now." He looked up, moon-face shining with perspiration. "Is anyone listening at three in the morning?"

"You are," pointed out El.

"True." Victor pitched another spade of tar out. Whitish bone fragments like splinters rained out as he did so.

Whose bones, Susan wondered dully, as she kept moving, her thoughts overwhelmed by the call flooding through her, pinging every sense, emotion, and nerve, a call not to be denied. If Victor dropped dead in his tracks and El was sucked under, she would remain, digging, until the call was answered.

El lowered another crude board next to him and stomped it in. She watched tar and dirt ooze up around it. "You're getting away from the lip," she said, suddenly frightened for him.

"I know what I'm doing. I'm still on solid ground, don't you worry." Harper shoveled in with a grunt and heaved a massive shovelful up. With a flex of his shoulders and a determined look on his face that reminded Susan of movies depicting Lincoln cleaving logs, he dug deep.

Suddenly the spade head moved on a sharp angle away from him, toward the center of the pit, as he drove it in. El went to his knees, off-balance, holding on.

"Something's got it," he panted.

Victor dropped everything and ran to Harper's side. He lay flat on the ground and held onto Harper's waist, anchoring him.

Susan went to her knees as well, as the song burgeoning in her reached a fever pitch of urgency. She watched with helpless fear as the tar pit threatened to drag both El and Victor in. "Poppa! Help me!"

Chapter 25

Susan fell back gasping as the two men wrestled to the edge of the pit. El's chin, then his elbows dipped into the tar. He yelled at Victor, who responded with a grunt and hauled him backward an inch or two, but still not out of danger. Poppa shinnied headfirst and grabbed Victor about the waist. His wiry strength showed as he began to anchor them both.

El dragged back on the wooden shaft, his knuckles white. Slowly, inevitably, the shaft began to emerge from the tar as he drew something to the surface. Victor tightened his embrace about El and wiggled backward, gaining a better perch. The cords in El's neck bulged with the strain, his mouth set in a half-open gasp as he exerted all the strength that he had to keep them from being pulled back in.

Tar bubbled. It roiled and leapt up as if in an immense cauldron. El gave a half-shout and hauled back with both hands, freeing most of the shovel from the goo.

Then the spade head came up, with a claw clutched about it, the tar running off it like water, revealing the scaled talons of an immense creature.

Startled, El almost dropped the shovel. Victor yelled in his ear, "Bring it in!" and he kept pulling back. Another claw emerged, free waving, flexing, and Susan stared in horror. It was like watching a child come into the world breech, seeing this thing emerge claw first. Victor, then El stumbled up out of the pit, a step at a time, dragging the weight behind them.

The bird's body began to ascend. El reached over the spade head and caught the clawed foot. It spasmed in El's hand and the free foot captured him. Harper yelped in pain and surprise. But it did not pull him back down the slope they had just torturously climbed and now the two men began to drag the bulk of the creature up onto the level ground.

Under the cloak of darkness, it was difficult to see what they had, what lay gasping across twenty feet of grass and dirt, tar dripping from it, obscuring it from sight. The two of them shed their waders, kicking free. Susan went to the creature. Victor sat down heavily, his chest heaving for breath, and turned a flashlight on it.

"Don't," said Susan sharply. Then, "Don't. It hasn't seen the light of day for centuries. Its eyes . . . hurt."

The spray of its tail feathers lay over and still drooped into the pit as Susan went to its breast. She dropped a hand onto it gently. She looked to El. "It's . . . breathing," she said.

"So this," Poppa said, breathing hard, hands on knees, "is the troublemaker. It doesn't look like much."

As the black goo sloughed away from it, its blue and gold feathers began to shine with a dim glamour. A sprig of feathers crowned its head, each with a golden eye. Its head was vaguely pheasantlike, yet noble. Its breast moved like molten gold under Susan's hand. None of them had ever seen its like before.

"Its wingspan," murmured Victor. "Thirty feet?"

"Maybe." El sat on his heels, his heart pounding like a drum in his chest. "Susan . . . it's old. It's not going to be able to meet any Chinese demon."

"I'm old," Irving argued proudly. "And I'm not doing so bad."

She looked at the bird, not noticing the eyes that opened and considered her, proud eyes of deepest blue like the lapis lazuli of its homeland, ringed by purest gold. "It's at the end of its cycle." She collapsed on the grass. "It wants to die." She cradled her head in her arms, trying to shut out the paean in her head. At her feet lay an elemental of fire and air and man's greatest wisdom, its spark all but extinguished, its desire for rest eternal burning brightest. And she was its last handmaiden. "It spent everything trying to free itself. It has nothing left."

The Phoenix lifted its head and curled its feet under itself, perching on the grass. Susan leaned back as the creature bowed over her and then lay its head across her shoulder.

El whispered, "My God, don't move. That beak could tear your head off."

"But it won't." She stroked its breast lightly again, making certain not to go against the grain of the feathers. It rumbled softly in her ear, not unlike Domino's contented purr. There was nothing fierce about this noble beast. Its presence felt as comfortable to her as one of Irving's well-worn slippers.

The Phoenix rested another moment, then lurched to its feet. It pulled its magnificent tail free of the tar, flicked it clean, and balanced itself. The pheasant, the peacock, the eagle, all had nothing on this, the king of its kind, the near immortal. El and Susan and Victor stood in its shadow. Poppa had backed away warily, his eyes creased in thought.

It dipped its beak down and caressed her. Susan staggered a little under its attention. She put her hand out to El.

"There's . . . something I have to do for him," she said.

Something in Susan's voice set Harper off. "No," he countered, fear in his voice.

"I must. There's no one else to do it for him." She put her hand to her temple.

Poppa lunged to tear her away from the creature. The Phoenix reared back, hissing. Its eyes went brilliant. It raised a taloned foot threateningly. Its spur at its heel loomed razor sharp as did a spur at the crest of its wing. A flurry of golden sparks rained down.

"Whoa," said Victor. "It's not shooting blanks yet."

As suddenly as the attack began, the Phoenix quelled. Its head snaked about, searching the night air.

It looked toward the museum, toward Wilshire Boulevard and the skyscraping buildings on the other side. Susan felt its alertness in the very marrow of her bones. A dull rumbling, nearly audible, pressured her ears. "Something's coming," she said.

Victor pulled off his earphones. "Incoming!" he yelped and steadied himself.

The ground rippled under her feet. With earnest movement, it rolled and shook. Glass chimed as it shattered and fell in sheets. A eucalyptus crashed to its side at the parking lot edge. The acacias and oaks shook like an ocean under a heavy wind. Birds rose with screams of fear and circled, unnerved, above the park.

Victor went to his knees. The Phoenix flung its wings out and ran, ostrichlike. Susan ran with it and El, with a cry of dismay, could only drag at Victor and follow. Poppa ran, his bowed legs bicycling with effort. They ran to the boulevard side of the museum, where the massive lake and tar pit with its diorama of prehistory reigned.

The lake boiled with tsunami tide. The fiberglass mastodon reared on its iron stakings and fell with a tremendous splash. The world seemed to come to a halt. The sidewalk roiled snakelike upon the street. Power lines fell to the ground and writhed in deadly sparks. Tall buildings swayed as if they had no girders to keep them straight. Glass shattered and fell in a rain of diamonds to the smoking streets. Susan stood, the Phoenix fanned at her back, its gold body illuminating the night, a false dawn, like the one only two hours away, cobalt wings the star-eyed night above.

Something dark heaved up from the lake-covered pit. It rose with a growl and a spit and lambent eyes of evil. Victor said something in startled Chinese as the demon came out of the darkness. The ground continued to shake and roll as all hell broke loose.

The beast struck the Phoenix and the bird went down, felled, and lay limp upon the grass. She put a hand to it, felt its shuddering breast. "Fight," she breathed.

The gold rimmed eye dimmed as it considered her. "You can't die like this! Fight!"

Poppa Irving wailed in dismay. "Susie! *Oi gevalt!* Get out of there!"

The beast coiled with feline grace on the asphalt-splashed grass, the wrought iron fence broken and scattered like kindling under its body. It put out a paw and pushed at the Phoenix's sagging carcass. The proud head lolled over and its beak gasped open, golden smoke roiling harmless onto the ground, spent. Susan's resolve quailed. She broke and ran and

the demon struck at her, drawn by her movement. Its hot breath fouled her own gasp as she
fell, wiggled out of the waders, and tore free as
the beast snagged up one of the rubber boots.
Blood was at the back of its eyes and shining
black upon its tusks. She could smell her death
on its breath. Susan lunged to her feet, racing
across the meadow grass, and heard the Phoenix crow thin defiance even as the demon beast
thudded after her.

Glass rained down from the side wall of the
museum. It cascaded down, a thousand million
droplets, and Susan hurled into the damage, the
demon at her heels. For a moment she thought
of safety, like a mouse bolting into a hole, but
the high roof of the museum offered none. She
skidded across the shattered glass. Alarms filled
the air. Tapestries rippled as if in a high wind.
Exhibit cases shuddered on their stands.

Three red clay Chinese gentlemen regarded
her solemnly. Susan curled her hand around the
talisman at her throat. They had held the demon back once. Maybe they could detain it
again.

She picked up a Chinese mud figure and
swung it into the case, breaking more glass, and
thrust her necklace inside as she leaned in.

The figures cames to life stiffly. They pushed
her aside, advancing with clip-clops upon the
museum floor as the demon roared, its head and
shoulders inside the building. It thrust out a
paw and slapped one away. The impervious clay

figurine toppled and spun away. Laboriously, it got to its feet and advanced again.

Time had rendered their hands empty. The archer went through the movements of pulling an arrow and bow, but it held nothing. The swordsman vainly pulled its clay sword from its sheath and the demon snapped, breaking it into pebbles that showered upon the floor.

The figurines of Huang's army could do no more than delay the demon.

Susan circled the battle, racing to the front of the museum where the quake had brought down the entire threshold. The statues bravely thrust themselves at the demon. It swatted. A terra-cotta arm, two thousand years old, powdered into dust. She spent a tear for the destruction. Susan forced herself through the rubble and made her way behind the demon, which continued to roar its rage and futility at the three statues battling it.

El caught her up. She tried to shake him off. "Let me go."

"We've got to get out of here."

"No. He's got to burn, and I've got to do it. I'm the only one who can." Her necklace was still entangled in her fingers. She slipped away from him. They sprinted across slick grass.

El felt his fear gutting him. Warnings of a slightly touched old man iced through him. He caught at her elbow. She twisted free and looked back as the demon roared.

"Hurry! It won't be decoyed long."

Victor knelt at the side of the felled bird. He

looked up. His gold lamé jacket was a poor glimmer next to that of the Phoenix's plumage. The reek of napalm rose in the night, napalm spread by Poppa in his earlier fervor. The Phoenix lay in a gelatinous puddle of it. Susan dipped her hand into Victor's jacket pocket and pulled out a book of matches. The gold lettering read: The Jade Pheasant.

"What are you going to do?"

Poppa got stiffly to his feet and took a tottering step, his face creased in fear. "No, Susan! No!"

"The only thing I can." Susan stepped away from both of them defiantly.

Irving fell on El. "Stop her!"

Harper stepped nearer. She took the book of matches and began to strike them, one by one. "Victor, stand back. El, Poppa." She smiled at them. "Remember me." She set herself aflame.

El felt his heart stop as she went up like a torch, splattered with tar and the artificial fabric of her clothing catching with a sizzle. Her hair stood on end, a candlewick ablaze. She stepped into the napalm and a hot wind exploded, taking her.

She raised a hand in salute, turned and walked to the Phoenix and embraced it. The two roared into white-hot fury. It answered her embrace with one of its own, wings shuttering her from sight.

Irving doubled over and dropped in El's embrace. El could hold himself erect no longer and went to his knees with the old man in his arms.

"Oh, my God," Victor said. He repeated it over and over as the bonfire thrust blindingly into the night. He turned his face away from the sight. He still had his shovel in his hand. A shadow dropped over him. He raised the tool for protection as the lion demon glowered over him. "El. El. We've got trouble."

Susan felt searing pain, then nothing as she stepped into communion with the Phoenix. It rose upward, broken and bleeding, and wrapped its wings about her. Coolness enveloped her even as the air itself burst into white-hot sparks and an inferno whirlwinded around her. *My God*, she thought, *what have I done?* She clung to the oddly frail bird-god.

In the center of the conflagration, like the eye of a hurricane, all was oddly calm, but the hot air took the very breath away from her and she gasped helplessly. Her clothes smoldered to soft gray ash and drifted from her, but her skin stayed the same, perhaps even younger, softer, than it had been before. It scarcely mattered. She would burn with the Phoenix and, unlike it, would not survive the immolation. She felt oddly complete, and thought of Pearl Moon, and the fate she had been sent to meet. Full circle they had come. El, she hoped, would help take care of Poppa. And Poppa, she hoped, would help console El. In her hand, the talisman itself finally began to burn, the gold coin of Huang dripping like wax as it melted, then the silk cord sizzling like a fuse and finally, the feather itself, catching and smoldering red. The remnants flew from her fingers, Susan letting it go before it burned her. She looked up and saw the bird's proud eyes, blue and gold, looking down on her, only the creature's head above the vortex of flame and then, it, too, disappeared.

Susan gasped louder for air. Her thoughts went weak and scattered, blown away. She could not breathe. She felt the uplifting form of the bird-god grow insubstantial, its support leaving her, and as she grew dizzy, there was nothing to save her. She toppled into the flames.

Victor parried the snapping jaws away. "El, get up! El!"

Harper stayed where he was, stricken, knowing that his heart had given out at last. But it had not gone with his efforts, it had gone with Susan's leaving. He came around and saw Victor dancing, jabbing with the shovel head as the huge jaws snapped and toyed with him. He lowered the sobbing old man onto the grass. The napalm blaze chapped his face. He sprang up to help Victor.

Old weapons for old evil. His head swiveled. The massive quake had pulled up the wrought iron fence which rounded the lake. How many months had he pulled schoolchildren off that fence? How many times had he freed stuck feet, knees, and even heads? He staggered back, yelling to Victor, "One more time!"

He grabbed a bar from the fencing and tore it lose with a heave. It came free with a rusty creak. He tore a second stake loose and then a third.

Victor let out a shriek of pain. El turned, and in one smooth motion, reared back, cocked his arm like a javelin thrower of high school days, and let loose a bar. It sang through the air, dull and rusty and blunt, straight into the demon's eye.

The glowing lantern spurted crimson and the beast roared with anger, clawing at its eye socket, reared on its bunched hind legs. El went to Victor and pulled him along the ground. The bruised grass was slick with dew. Victor clutched his chest.

"I think," his friend said, "I lost a rib."

El peeled back the jacket and shirt. It was damp with blood, but the flap of skin hanging loose covered only the lower two ribs, skinned loose, nothing more important injured. He put the shirt back. "It's a flesh wound," he said. "Hold this."

He put a bar into Victor's fist.

"What's this for?"

"To give him a real toothache if he tries to swallow you." El straightened. As the beast sat in furious injury, pawing at its gory socket, he picked up the biggest piece of iron he could. His heart thudded in warning, but Harper ignored it. El took a running leap, and pole-vaulted the end of the railing into the exposed underside of the beast. Its bellow resounded as El fell to the ground and puffed to catch his breath.

A chunk of demon flesh dropped from the head and lay smoking on the ground. El scrambled away as the demon came to all fours.

It spoke. The ground vibrated with its voice and, by God, it knew English, El thought as he crawled back to Victor and took up a stance, another rail grasped in his hands.

"Run, juicy flesh," the beast howled. "The chase is sweet."

"No," answered El. "Come and get us. You're not doing so well." He braced the butt end of the wrought iron.

"I have consumed legions," bellowed the demon.

"And been put down for centuries," wheezed Victor. He stood up, trembling, fell to one knee and stayed. "We know where you came from. Huang Ti is dead, but his triumph is remembered."

The demon put his head back and shrieked defiance at the heavens. There were cars on Wilshire Boulevard behind him that wheeled to frantic stops, headlights gleaming, and then, whirled away, shocked by demon sight when even a massive quake had not deterred them. El watched, bemused, feeling an odd detachment from the scene. Susan was gone. He had nothing to anchor him to this earth any longer. He cared for nothing but vengeance. He cocked his arm for another spearing.

It paced a step closer. Harper measured the distance between them, did not like it, and stepped back, hauling Victor with him though his friend hissed once sharply in pain. He took another step, the single glowing eye of the beast cutting across them like a studio beam. He winced in its glare.

Feathery ash drifted across El's feet. The afterstink of burned napalm and flesh filled the air. He knew instantly where he stood. A lump built in his throat, but he swallowed it down. Susan was gone. The Phoenix was gone.

The beast laughed, a cruel, echoing laugh. It crouched upon its haunches, twitching, and El knew it would leap upon them, and that the iron he held might injure it—but it would never stop it.

He tightened his grip anyway and said to Victor, "It's been nice."

"Hasn't it though," his friend replied. "Good *joss* to you."

A shower of sparks rained around them, growing in intensity and brightness and El felt something ascending at his back *out of the ashes*, though he dared not look.

Then a young voice, raw but powerful, challenged the demon. "Come meet me," it said.

Wings fanned about them. El saw from the corner of his eye, the blue and gold plumage of a vastly different creature, a bird of fire and air and energy, of the raw, untried and unafraid nobility of the young.

It took a step forward and tottered before them. The demon spat and swatted at it. The bird ducked, and the paw swiped through its raised crest. Sparks sizzled and shot up at the contact. The young bird-god had not the strength it thought it had.

El yelled, catching the Chinese demon's attention. He filled his second fist with iron and ran at it, jabbing at the snapping muzzle. The demon expanded, its flesh growing insubstantial. Its wounds smoked and sucked back inward, healing as if never touched.

The Phoenix crowed. It spewed a fountain of flame that seared past El, he felt its heat like a flamethrower, and the demon gave a yelp of pain.

Irving was at its rear. He rose upward, though bent by age, and gave a cracking yell. "For Susan, you son of a bitch!" the old man cried, and swung a length of fencing at its hamstring with all the might he had.

The Phoenix puffed its chest out and crowed again, but its beak issued only a cloud of smoke. The youngling fell back, eyes flashing, wings bating. El saw with astonishment that the creature grew with every breath of air it took, wingspan flinging outward as it gained its full growth.

He stabbed the Chinese demon again, to keep it from whirling about on Irving. Victor got up and drove an iron bar deep into its flank where it sank into the quicksand of its flesh. The beast slapped around, upending El with its quickness.

His feet went up and his head went down. Then he landed and the world flashed before his eyes.

With a growl, the beast was on him. The jaws snapped once, tearing the last iron bar from his fingers and flinging it aside.

El sucked in his breath. The fragile cage of ribs that curled about his heart held, and so did the repaired pump, the wonder of muscles and organs, empty of love though it was. He held together. It would be the demon not his own failure which would kill him.

The Phoenix licked the air, its pointed tongue lashing, ablaze. The demon answered, backing off El. El rolled away weakly. With a cry of challenge, the Phoenix launched, in a comet tail of fire and sparks, and the demon bounded after it.

El cast his bar anyway, heard it thud home at the base of the demon's neck, as they took to the sky. The effort exhausted him and he toppled, as did Victor, onto a bed of soft ash.

He rolled over with a sob. His arm struck a mound under the ash. As the sky lit up with glitter and glistening and roars, he uncovered a patch of flesh. It was clean and supple, like a newborn babe's.

"Vic," he said thinly. "Victor!"

He began pawing away the ash. "Irving!" he shouted as his certainty grew.

Susan lay naked beneath it, her face pale, her hair a gold so thin and fine it was almost ethereal, her eyes closed.

Victor snaked off his jacket and threw it around the girl's body as El embraced her tightly. Susan gave a shuddering breath, then gulped for a second. Irving threw his trembling arms about them both, a stream of undecipherable Hebrew showering them.

Her eyes came open.

El kissed her soundly. She quivered within his hold, eyelids fluttering.

Then, "El?"

Too full to answer, he held her as tightly as he could.

"Poppa?"

Tears blinded the old man's eyes. His voice shook. "I never saw this," he said, and stopped, emotion choking him.

The night rumbled with dark clouds and lightning. They looked up, to see the demon and Phoenix, both grown massive, curling about one another, yin and yang of power. The sky exploded as they struck one another. Lightning stalked the hills. And then, a massive burst, a sun gone nova, turned the velvet dark completely white. It faded slowly, lingeringly. Susan peered through blinded vision. Showers of fire rained earthward, and when the clouds wept, it was with tears of earth and water. Red clay streaked the streets with puddles and rain into the gutters, dissipating.

The rains began. The hills above Malibu washed out from the deluge and the streets of L.A. adding flooding to their earthquake woes. El and Victor and Susan and Poppa stood in the rain and watched the fire dancing in the heavens.

"Who's going to win this time?" Susan asked, of no one in particular. She hugged Victor's coat about her.

Victor turned almond eyes on her. "In the true balance of yin and yang, no one should. But I'm rooting for the Phoenix."

A tremendous crash split the heavens. Fountains of yellow-white sparks gouted upward and then all was silent.

Dawn began to disperse the last of the dark clouds. For a split second, two suns rode the sky. Then the smaller, younger, more curious one coalesced. It darted earthward toward Hancock Park, did a looping swirl through the sky and winged out of sight.

"Where does a Phoenix go?" asked El.

Susan linked arms with him. "Anywhere it wants to?"

He looked at her. The laughter was slow in coming, rumbling upward, but erupt it did. He did not bother putting a hand to his chest. If his heart had lasted this long, it would probably go the distance.

Victor coughed. He said, "I could use a few stitches here and there. And, I don't know about you, it's not that uncommon a sight on Wilshire Boulevard, but you might not be comfortable standing around half-naked. Also, the earthquake damage crew should be here any minute and I'd just as soon not have to answer any questions." He looked toward the rising sun.

Poppa patted him on the back. "You'll come to the wedding?"

"What wedding?"

Poppa raised gray eyebrows at El and Susan. Victor laughed. Then he sombered.

"Tam Chen should be home today. I have work to do," he added.

They leaned on one another as they walked to the car. The ground zero effect of the earthquake had left small crevices in the walkway and lawn. Hancock Park would be rough jogging that morning, but as El looked around, it was nothing that wouldn't heal, given time.

"I have a job," El said to Victor. "Two, actually. But they don't suit me anymore, somehow."

"Me, too," said Susan seriously. "Il Mode is gone. Angelo. And I am, I think. Tempered. Certain things in life are too precious to waste." She looked at Victor. "What do you do besides cook Chinese?"

"Ah," said Victor. "There's a whole side of me El knows nothing about." He opened the car door for them, eyes sparkling in the rain-washed dawn. "But I'd be glad to tell you about it . . . if you're interested. It may take some time and commitment."

Poppa said, sliding in, "It sounds interesting.

Did I ever tell you I used to be in the Resistance?"

Susan threw him a fond look, as Harper hooked her about the waist, refusing to let her go.

"We've been baptized by fire," El said. "We're ready."

DAW

Enter the Magical Worlds of

Tanya Huff

DAW

Melanie Rawn

THE DRAGON PRINCE NOVELS

☐ **DRAGON PRINCE: Book 1**   UE2450—$5.95

He was the Dragon Lord, Rohan, prince of the desert, ruler of the kingdom granted his family for as long as the Long Sands spewed fire. She was the Sunrunner Witch, Sioned, fated by Fire to be Rohan's bride. Together, they must fight desperately to save the last remaining dragons, and with them, a secret which might be the salvation of their people. . . .

☐ **THE STAR SCROLL: Book 2**   UE2349—$5.95

As Pol, prince, Sunrunner and son of High Prince Rohan, grew to manhood, other young men were being trained for a bloody battle of succession, youths descended from the former High Prince Roelstra, whom Rohan had killed. Yet not all players in these power games fought with swords. For now a foe vanquished ages ago was once again growing in strength—a foe determined to destroy Sunrunners and High Prince alike. And the only hope of defeating this foe lay concealed in the long-lost Star Scroll.

☐ **SUNRUNNER'S FIRE: Book 3**   UE2403—$4.99

It was the Star Scroll: the last repository of forgotten spells, the only surviving records of the ancient foe who had nearly destroyed the Sunrunners. Now the long-vanquished enemy is mobilizing to strike again. And soon it will be hard to tell friend from foe as spell wars to set the land ablaze, and even the dragons soar the skies, inexorably lured by magic's fiery call.

THE DRAGON STAR NOVELS

☐ **STRONGHOLD: Book 1**   UE2482—$5.99
☐ **STRONGHOLD: Book 1 HARDCOVER**   UE2440—$21.95
☐ **THE DRAGON TOKEN: Book 2 HARDCOVER**   UE2493—$20.00

A new cycle begins as a generation of peace is shattered by a seemingly unstoppable invasion force which even the combined powers of High Price Rohan's armies, Sunrunners' magic, and dragons' deadly fire may not be able to defeat.

DAW

Mickey Zucker Reichert